HONOURABLE INTENTIONS

GAVIN LYALL

CHAPTER ONE

Aunt Maud's house in Cheltenham was really quite large, in a rambling way; it just seemed too small for the possessions she and her late husband had accumulated. Every small table was draped with a fringed embroidered cloth and then jammed with framed photographs, bowls of potpourri, vases and little silver knick-knacks – each with a very dull history. Every wall was coated with elaborate frames, in which were incompetent landscapes. Each door had a heavy velvet curtain with a brass rail on it, to keep out draughts, and every window curtain was as elaborately draped as a rococo Madonna. It would have been a bad place for kittens, drunks and children, if one could conceive of Aunt Maud allowing such creatures in.

It smelt of dust and old ladies, the other of whom was Ranklin's mother.

"You still haven't married, Matthew," Aunt Maud told him. "I imagine you want your family name to continue." Her tone made it clear that she couldn't imagine *why*. "You're not getting any younger."

"I'm thirty-nine," Ranklin said. Though with his round, innocent face he looked ten years younger, something that no longer bothered him.

"I suppose you're putting it off in the hope of being promoted to Major. An Army Captain's pay can't be all that generous, judging by how much you give your poor mother." His mother was sitting on the far side of the fireplace, silently doing embroidery, and Ranklin was depressed to see that she was beginning to adopt Aunt Maud's style: severe floor-length dresses in grey or muddy colours over prim white blouses with high collars fastened with cameo brooches. Damn it, as a child he had thought her the prettiest woman in the world.

But now age was bringing out the family resemblances: the same lack of chin, the pursed lips, the slightly hooked nose, along with grey hair drawn into a severe bun. Soon they would be just two dusty, old and near-identical sisters whose marriages had been episodes, long passed.

"And are you still living in Whitehall Court? I am given to understand that that is a very expensive address. No wonder you can't afford to send your poor mother a proper allowance."

"The War Office pays for the flat. It's right across the street so I can act as a sort of caretaker."

"And do you do anything else besides *caretaking?*"

"They send me abroad from time to time."

"Where to?"

"I've been to France, Germany, Italy—"

"Oh, only the Continent? The Captain thought of those places as being *local.*"

Aunt Maud was the widow of a Navy Captain and didn't think it odd that he had left her with a comfortable inheritance. Ranklin, who knew that a Navy Captain was unlikely to have earned more than £500 a year, thought it distinctly odd. He wondered how often the Captain, while earning a DSO for suppressing Malayan pirates, had shared in their booty or taken a bribe to look the other way.

"But just what is it you *do!* Mind, I've never been clear about what the Army *did.* Now, the Navy's task is quite clear: preserving the Empire and keeping the world trade routes open."

Ranklin had had enough. Ignoring his mother's pleading look, he said: "Trade? Oh, I don't think the Army has anything to do with *trade.*"

They were now in for five minutes of penal silence, quite likely timed to the second by Aunt Maud, before she would decide she had not heard that. Not forgiven it: forgiveness was a word she understood only in church, and there only in the abstract.

But suppose he had told the truth – that he was attached to the Secret Service Bureau and its unofficial (and reluctant) deputy chief? Aunt Maud would have said that he was as big a fantasist as his brother had been and that there was something odd about Ranklin blood.

In fact, his father had been a conventionally successful farm-owner – *not* farmer, that sounded too muddy for a Gloucester-shire squire – who had died soon after the Captain, ten years ago. So Ranklin's elder brother Frederick had inherited earlier than he had expected, and when agricultural prices began to slide, he started dabbling in gold shares, being warmly welcomed by those who understood such things.

When Frederick found *he* hadn't understood, being a man of honour, he killed himself with a shotgun. He might have done it where his mother was less likely to find his near-headless body, but perhaps he had other things on his mind. A lot of legal fees later, Mrs Ranklin had come to Cheltenham while Matthew was about to become bankrupt and resign his Army commission. Going off to fight for the Greeks in the 1912 Balkan War was simply opportunism: his only skill was in commanding artillery.

Still, a bankrupt mercenary soldier does seem rather caddish, and this had attracted the recently-formed Secret Service Bureau. Becoming unofficial second-in-command was partly because he was older than the other London-based agents, and partly because he wasn't as much of a cad as the Bureau's Chief had hoped. However, since he needed someone who would run the office without embezzling the furniture, he gave the job to Ranklin.

The five minutes' rigid silence ended with: "Perhaps you are pinning your hopes of promotion on there being a European war, Matthew?"

Ranklin considered his answer carefully. The world had scraped through 1913, when things had looked very sombre, but everyone seemed to agree that the first months of this year had seemed brighter. But the danger time wouldn't come until late summer, when the harvest was in and reservists could be called up.

"We're all still arming," he said. This was indisputable, even by Aunt Maud.

"Exactly!" she said triumphantly. "I don't approve of Winston Churchill, but he does seem to understand that this country depends on the Navy."

"Perhaps the trouble is that the Navy can't really influence what happens on land."

"Fiddlesticks. The boy," Aunt Maud turned to Ranklin's mother, "seems never to have heard of *blockade*."

"I think submarines and mines have made—"

"And what will happen when we've trounced the German fleet?"

"Er... I'm afraid I don't know."

"If they haven't had the sense to give up already, you and your *Army* will land a few miles from Berlin and march in."

Oddly, she wasn't alone in planning this. Lords of the Admiralty had had the same farcical idea for decades. Ranklin did his best to look apologetic. "I doubt the Army's big enough for that."

"I know, I *know*. And that is why we have had to ally ourselves with the *French*." Clearly an exceptionally Satanic sect. "Our natural enemy! King George should have got rid of the Liberal government first thing. And then told the French to go about their business. His Majesty had a naval upbringing, you know, but quite clearly he would not have made a good Captain."

"Really? I do believe Mr Lloyd George—" He hadn't bothered to think up what he believed, knowing he'd never get to say it. His mother winced, but it was too late.

"Lloyd George is an anarchist! A charlatan! A *Methodist*! I have Heard Things about him that I Will Not Repeat!" But she would be in a better mood afterwards. Mention of Lloyd George always acted like an enema on Aunt Maud.

* * *

BEFORE HE LEFT on Tuesday morning, Ranklin gave his mother an envelope holding thirty pounds in notes. As usual, she said it was too much and he said he was sorry it wasn't more. But it didn't make any difference: she would just hand it over, gratefully, to Aunt Maud. Then he kissed them both and walked off towards the station.

There was a horrifying inevitability about that house. It was utterly alien, yet it was on his road. He could never imagine himself starving in a damp London basement, but could all too well imagine the dust settling on him among the worthless bric-á-brac of Cheltenham.

* * *

WHITEHALL COURT LAY between Whitehall and the river, comprising mostly expensive service flats and small clubs. The Bureau also had its offices there, in a rambling set of attics and garrets on the eighth floor, rooms built originally for junk and servants.

Ranklin came in through the outer office and said: "Good afternoon, Miss Stella," to the senior lady, and she looked up from her typing machine and said: "Good afternoon, Captain, did you have a pleasant Easter?" Ranklin lied politely back and the two other ladies smiled and bobbed their heads as he went on into the agents' room.

By now this had itself taken on the air of a club, albeit a rather bohemian one. One side of the room had a sloping outer wall, pierced by two dormer windows. The floor was bare boards – quite good boards, since the building was only fifteen years old – with various rugs over the draughtier places. The Commander, whom everyone except Ranklin called Chief or even "C", had donated some basic furniture, and the rest had accumulated on the principle of "if you want a comfortable chair, you're welcome to bring one in".

Beside one of the dormer windows Lieutenant P was rumpling through a stack of morning newspapers, pausing now and then to cut out an article. Like most men, he used scissors very clumsily. Standing by a small table was Lieutenant Jay. He was really Lieutenant J, but six months of token secrecy had actually worked, and nobody could remember what his name really was, so he had become Jay. This had not happened to Lieutenant P. Jay was trying to brew coffee with a new infernal machine and spirit stove he had bought. No, not bought, not Jay – just acquired. Despite his family supposedly being very rich, Jay had a talent for acquiring things that would be the envy of any quartermaster-sergeant. Both agents paused to smile and nod at Ranklin and that was all.

The office didn't look much; it certainly wasn't the busy warren of panelled rooms that writers of shilling shockers imagined the HQ of the British Secret Service to be. But most of all, it wasn't as old: probably the biggest secret that the Bureau kept was that it had only been founded four years ago.

Waiting for him on what by tradition had become his table was a parcel of books – *Wer ist* (the German *Who's Who*) and the Italian *Annuario Militare* – which the Commander had grudgingly accepted they should buy. He put them in the glass-fronted bookcase that was their library, added their names to the exercise book that was their filing system, and sat down to fill and light his pipe.

The soundproof baize door to the inner office was wrenched open and the Commander stumped out, waving two sheets of paper. He headed for Lieutenant P.

"You say here the attaché's mistress is..." he read from the report "... 'olive-skinned'... Was she green?"

"No, of course not, sir."

"Black, then?"

"No, sir."

"Those are the only colours I've ever seen on an olive. Did you mean she was *swarthy?*"

"Er... that sounds rather unshaven, sir."

"Any reason to believe she does shave? – her face, anyway?"

Lieutenant P shook his head.

"Very well, then, she was *swarthy*. Say so next time." He noticed Ranklin. "Ah, you're back." He pulled out his watch. "We're due at the Cannon Street Hotel for tea at four. Your girlfriend wants us to meet that lawyer Noah Quinton. Says it's of national importance. It had bloody well better be."

Ranklin puffed and nodded contentedly. He was home.

CHAPTER TWO

The Cannon Street Hotel wasn't quite in the heart of the City but a bit south of that; say the liver. So, it was geographically Corinna's territory, and the hotel was prepared to overlook its City prejudice against women – save as rich widow shareholders at the many company annual general meetings held there – because she was the daughter of Reynard Sherring. And Sherring controlled a private bank that, even at the flood tide of joint-stock banking, was keeping its head a million or two above water.

Shortly before four, Ranklin and the Commander were sipping tea in the drawing room of the hotel which, true to the current fashion, ran to a high ceiling, cushioned wickerwork chairs and potted palms.

The Commander looked at his watch. "She said four o'clock, didn't she?"

"That's what you said."

"Is she usually late?"

"I wouldn't say she was, yet."

The Commander watched five seconds tick by. "Dammit, she

could perfectly well have told you whatever-it-is. No need for me. I've got things to do."

Like keeping the Bureau from getting involved in the mess that was Ulster. There was a good case for this, but the danger was that the spring of 1914 was turning out to be rather quiet on the Bureau's true international stamping-ground and they didn't have enough to do.

Ranklin shrugged and another five seconds passed.

Then the Commander demanded: "I know she's a partner or something in her father's bank, but does she really understand banking and finance and...whatnot?"

"I imagine so. But *I* don't, so I can't judge."

"She's one of these *clever* women, then."

"Certainly." Ranklin realised they were passing the time with a little game of make-the-other-lose-his-temper-first.

"Handsome gal, though."

"I didn't know you'd met her." Did he lose half a point for being surprised?

"Oh yes. At a dinner party at the Grenfells'. We got on rather well."

Perhaps that was supposed to make Ranklin jealous. But he could well believe that Corinna had been intrigued to meet the Bureau's Chief. Of course, his identity was a closely guarded secret, but equally of course, that didn't apply to *Certain People*. Moreover, the Commander – a genuine naval rank – fancied himself as a ladies' man. By now in his mid-fifties, he was a stocky man with a face like Mr Punch, nose and chin seemingly trying to meet. He had a complexion that he probably hoped looked weather-beaten old seadog, but was really just ruddy, and the Navy had long ago beached him for incurable seasickness. He had once been heard calling espionage a "capital sport", but probably that was just a sop to the type of Englishman who took nothing seriously except games.

On the whole, Ranklin thought he was probably right for his job. He had a lot of enthusiasms – gadgetry, motorcars, pistols – a love of secrecy, and apparently no scruples. Certainly, he betrayed his rich wife, who lavished Rolls-Royces and yachts on him, as skilfully and naturally as he did foreign governments. Ranklin wished he thought these two talents weren't connected.

When Ranklin hadn't reacted, the Commander provoked further: "Bit tall for you, I thought."

"I don't know... Can't have too much of a good thing."

That gave the Commander the choice of being even more vulgar or pretending to be upright and shocked. Cannily, he did neither. "Ah, your intentions aren't honourable, I see. Just animal passion."

"As technically my commanding officer, would you give me permission to marry an American citizen?"

"Certainly, if it was just for her money. If I thought you were sincere, I'd sack you."

Ranklin decided it was time for a change of subject. "What do we know about Noah Quinton?"

"As a man or as a lawyer?"

"Either."

"I understand he doesn't come of one of the academic-professional families. First of his line. Lower-middle-class, East London, Jewish... Perhaps not *very* East London." The Commander wasn't speaking geographically. "It's said he's a good man to go to if you want to win and don't mind how."

In answer to Ranklin's raised eyebrows, the Commander added: "I don't say he breaks the law. Just got a reputation for sailing close to it."

Ranklin wondered if he'd been naive in thinking that that was just what lawyers were for. While he was still wondering, Corinna and Noah Quinton arrived.

Corinna, who liked to be called Mrs Finn and thought of as a widow for entirely immoral reasons, was indeed tall and attracted words like "striking" and "handsome". Or "vivid", because her eyes and mouth were exaggerated like an actress's and her hair was very black. With all this, she could carry off strong colours and did, while most of London was wearing pastels and fussy little hats. Today she wore a black matador hat and was wrapped in a cape of purple wool that completely hid, and therefore hinted at, her shape beneath.

Probably it was too warm for the day – a fine Easter was stretching on, with temperatures nearing sixty degrees – but when did being hot or cold affect how a woman wanted to look?

The Commander pre-empted her to the introductions. "I'm Commander Smith and this is Captain Ranklin. *Army* Captain, of course."

Corinna smiled. "May I present Mr Noah Quinton?" They shook hands and Quinton said: "And you represent the Government?"

"Whatever Mrs Finn told you," the Commander said blandly. They all sat down, a watchful waiter hurried up with a fresh pot of tea, and Ranklin poured.

If you had met Quinton anywhere, you would have thought: Ah, a sharp lawyer. But how else was a lawyer allowed to advertise? He was dapper (attention to detail), quick of movement (and thus of thought), and looked you in the eye with a smile (he believed what you were telling him). Actually, between his curly grey hair and small grey beard was a rather ferrety face, which his heavy-rimmed glasses helped humanise, but he was constantly putting those off and on.

"We're all busy me...people," the Commander said briskly. "So, I believe you have something you feel we should know."

"Yes." Corinna took a deep breath. "My father, Reynard Sherring, is honorary treasurer of a small fund set up by Americans in London to help out American citizens in trouble here. Our consulate passes on people they think are deserving of our help. Last week they told us about a young American in prison over in Brixton. It seems you're holding him for the French. They want him extradited on an arson charge."

"What did he burn down?" the Commander asked. "Allegedly."

"Oh, only a police station-house." The Commander's eyebrows vibrated at that "only", but Corinna sailed on. "It doesn't seem to have been more than singed, anyhow. So, I run the fund when my father isn't here, and I was…well, I was kind of bothered by something the boy said to our vice-consul and a letter the boy's mother wrote him. He was bothered, too. The vice-consul. So, I asked Mr Quinton to take on the case. Frankly—" she flashed Quinton a searchlight-strength grin to disarm him "—I was hoping the boy would say more to him and he'd pass it on to me, but…"

"Without my client's permission, it would have been quite unethical for me to do anything of the sort," Quinton said tonelessly.

Corinna said cheerfully: "But it seems he hasn't said any more anyhow, so our ethics are unsullied." She could be deceptively feminine and vague when she wanted. In truth, she must have dealt with lawyers in half a dozen countries.

There was a pause, then the Commander said: "Are we going to hear what the chap said?" at the same time as Ranklin's "Does the lad have a name?"

Corinna chose to answer Ranklin. "Grover Langhorn, aged twenty-three; he worked as a waiter at a café in La Villette – the nineteenth *arrondissement*." She flicked on a fastidious expression: the nineteenth was the area Paris didn't talk about, like an uncle who had gone to the bad. All Ranklin knew of it was that it was in the north-east of the city and had acres of abattoirs.

The Commander, who didn't like coming second, said: "*Grover* Langhorn?"

"As I'm sure you remember," Corinna said sweetly, "we had a President called Grover Cleveland around the time this boy was born. And what he told the vice-consul was that if he was going to be sent back to France he'd tell something scandalous about your King."

Ranklin felt his own expression must be a mirror of the Commander's: blank puzzlement. Agreed that it would be impossible to top the late Edward VII's mark for scandalous behaviour, George V didn't even seem to be trying. His appearance was entirely the opposite: that of a dutiful family man. Could he have told a *risqué* story from his naval days in mixed company? At full stretch, that was the worst Ranklin's imagination could reach.

Finally, the Commander asked: "Is that *all?*"

"Not quite." Corinna dug in what she called a "purse" and anyone else would have said was a moderate piece of luggage and unfolded a sheet of pale violet writing-paper. She passed it across.

> *18 rue Castelnaudry*
>> *Paris 19*
>> *April 3erd*
>> *Dear sir*
>> *My son Grover has been arested by the London police becaus the French say he set fire to the police baracks but I know he did not do this but they will lock him up for ever if he is sent back here becaus of perjery so pleas see him & listen very carefuly to what he tells you becaus it is true*
>>> *yrs faithfuly*
>>> *Enid Langhorn (Mrs (widow) born Bowman).*

"Let me get this quite clear," the Commander said. "Was this sent to the American Consul here?"

"She was English and married an American merchant seaman back...whenever. And the letter was sent to the American *consulate*. It was opened by one of the young vice-consuls – a sweet boy, you'd love him – and it was he who saw Grover and then got in touch with me. As he'd sort of handed the case over to me, he gave me the letter as well. He said that it probably wasn't the sort of thing to leave lying in a file anyhow. Between you and me, I don't think he feels America should be mixed up in the scandalous behaviour of royalty.

"You can keep it," she added. "Unless Mr Quinton wants it."

Quinton shook his head firmly and the Commander, after one last frowning glance, tucked the letter into an inside pocket. He seemed uncertain about what to say next.

So Ranklin said: "Perhaps Mr Quinton would care to say something about extradition procedure – in general, of course, not in regard to this case."

Quinton's smile flickered quickly and then he said: "Extradition's rare, so not many lawyers bother to know much about it. It's really an uneasy mix of law and international politics. Our courts can decide that a man should be extradited, but then the Home Secretary – although it would really be a Cabinet decision – can overrule them and decide he shouldn't be. However, not vice versa: if the courts decide someone should *not* be extradited, that's an end of the matter."

The Commander said: "Be a bit of a snub to that foreign government if the Home Sec chose not to extradite when the courts had said he should."

"Quite so," Quinton nodded. "Just what I meant by an uneasy mix with politics. And that aspect goes a little further: the court can hear evidence to show that the alleged crime was a *political* one – something that would be irrelevant in a normal trial – and if they decide it *was* political, set the prisoner free."

The Commander frowned. "But suppose—"

"*Even* if the charge is murder. There was something of a landmark case some thirty years ago, Castioni. He killed a man during the overthrow of the local government in one of the Swiss cantons and fled to England. The judges decided the killing had been a political act and refused to extradite... Perhaps I should point out that treason, spying, subversion and so on aren't even extraditable crimes, of course. Nobody gets sent back to, say, Germany because he's been doing naughty things to their government."

Perhaps Quinton was just trying them out: Corinna certainly wouldn't have told him who they really were. The Commander was clearly less certain about her, but she ignored him and asked: "Burning a police station-house…is that political? Sounds as if it could be."

Quinton didn't answer; instead, he said: "Why doesn't someone ask about anarchism?"

Knowing the Commander now wouldn't, Ranklin asked: "What about anarchism?'

"Interesting that you should ask that," Quinton said. "Because there was a case just a few years after Castioni: Meurnier, this time, a French anarchist. He blew up a Paris café and killed a couple of people and claimed that had been political. Mr Justice Cave – as he then was – came back with a rather crafty judgment. In effect, he said that a political act is one aimed at replacing one party or system of government by another – but that, since an anarchist didn't believe in *any* form of government, all his actions must be directed against private citizens, and he sent Meurnier back."

"Does that mean," Corinna asked, "that nothing an anarchist does can be political?"

"That would be one possible reading of the judgment."

A grimy light began to shine on Ranklin's thoughts. "This café in La Villette – do you know what sort of place it is?"

Quinton smiled but retained his legal caution. "I understand that it is said to be a haunt of anarchists."

* * *

THE COMMANDER GROWLED: "If this damned American is an *anar-*

chist then all that stuff about royal scandal is probably just trouble making."

Quinton said: "Nothing in the depositions offers any proof that he is an anarchist."

"But if he was working as a waiter there—"

"Would you assume that every waiter at a poets' café is a poet?"

Corinna said: "But Mr Tippett the vice-consul said the boy—"

"That is not evidence."

With Corinna and the Commander both rebuffed, that left Ranklin to steer the conversation into a more soothing, general channel. "You were going to explain to us laymen the normal progress of an extradition case..."

"'Hearing' is the proper term. Yes. It starts with a request through diplomatic channels for us to arrest the chap. When we've done that, he makes a brief appearance at Bow Street police court to be remanded to Brixton. Then the foreign government sends over depositions and perhaps witnesses themselves – there are two in this matter – for the magistrate to decide whether they have made a *prima facie* case of an extraditable crime for the prisoner to answer. We've reached that point now, with the hearing due tomorrow."

"Tomorrow?" the Commander and Ranklin said simultaneously.

"I came a little late to this matter—"

"I was slow off the mark myself," Corinna confessed. "And the consulate didn't—"

"It seems," Quinton said firmly, "that the lad didn't take the matter very seriously until someone else read the French depositions and explained how strong a case there was."

"Is it strong, then?" the Commander asked.

"I think..." Quinton sounded a little reluctant but now he was embroiled in the real case and couldn't turn back – which was roughly what Ranklin had hoped. "I think it might be torn to pieces by a good, well-prepared advocate at a full trial – in

France. Whether I can do as much tomorrow, I wouldn't care to say."

He looked pensive and Ranklin prayed for the Commander to stay quiet. And for once, he did.

Quinton went on: "The prosecution only has to show there is a case to answer – the defence doesn't have to answer it. But the boy wants me to: he wants above all not to be sent back to France. He's convinced the police are fabricating evidence against him."

"And are they?" the Commander asked, brightening up at this hint of illegality.

"There's one witness in particular whom I'd like to see cross-examined within an inch of his life. But to do that properly, I need more preparation. If I do a half-cock job and the boy gets extradited anyway, I'll just have shown the prosecution the holes in their case, so they can patch them up for the full trial. But my client seems ready to risk that."

Corinna said: "What about it being a political crime anyhow?"

"I shall argue that as well. But I can't see a Bow Street magistrate ruling on that. I think he'll leave that to a higher court."

The Commander asked: "Can you appeal the magistrate's decision, then?"

"In effect. It'll be a *habeas corpus* hearing in the King's Bench. When," he turned to Corinna, "your fund will have to stump up for *Counsel*. But I think I can find one who'll say what he's told and not have ideas of his own."

Mr Quinton, one suspected, did not share the high opinion that barristers had of themselves.

The Commander said: "I think we're getting bogged down in legalities. Frankly, it's no skin off our nose whatever happens to the lad – that is, I'm sure he's safe in Mr Quinton's capable hands. What concerns me is whether he's going to say anything in open court. Is he?"

"If he listens to me, he'll say nothing bar his name," Quinton said very firmly.

"Good. And meanwhile, if he tells you anything more about this – alleged – royal scandal, you'll be sure to let us know?"

Quinton frowned. "Whatever a client tells his solicitor is in the strictest confidence."

"Good Lord, man, this is a question of your duty to the *King*!"

Quinton stiffened. "I agreed to come to this meeting on the understanding that you would take this aspect out of my hands. It isn't germane to the boy's case and is the sort of thing I prefer not to be told. And if told, not to hear."

"I would have hoped your patriotic—" the Commander began, but Ranklin cut in:

"I'd better come and hear what happens at Bow Street myself tomorrow. Will I get in?"

"I'll make sure you do. But I can't promise you'll hear anything from the public seats. Meet me outside at lunchtime and I'll explain what's been happening. Now, if you'll excuse me…Mrs Finn…" He bowed over Corinna's hand, shook hands with the Commander and Ranklin, and walked briskly away.

Watching him go, the Commander said thoughtfully: "D'you think I overdid the duty-to-your-King bit?"

"Perhaps," Ranklin said.

Corinna said: "He's supposed to be good."

"I imagine, madam, that by that you mean 'effective'."

"Isn't that what we all mean?" She was quite unabashed. "Well, I've done my *effective* deed for the day." And she leant back in her chair and looked at them expectantly.

The Commander looked puzzled. Ranklin said: "Not quite. That letter the lad's mother wrote had a Paris address. When you sent someone from your Paris office to check up on her, was she still there?"

Corinna said dreamily: "If I had three wishes, d'you know what the first would be? To have someone push that terrible little crook Lloyd George under a bus. Having a Chancellor of the Exchequer who—"

"Sorry we can't oblige you there," Ranklin interrupted. "What's the second wish?"

"Are you truly offering to do me a favour?" Her surprised delight was quite false.

"No, ducky, we're not, but let's hear it anyway."

"Well, *since* you mention it...at the moment, the Treasury doesn't place many bonds in the US, but it does so exclusively through Morgan Grenfell. Now, if you happened to be speaking to anyone with influence, you might just *mention* that the House of Sherring has its main office on Wall Street and would be only too happy to help out."

Looking grim again, the Commander came in with a surprising knowledge of financial politics – surprising to Ranklin, anyway. "Madam, I can only see us needing to sell more Treasury bonds abroad in an exceptional circumstance – such as a European war. And a long one."

"Is that truly so?" Corinna was an innocent little girl again. "Dear me. Still, it helps to be prepared, don't you think? So, you will remember?"

"Are you *blackmailing* us, Mrs Finn?"

"Me, sir? Blackmail? What a terrible thought. No, I'm just doing what is known in my humble trade as a 'deal'. A *quid* — or dollar – *pro quo*." She shifted her smile to Ranklin. "Yes, I sent our people to see Mrs Langhorn, but she'd gone, bag and baggage, and no forwarding address. It was just a *pension*, and a pretty lowly one, anyway. But another thing Grover told our vice-consul: she was born English, Miss Bowman."

"Thank you. And would it now be too much to ask that you leave the rest to us?"

"Delighted. I must get back to the office. Thank you *so* much for the tea, and it was a pleasure meeting you again, Commander...*Smith*."

Ranklin walked with her to the hotel lobby. "Thank you again, but...may I offer a word of warning?"

This was still her home ground; she nodded cheerfully.

"You held things up for at least a day sending your Paris people to see the lad's mother because, if I know you, you wanted the *full* story before you came to us. So, here's the warning: don't try to be clever when it comes to our monarchy. No deals. Just hope for gratitude."

"I've heard you say things about your kings that I'd never dare."

Ranklin nodded. "We all do. It's fashionable. But there can be a very sudden closing of ranks, too. I'd hate to see you caught on the outside."

* * *

WHEN HE GOT BACK to the Commander they sat in silence for a while. Then the Commander said: "Is she usually so..." He was obviously trying to think of a (relatively) polite synonym for "mercenary".

"She has an instinct for doing deals; she's a banker. But banking is a secretive trade, too."

"Hm." The Commander felt in his pocket and took out the violet-paper letter. "The woman's spelling suggests she's either daughter of a duke or a dustman. I'd guess the dustman. And obviously she's in on it: tipping off the American Consul to start the ball rolling, and then vanishing. I presume it's all to get us to let her son off... What else have we got?"

"D'you think we should be taking this seriously, then?"

"That's the first thing to find out."

"But we don't even know what it is that the lad's threatening."

"Then *that's* the first thing to find out."

"And whether we're really the right people to tackle—"

"Damn it, it was *your* girlfriend who dumped it in our lap. If we go to the police that's just spreading it. And they probably wouldn't do anything because he hasn't committed any offence – over here, that is. And I don't propose to give it to Kell and his people." Relations with their sister counter-spy service had recently become a little strained.

Ranklin nodded unenthusiastically. "Well, I'll go along to Bow Street tomorrow; I don't know if I'll learn anything, but... Should we ask O'Gilroy to have a look at back numbers of the Paris papers?"

"Good idea. Send him a telegram – but don't let him know why we want to know."

Ranklin let that slur pass; anyway, the Commander was still thoroughly irritated by Corinna and didn't care about Ranklin's feelings. "I know you've usually worked with him and trust him, but we want to keep this as small as possible. Anyway, as an Irishman he probably thinks royal scandals are a good thing."

"Don't we all – as newspaper readers? But do we want to get in touch with the lad himself?"

"How?" the Commander growled. "We can't go along to Brixton and demand to see him, we'd have to go through Quinton or the American consulate—"

"—or we could try slipping O'Gilroy into his cell on a fake dynamiting charge and let them swap grievances and brigandry techniques. There, O'Gilroy can be as republican as he likes."

As Ranklin expected, the prospect of behaving dishonestly cheered the Commander up immediately. "Ye-es... All right: get him here by tomorrow night, bringing whatever he's got about the arson, and if the whole thing hasn't fizzled out by then...we'll see."

Ranklin nodded, hiding the uplift he got from prospectively having the Irishman back. O'Gilroy was, unofficially, their Man in Paris. He was there mainly because he had to be somewhere, and London was too full of other Irishmen who wanted to cut his throat. He wasn't much good at French politics, but there was no shortage of self-styled experts on that; what O'Gilroy now knew was the Paris streets. Ranklin felt he himself belonged there, too:

The Bureau's job was abroad, and Paris was eight hours closer to anything happening on the Continent.

The Commander may have suspected how he'd been led to his decision, because he went on looking at Ranklin. "You know, you're not a *bad* second-in-command." Then added explosively: "But by God – you've got a bloody funny taste in girlfriends."

CHAPTER THREE

"My name is Detective Inspector Thomas Hector McDaniel of Bow Street Police Station." Ranklin was particularly glad to hear those words, the point being that he *could* hear them, after three-quarters of an hour of straining and guessing.

Popular myth has it that courtrooms provide scenes of natural drama. Not this one: most of that morning would have been upstaged by a public reading of the London Street Directory. He couldn't even study Grover Langhorn. Jammed among the spectators at the back, Ranklin was facing the magistrates' bench, but so was Langhorn, standing in the raised dock in front of him. By the end of the morning, Ranklin knew he would recognise that slight and shabby back view of baggy check trousers and dark blue donkey jacket for the rest of his life, but he had yet to glimpse the face.

Moreover, once Langhorn had agreed he was who he was supposed to be, he apparently became irrelevant to the routine going on around him. Documents were passed, mulled over and agreed upon, men in old-fashioned frock coats, one being Noah Quinton, bobbed up, murmured things, and sat down when the magistrate had murmured back.

Then came Inspector McDaniel (it was odd how many London policemen had obviously been born elsewhere; were native Londoners too finicky or too corrupt?). He was bald-headed, walrus-moustached, as well fed as any lawyer, and probably as familiar with courtrooms. He gave his evidence loudly and confidently, pausing after each sentence so that the clerk could write it down. "Acting on information received" he had proceeded to 29 Great Garden Street... He there saw a man who admitted he was Grover Langhorn... Yes, he is the man standing in the dock there... He then arrested said man on a warrant issued by the Bow Street magistrate on the second of April...

The slow delivery let Ranklin's attention wander to the others crammed beside him in the public seats. He had thought carefully about how he should dress that day, but after dismissing the idea of posing as a Cockney as impossible, and a farmer-in-town-for-the-day from his native Gloucestershire as improbable, he had just dressed as himself. He knew he would look vaguely official – just how, he wasn't sure, but he had to accept it – but hoped the case would attract vaguely official attention anyway. And so it had: those around and altogether too close to him were definitely official-looking; he thought he recognised at least one face from the Foreign Office. Indeed, the one man who stood out was wearing a non-London check suit. He was taking assiduous notes.

Ranklin came back to earth when he realised the bowling had changed and Quinton was asking the questions: "Did my client say anything when you arrested him?"

Quinton's courtroom voice was monotonous and uninflected.

"Yes, sir, he asked me how I found him there. He also—"

"And what did you reply?"

"—*he also*," McDaniel said firmly, "stated that this was supposed to be a safe place for him to hide. I made no reply to these statements."

"Did he say anything else, then or at a later time, apart from confirming his name?"

"No, sir."

Quinton sat down again. McDaniel stayed where he was while his evidence was read back to him, then the court relapsed into muttering over documents. Ranklin was looking at the time – it wasn't easy to get his watch out in a crush like in a crowded underground train – when another witness popped up in the box and identified himself as *Inspecteur* Claude Lacoste of the Paris *Préfecture* attached to the eighth district, which included the nineteenth *arrondissement* – La Villette.

By contrast with McDaniel, this was a man with a clean-shaven round face who might have been chosen for his all-round averageness (and had been, Ranklin discovered later: French logic said that only men of average looks and height could become Paris detectives). But his manner was quiet and confident, someone who knew his job. He spoke English with a strong accent, but fluently enough to manage without an interpreter.

Yes, he could identify the accused as Grover Langhorn... He had been employed as a waiter at the *Café des Deux Chevaliers* since last autumn... It was a haunt of anarchists—

"I fail to see the relevance of that," Quinton interrupted.

The magistrate looked enquiringly at the prosecutor, who was just another half-bowed back to Ranklin, but Lacoste beat him to it: "It is the only reason why I am familiar with the establishment, M'sieur."

Quinton shrugged dramatically – by the dramatic standards of the day so far – and sat down.

Yes, on the night of 31 March there had been a fire at the police barracks... It had quickly been established that it was deliberate, caused by petrol... A fire-warped five-litre petrol tin had been discovered at the scene... He had led the investigation... He had questioned certain persons... There are few places in La Villette which sell petrol, there being few motorcars in the area... At one garage, however, he had learned that at about six o'clock in the evening four days earlier... Yes, 27 March... the accused had purchased a green tin of petrol...

There was a break while the prosecutor assured the magistrate that there was a sworn statement by the *garagiste*, one from the café proprietor, two from patrons, and one from an eyewitness, representing Lacoste's investigation.

...As a result of all this, Lacoste had sought to question Langhorn... He could not be found... It had been suggested he might have fled to England... (there was something missing here, Ranklin thought: somebody had either volunteered the suggestion or been persuaded to volunteer it by method or methods unknown. Such thoughts wouldn't have occurred to him eighteen months ago.) Consequently, an extradition warrant had been sought...

In his own job, Ranklin demanded bare facts and came down brutally on colourful phrases. But here he felt cheated at being told of an arson attack followed by a police trawl of the local underworld, hasty flight and legal pursuit – and all made as dull as a railway timetable. Perhaps Quinton's cross-examination would help...

"The fire at the police station – what part of the building did it damage?"

"The kitchen, M'sieur."

"So, it could hardly have been an attempt to free any prisoners held there, for example... Do you have any reason to believe that my client is an anarchist?"

"He is a waiter at a café of anarchists, M'sieur."

"Just an employee – one who is paid to work there?"

"I know nothing of his pay, M'sieur."

"But still only an employee?"

"So, I believe, M'sieur."

"And would you expect every waiter at – say – every poet's café in Paris to be a poet?"

"No, M'sieur."

"Has my client ever expressed anarchistic views to you or within your hearing?"

"No, M'sieur."

Ranklin was not tempted to whisper to those beside him that here Quinton was paving the way to claim that this was a political crime and his client was *not* an anarchist. But he didn't mind them noticing his knowing nod and smile. Then he remembered he was here on duty and trying to be anonymous, and shamefacedly went back to thinking about the case.

Probably Lacoste would have pointed out that in a scruffy, dangerous little café in the nineteenth *arrondissement* an anarchist clientele wouldn't have tolerated for a moment a waiter who didn't share their views. But Quinton had given him no chance to say so, and presumably magistrates weren't allowed to think such things for themselves.

Once Lacoste had stepped from the witness box, the court returned to murmuring over documents. In front of him, Langhorn moved nervously from foot to foot, never quite standing straight. An Englishman might have stood to attention or he might have leant on the dock rail; he wouldn't have stood in that loose, rangy way. Perhaps it was something to do with Americans walking with their hips thrust forward – Corinna had once demonstrated that for him, stark naked. It had been most instructive but not a suitable memory for a police court—

From what Ranklin could hear, the depositions from the café proprietor and patrons had Langhorn asking to go off duty at ten that evening and not reappearing until about one o'clock. Obviously, it was not a café which relied on early-to-bed working citizens for its customers.

Several times Quinton bobbed up asking for clarification of some point, in a manner that looked to Ranklin like time-wasting. It apparently struck the magistrate the same way, because the last time he gave Quinton a sour look, weighed the yet-to-be-accepted depositions in his hand and said: "It looks as if we're going to have to postpone hearing the next witness until after lunch. Perhaps that won't inconvenience you too greatly, Mr Quinton?"

Quinton fawned decorously, and once they had polished off the depositions, they broke up.

* * *

STANDING like a rock amid the hurrying crowd spilling out from the court was a man in dark blue chauffeur's kit asking people if they were Captain Ranklin. It was a distinct shock to Ranklin to hear his name used so publicly when he was working – it reminded him again of how far he had come in eighteen months – and he hurried to hush the man up.

"Mr Quinton's just having a word with his client, sir, so he said would you care to wait in his motor?" He led the way to a spacious black Lanchester parked at the kerb, ushered Ranklin into the back seat, and opened a small built-in cabinet behind the driver's partition. "Whisky, sherry or beer, sir?"

Quinton arrived nearly ten minutes later. But instead of driving off, the chauffeur handed in an attaché case and spread a napkin over Quinton's lap. From the case, Quinton took a china plate, then unwrapped a game pie and several small dishes of salad and pickle. His movements were quick and precise. The last item was an opened but recorked pint of claret. During this, he said: "Could you hear anything in court? What do you think so far? You talk while I eat."

Privately, Ranklin thought that having your lunch in a parked car was a bit showy when you could just as well have been driven back to your office or a chop-house. Perhaps it was another form of advertisement, or perhaps it just came of being born poor.

"It seems," he began slowly, "to be mostly what I think you call 'circumstantial' evidence – though unless you've got someone who saw Langhorn strike a match, I imagine that's what you'd expect. So far, all we've got is that he bought the petrol—"

"He bought *some* petrol."

"Sorry, some – and was off duty at the relevant time. I imagine this afternoon's witness will implicate him more deeply... Is he the one you want to tear apart in cross-examination?"

Quinton, his mouth full, just nodded.

"And, of course, he fled to London. I don't know how much inference one can legally draw from that, but I don't see how anyone can ignore it."

Quinton swallowed. "A fair enough summary. Any gaps or weaknesses?"

"Simply as a story, I'd like to know who told the French police he'd gone to London and who told our police where to find him."

"You'll see winged pigs first. That's the police on both sides protecting informers." He was about to take another mouthful when there was a scuffling sound outside and they looked up to see the chauffeur trying to hustle away a dumpy girl in a big hat and ankle-length coat the vague colour of an Army blanket. Quinton said: "Oh, damn it," handed Ranklin his lunch and got out of the car.

Ranklin watched through the open door and tried to listen, but in the busy street all he heard was that they were speaking French. Quinton had called off the chauffeur and seemed to be pacifying the girl. Her features weren't exactly coarse, just not refined, except for an upper lip in an exaggerated medieval bow shape that gave her a natural pout. Right now, she was pouting fit to bust, her dark eyes adding sullenness. She also had an unnaturally upright stance, as if she were balancing her big hat rather than wearing it. A few untidy strands of brown hair dangled from under it.

After a time, Quinton gave an exaggerated hands-and-shoulders gesture and turned away. She went on pouting but didn't follow as he climbed back into the Lanchester.

"That's the girlfriend of the accused. Apparently spent her own money following him over here." He shook his head. "Young love's seldom any use in court." He reclaimed his lunch and added: "She says she was in bed with him at the time the offence was committed."

At least this promised a more interesting afternoon in court, and Ranklin cheered up. "She's going to say that?"

"Of course, she's not." Then, seeing Ranklin's disappointment, he went on: "Captain, this world spends half its time denying it was fornicating when it was, and the other half claiming it was fornicating when it was doing something worse. Every magistrate's heard it a thousand times. She'd only label herself a whore and thus unreliable as a witness."

Ranklin nodded, understanding, but a little regretful. The girl was standing back on the pavement, still unnaturally upright but now looking lost and somehow alien. A man raised his hat to her and made some inquiry. Ranklin couldn't hear it or her terse reply, but the man recoiled and walked away quickly.

"D'you know her name and address?" Ranklin asked.

Quinton looked at him warily. Ranklin said firmly: "Government business."

"Her name's Mademoiselle Berenice Collomb," Quinton said, "and she doesn't speak any English. I've no idea where she's staying in London."

Ranklin wrote down the name, then asked: "And you said that Langhorn isn't going to say what he was doing, either?"

"He is not."

Ranklin thought this over for a moment, then: "May I ask: is he innocent?"

There was no change in Quinton's expression. Just the sense that he had withdrawn into himself and was thinking that just when Ranklin had been showing signs of intelligence, here came the usual naive old question.

So Ranklin asked it again "You're a man of experience: does your experience tell you he's innocent or guilty?"

Clearly, Quinton's experience had been carefully trained to

avoid such emotive thinking. "If you're asking whether or not he'll be extradited—"

"I'm not. I'm asking—"

"—on the face of it – and that's what *prima facie* means – the case against him is good so far. I still think it may fall apart in a French court, but that's not my concern. He wants me to save him from being extradited, so that's what I'm trying to do. No evidence has been given that he himself is an anarchist, and a rather half-hearted attempt to burn a police station seems only explicable as a political gesture."

"Thank you. Now may we go back to my original question?"

Quinton looked at him for a while, then shrugged quickly and spoke just as quickly. "All right, he's acting as if he were innocent. He'd like to get this over with: stand up, say his piece, be believed and walk out a free man. But that's no way to conduct a defence, as any experienced criminal knows. You take your time: time for something to turn up, for witnesses to forget – sometimes even be persuaded to forget. So, yes, Langhorn's acting as if he were innocent – of this charge.

"But there are degrees of innocence. If I let him be cross-examined this afternoon, I'll tell you just what he, in that innocence, would admit. First, that of course he's an anarchist. Second, that he left a good, respectable job (did you know he'd been a steward on an Atlantic liner?) to work in a filthy dive among other anarchists and known criminals – I've learnt that much about the *Café des Deux Chevaliers*. And lastly, that he thinks the police are the sheepdogs of cruel government shepherds herding the workers to slaughter, and thoroughly deserve burning. That is not my own phrase. Now you should see why I don't want that on the record. And perhaps it answers your question."

"Very fully, thank you."

"And incidentally, remember that someone *did* set fire to that police station, and if Langhorn didn't do it, he probably has a very good idea who did. As I said: degrees of innocence."

There was a gentle rap on the window and Quinton looked up with an impatient sigh. But it was just one of his clerks with a couple of papers to sign.

Ranklin asked: "Then we won't be hearing any of Langhorn's story?"

Quinton smiled briefly. "Oh, we've got nothing to hide. He needed the petrol because he's helping put a motor in a boat in the nearby canal, as I shall tell the court. And at the time of the fire, he was *resting* in his room. But this isn't a case that turns on an alibi. The facts all depend on this afternoon's witness."

"And Langhorn hasn't said any more about his threat...?"

"Captain, I hope you aren't relying on me for any more explanation of that. As I suggested yesterday, I have a certain amount of experience at not being told what I don't want to hear."

Mildly annoyed, though without any justification, Ranklin said: "Never mind. Tomorrow we may well have our own man sharing his cell."

"In Brixton? You won't, you know. Things have changed since Dickens's day. Whenever I go down there, each prisoner has a cell to himself and a number of empty ones left over. They don't like prisoners on remand talking to each other and cooking up mutual alibis."

Blast. And the Commander would say it was another of Ranklin's half-baked, unthought-out wheezes, quite ignoring how eagerly he'd adopted it himself.

Pleased at ending the conversation on a winning note, Quinton smiled and said: "We'd better be getting back. Wish me luck."

"*Hals und Beinbruch,*" Ranklin murmured, and if Quinton really had broken his neck and legs at that moment, he wouldn't have minded at all.

* * *

THERE WAS a public telephone in the ante-chamber to the courts – probably for journalists – and Ranklin caught it at a free time. He called the office and made some arrangements. Then he had at least twenty minutes before the court restarted. He should have lunch, but there was hardly time enough, so he went outside again to light a pipe.

By the doorway was the man in the check suit, and by now a foreign-looking hat, who had been taking so many notes. He was a little taller than Ranklin, a little older, wore a neat grey-flecked black beard and was smoking a small cigar.

They looked at each other, smiled tentatively and then it became impossible not to speak.

"Are you a reporter?" Ranklin asked politely.

"Of a sort."

"For whom?"

"*Les Temps Nouveaux* of Paris." The man had an unidentifiable Continental accent. But that wasn't rare: Continental frontiers were porous and cross-border marriages common. "And yourself?"

"Oh, I'm keeping a watching brief for the American fund defending this lad. Sorry, I should introduce myself: James Spencer."

"Feodor Gorkin." They shook hands, and Gorkin consulted his watch. "The court does not reconvene for half an hour. Do you like a drink?"

"Happy to."

In Covent Garden you're never more than a few steps from a public house, but Ranklin let Gorkin choose which. As they walked the few steps he was trying to dredge up what he knew of *Les Temps*.

"I say, *Les Temps Nouveaux* – isn't that the anarchist..." he searched quickly for an alternative to "rag"; "...er, – publication?"

"It is. I think that is why I am not permitted to sit with the other journalists."

"Ah." Ranklin put on an innocently puzzled expression – easy for him. "I can't make this lad Langhorn out. A waiter in an anarchist café, but no mention of him being an anarchist himself."

"What does Mr Quinton say?"

"Yes, I was talking to him—" since Gorkin had obviously seen that already "—but he wouldn't say much. You know lawyers, I dare say. Some stuff about if you're an anarchist you can't claim you committed a political crime. I'm not sure I follow that, but I don't follow most of what lawyers say..." They were at the bar now. "What would you like?"

They sat down, Gorkin with a brandy and soda, Ranklin with a whisky, and nodded to each other and drank. Gorkin might be ten years older – it was difficult to tell with people of different backgrounds – with a face that was very calm and dark eyes that were quietly watchful. Ranklin said: "Is this *affaire* causing much interest in France, then?"

"But yes. The burning of a police station, the *Préfecture* takes that most seriously. I think they will do anything to get a conviction."

"Ye-es, I suppose it strikes at the whole edifice of law and order... But that's what anarchism's about, isn't it?"

"Striking at law, yes. Laws are not needed, and every law breeds another law until, you say yourself, you cannot understand what lawyers talk about. But order, people will make their own order, without leaders, after government has collapsed."

"Government collapsing? What makes you think...? But then you'd have..."

"Anarchism, not anarchy."

"Oh." Ranklin hadn't planned on getting into a political argument; he was just, suddenly, there. "But I thought you wanted a revolution?"

"That is one way to make a government collapse, yes."

"But do you really think a revolution is likely?"

"Unless government collapses of its own weight, it is

inevitable. Do you know how much your factory workers and farm labourers are now paid?"

"Pretty damn little, I imagine," Ranklin admitted. "But people get killed in revolutions."

"People are killed in wars between nations now. But never the generals and politicians who decide to have a war, just the workers who can gain nothing even if they win."

Ranklin had his puzzled frown working overtime. "Well, I suppose so… But you can't mean in Britain. We haven't had a war for a hundred years."

"Not in South Africa? And other parts of Africa? And all the time in India?"

"Oh well, those are just…"

"Just imperialist wars?"

"Oh, dammit all…" But he didn't want to get embroiled in arguing a defence of empire: Gorkin must have had such discussions so many times before that he always had the answer ready, soft, polite and smiling. It was like playing chess against a master.

So, he switched tack. "But whoever we were fighting, *they* all seemed to have leaders. Don't revolutions throw up leaders, too?"

Gorkin nodded and sighed perfunctorily, as if he always did when about to make this point. "It happens, and it is always a mistake. When a revolution creates leaders, even elects them, the revolution is finished. Anarchists know that people are truly sociable, that if they are left alone they will work at what they do best for themselves and for others. You do not believe this."

"I think people need a framework."

"But then the framework, as you call it, becomes a shell like a… a lobster and holds everyone in, makes them slaves to that shell. Is it not so in England? With your King and your ministers and Parliament and law, your judges and generals, all this becomes your nation that you worship and cannot ever say is wrong. And yet—" he smiled sadly "—it began so harmlessly as just *a framework* to make life more efficient."

The King can do no wrong, Ranklin recalled. Did that still hold good? Certainly, Parliament could do no wrong: it was the final arbiter of such matters. On earth, anyway. "I imagine," he said, "that you don't believe in God?"

"I think that does not matter so much." Gorkin finished his brandy and checked his watch again. "Just look about and ask: does God believe in us?"

As they walked back towards the court, Ranklin's thoughtful frown wasn't all acting, and he asked: "But thinkers, intellectuals perhaps like yourself, aren't you leaders?"

"There will be no laws to make people do as we suggest."

Ranklin nodded.

Gorkin said: "I should enjoy to continue this discussion. Perhaps if you care to call while I am in London...?" He took out a card and wrote an address on the back. Glancing at it, Ranklin noted that Gorkin was a "Dr", but of course that didn't necessarily make him medical; on the Continent, it only meant a university education. He handed over a James Spencer card of his own, with the address as just Whitehall Court.

RAYMOND GUILLET, meat porter aged twenty-five with an address in the rue Petit, looked the part: blunt and hefty, with cropped fair hair and a tiny patch of moustache, dressed in his Sunday suit of shiny black. Above all, he looked *genuine*: a proper workman, worlds away from what Ranklin imagined anarchist café society to be.

Even through an interpreter and with the need to write everything down, it didn't take long to extract Guillet's story. At about half-past eleven he had been returning home when he passed Langhorn, the waiter from the *Deux Chevaliers*. He knew him because he was the only American he had ever met; everybody around there knew him. That night, Langhorn had been carrying a green petrol tin in the direction of the police station.

When the story was finished, Quinton stood up slowly and said: "Half-past eleven at night."

Guillet agreed.

"How did you know the time?"

"I have a watch." There was a silvery – though probably nickel – chain across Guillet's waistcoat.

"Good. Will you show us how it works?"

Ranklin looked on, puzzled, as Guillet fumbled the time-piece from his waistcoat pocket and offered it.

"No, show us yourself. Just open it and re-set the time to an hour ahead."

Then Quinton's tactic became clear. Guillet took two tries to open the case and was quite unable to set the hands.

The lawyer watched with a slight, patient smile. When Guillet's struggle had got almost unbearably painful, he asked: "Is that your own watch?"

The relief on Guillet's face was obvious. "No. I borrowed it. My own is broken. Since two days ago."

"And is this one very different?"

"Yes, quite different."

"Perhaps now you would show it to his worship."

The usher passed it up to the magistrate, who fiddled with it for a few seconds then handed it back impassively. It was quite obviously a standard watch.

But Quinton didn't labour the point any further. "What time do you start work?"

"At four in the morning. Usually."

"Yet on that evening, little more than four hours before you were due to start work, you were still out on the street?"

"Sometimes I stay up late."

"Where had you been that night?"

"In a big café in the Rue Manin."

"Whereabouts in the Rue Manin?"

"Towards the Rue de Crimée."

Quinton pushed his glasses up onto his forehead and peered short-sightedly at a guide-book map. "Ah yes. And to reach your lodging you turned down the Rue du Rhin... Do you then turn left or right into the Rue Petit?"

"Right."

"And coming up the Rue du Rhin, you saw Mr Langhorn carrying a tin of petrol – is that what you said?"

"Yes."

"But obviously you could not see the petrol, could you? How do you know it was not an empty tin?"

"He was leaning with the weight of it."

Quinton appeared foxed by this. He frowned, play-acted himself carrying something heavy, then seemed to get the point. Guillet smiled and relaxed.

"What was the weather like?"

"It was clear. It had rained earlier in the day but not for several hours. Now the streets were mostly dry," Guillet replied confidently, as if that had been an expected question.

"Why did you say he was going towards the police station rather than anywhere else? Was he on that side of the road?"

"Yes."

"And you were hurrying home to bed, weren't you?"

"Not hurrying, no."

"But you didn't pass close to him, did you?"

"Yes. Very close."

"Very close? How close?"

"Less than a metre."

Quinton nodded. "Why did you cross the road?"

Guillet was baffled and suddenly suspicious. "I did not say I crossed the road."

"You turned *right* into the Rue du Rhin, you were going to turn *right* out of it. Why did you cross to the other side, the police station side, where you said Mr Langhorn was?"

Quinton's opposite number, the prosecutor whose name Ranklin hadn't caught, stood up and said mildly: "Your worship, I feel that Mr Quinton is hectoring the witness."

The magistrate nodded but spoke to Quinton: "May I see your map for a moment?"

Quinton passed it to the usher, pointing out the locality, and it went up to the magistrate. He peered closely for a time, then looked up. "Well, Monsieur Guillet?"

"I made a mistake. Langhorn was on my side of the road. But still going up the hill towards the police station."

"A mistake," Quinton said, and after waiting a moment, the interpreter said: "*Une erreur.*"

Quinton selected one of his papers and glanced at it, then: "The street lighting in the Rue du Rhin is turned off at eleven o'clock, is it not?"

"I do not know... No, it can't have been."

Quinton frowned and consulted the paper again. "You say it was on?"

"I think so." Even at that distance, Ranklin could tell Guillet was sweating.

"Now you only think so?"

When Guillet didn't answer, the magistrate said: "What authority do you have for suggesting that the street was no longer lit at that time, Mr Quinton?"

"None whatsoever, your worship," Quinton said blithely. "I had hoped to get an official answer to my query to the relevant authorities by this time but, perhaps owing to the Easter holidays..."

The magistrate frowned down at his papers, thinking. Finally, he said: "So far, I cannot say that this witness has made an entirely favourable impression... This seems to me to be one point of fact which we should have cleared up… Do you think you would have an answer by tomorrow?"

"I would hope so, your worship, but I am quite prepared—"

"No, I'd like to see this sorted out before we proceed any further. I'll adjourn the hearing until ten tomorrow morning."

Quinton bowed perfunctorily, but as he turned away from the bench, his face was a black scowl. He'd had Guillet on the run, and now the witness had time to get his second wind and some intensive coaching. Ranklin sympathised but had no time to commiserate.

CHAPTER FOUR

Outside the court, a Miss Teal from the Bureau's outer office was waiting. She was a spinster of a certain age and impeccable background – indeed, the whole Bureau came of good backgrounds; it was the foregrounds of its agents which had become a little muddy.

Ranklin took her arm and whispered urgently: "I'm James Spencer and we're hired by the American consulate to safeguard Langhorn's interests. That's the girl over there, her name's Mademoiselle Collomb. Offer her a taxi-ride to her lodgings, a cup of tea, any help we can give."

Miss Teal moved in, radiating respectable purpose – which was why Ranklin had telephoned for her. And once she had had time to establish their bona fides, he followed up.

"*Mademoiselle Collomb? Je suis James Spencer...*" He took over the fabrication about the consulate and Berenice listened with a subdued, suspicious pout. But at least listened, and perhaps his reasonably colloquial French helped. He finished up: "And do you understand what will happen next?"

A shrug and a brief shake of her head.

"I have talked to M'sieur Langhorn's lawyer. He—"

"Lawyers." She spat the word.

Ranklin smiled deprecatingly. "But in matters of law, we are in their hands. Now—"

"Then why did he not let me tell the truth? Why did that meat porter tell those lies? You are all the same as the *flics:* bourgeois liars."

Ranklin suddenly saw that their feigned respectability had been a mistake: if Berenice was an anarchist, too, then he and Miss Teal were just more shepherds chivvying the toiling masses to the slaughter-yards – or whatever. Still, he now had to play the hand he had dealt himself.

"I have no concern with politics, only justice." And he said it with a pained expression that constituted a third lie. "I can only try to explain what *Maître* Quinton explained to me. So, would you like a cup of t-coffee?"

She shrugged sullenly but said, "If you want."

As they turned towards the Strand, Ranklin saw Gorkin watching them from the court steps. But there was no reason why Mr Spencer shouldn't be talking to the girlfriend of the accused; he could have been more secretive if need be.

They weaved through a blue tide of policemen spilling out from the station next door, Berenice scowling and muttering while Ranklin kept up a flow of small talk. "Are your lodgings comfortable?"

"I am staying with *camarades.*"

"And do you know London well? A varied city. Not so beautiful as Paris, of course."

"Do you know La Villette?"

"Ah... I have passed through it..."

"Beautiful, hah?"

"Er, no..."

They found one of the shiny new tea-shops and Ranklin ordered two coffees and a tea for Miss Teal. Berenice pouted at the hygienically genteel surroundings and the waitresses in their demure little aprons and frilled caps – badges of servitude, to her, no doubt – and demanded: "Do they have any absinthe?"

Miss Teal's expression would have done credit to an elder of the Scottish kirk, and Ranklin took the opportunity to side with Berenice. "I fear not; the English do not understand these things. But may I offer you a cigarette? – it is probably just as forbidden, but..."

She puffed hungrily, which might have been affectation, but with fluency, which couldn't be. Looking at her across the table, Ranklin saw that her coat wasn't just the colour of an Army blanket but worn to the same near-transparency the Army demanded before changing it. And she had probably dressed in her best clothes to travel to London. He guessed her age at about twenty but knew he could be wrong either way by several years. With such a patchy skin – which might be more the nineteenth *arrondissement* than adolescence – nothing would make her pretty, but more expression and less pout might dispel the expiring-fish look.

He lit his own cigarette. "So, may I try to explain?"

Another sullen nod.

"*Maître* Quinton hopes the meat porter will not be believed and Grover set free. But also, if he can show that Grover has not been proved to be an anarchist, the arson may be seen as a political act – and again he will be freed."

"But he did *not* set fire to the police barracks."

"Yes, yes, but *Maître* Quinton will not be admitting that he did. The act itself, whoever did it, should be accepted as political as long as Grover has not been proved to be an anarchist." Even as he was saying it, he realised that, logically, that was sheer balls. Surely whether an act is political or not must depend on the motive of whoever commits it, and thus on knowing who that person is. Oh well, probably a lawyer could talk his way out of that.

Berenice wasn't impressed, either. "Then they will let him go if

45

he is not an anarchist but send him back to Paris if he is? So, being an anarchist is against the law?"

"No, you can be and say what you like here in England – er, within the law, of course."

"But he must pretend not to be an anarchist to be set free?"

"It more or less seems that way," Ranklin said, getting annoyed with himself, the law and anything else within reach.

She shrugged vigorously, almost toppling her hat. "The law, the law, the law. It is hypocrisy... And you ask why we do not believe in it?"

Ranklin *hadn't* asked but was tempted to lean over and clout her across the chops as a demonstration of what a world without law was like; however, he knew that was – mostly – just his annoyance. He confined himself to saying: "You could have stayed in Paris. But tell me, if Grover is returned for trial in France, what does he fear?"

She pouted at his innocence. "The *flics* paid that meat porter to lie. Naturally, they will pay him again." When he looked appropriately gloomy, she went on: "I know where he stays – at the *Dieudonné* at R-y-d—"

"Ryder Street, I know. French hotel."

"Last night I tried to see him, to ask him why he has sold another worker to the police, but they would not let me." A threadbare and probably angry female...even a French hotel would draw the line somewhere.

"Terrible." Ranklin shook his head. "But something I don't understand: the American Consul who saw M'sieur Langhorn said that he claimed to know of some royal scandal..."

Berenice suddenly smiled. It didn't make her pretty, but for a moment she looked more *gamine* then *poisson*. "Oh, that stupidity. Him and his silly mother with her fairy tales."

"Oh?"

"She told him he is the son of your English King and so he is the next king."

* * *

"WELL, THAT'S WHAT SHE *SAID*," Ranklin reported into a stunned silence. They had gathered in the Commander's office: The Commander himself and Lieutenant Jay, who was there because Ranklin had insisted they needed another pair of hands, and particularly feet. Right now, however, Jay was coming out of his concussion into delighted but stifled laughter.

The Commander, not in the least delighted, said: "The boy must be barmy."

To distract attention from young Jay, Ranklin said: "Of course, I suppose you can't be sure who your father really is; by definition, you aren't around at the time. It's the mother's word that matters, and this could tie up with the letter she sent to the consulate. And her being English originally, I suppose."

"Any chance of getting hold of a birth certificate?" the Commander growled.

"What's the betting that it doesn't say the Ki – no, Prince George in those days – is the father?" Jay asked cheerfully.

Ignoring that, Ranklin said: "The boy must have been brought up in America, but I don't know where he was born."

There was another long silence. The Commander broke it again by growling: "But he's such a bloody *dull* king."

"But equipped with all the normal urges," Lieutenant Jay smiled. He had a pleasant smile, along with slimness, dashing, clean-cut good looks, longish fair hair – all refined through a line of ancestors able to afford the most beautiful women of their day. He could no more pass for a coal-miner than a kingfisher could, but then, the secrets of Europe weren't kept in coal-mines but in chancelleries and drawing rooms. And in such settings, it was difficult to see where Jay ended, and the Louis Quinze furniture began.

But that was only the half of Jay that you saw. The other half, which should include concepts of honour, scruples, honesty, was unseen because, Ranklin suspected, it didn't exist. He would trust Jay with his life, but not much else.

The Commander added: "You didn't get much out of this French floozie, did you?"

Ranklin wasn't standing for that. "Damn it all, if I'd started cross-examining her, she'd have seen I was taking it seriously and then *she'd* take it seriously. And God knows what she'd do or say to get her lover out of jail." He stared defiantly at the Commander.

"All right, all right," the Commander soothed – but then another thought struck him. "If this girl told you, what's to stop her babbling to anybody else?"

"Me," Ranklin said, still belligerently, "telling her she was likely to make Grover more enemies than friends over here if she did."

"Good. Excellent... Then I suppose we have to look into the chances of this being true."

Jay stared. "That this lad's the next *king*?"

"Of course, he's not. He's an American citizen."

"Oh, that can't be any bar. We took William and Mary off the shelf from Holland, and the Hanovers from Germany and the present House of Saxe-Coburg from...well, Saxe-Coburg, I suppose." The long-established British families could regard the Royal Family as very much Johnny-come-latelies.

"The first thing," the Commander said firmly, "is to discover whether there *might* be anything in what the lad says about his father. What's his age again?"

"Twenty-three," Ranklin said. "And his birthday was given in court as November the twenty-first, so his date of conception must have been in February 1890."

There was a pause while they checked his arithmetic.

Ranklin went on: "If the mother met and married an American merchant sailor in this country, that could be Southampton. American passenger ships come in there. And it's just round the corner from Portsmouth, where quite likely Prince George was stationed in the Navy."

The Commander made an expression of distaste; things were fitting together too well. He nodded at Jay. "Get down to Somerset House first thing tomorrow and look for a marriage certificate from Southampton or Portsmouth for Langhorn-Bowman... But that apart, it must be easier to trace the movements of the King – Prince George, as you say – than the woman."

"Not all that easy," Ranklin warned. "At the time he was doing mostly just normal naval things—" now the Commander's expression turned sour; after all, he should know what "normal naval things" included, "—not worth reporting. But someone can try going through the Court pages of *The Times* for that spring—"

"Never mind that," Jay said, "what we need is my old nanny."

The Commander stared, then exploded. "Are you suggesting we include *HER* in this...this gathering?"

"No, of course not, sir. But she was – still is, I'm sure – a terrific monarchist. She followed the doings of the Little Princes, as she called them, almost day-to-day. Used to fill dozens of scrapbooks with bits cut out of newspapers and magazines. My father thought she was potty and she thought he was bound for hell-fire."

"Both right, I dare say," he added thoughtfully.

The Commander demanded: "Can you lay hold of the right scrapbook, d'you think?"

"Perhaps this evening. She's with a family in Berkeley Square now."

"Get round there as soon as we're finished." He shook his head mournfully. "The Secret Service Bureau borrowing some dotty old nanny's royal scrapbook. God Almighty... What else?"

Ranklin said: "We'll have the Paris view of the crime itself when O'Gilroy gets in tonight. And after that, he'll be sitting around with nothing to do while we buzz about like bees."

The Commander looked at him. "And you still want him to join our select throng, don't you? I'd've thought the last thing we want in all this is an Irish renegade."

"Odd, ain't it?" Jay mused. "The Irish want a republic but the Englishman they hate most was our leading republican and regicide, Cromwell."

"Don't try to make sense of history," the Commander warned, "particularly not in Ireland."

Ranklin said: "And when we're finished here, I want to try and get a word with the Paris meat porter who gave evidence today."

"D'you think it's worth the risk? I don't want us getting sidetracked by the crime itself. It's hardly relevant, now."

"It's very relevant to Grover Langhorn, and it's what he might say next that worries us." Ranklin looked at the Commander and shrugged; the Commander looked and shrugged back. Permission, reluctantly, granted.

Serious for once, Jay said: "Surely it's still what the mother might say that really matters... And incidentally, why isn't she over here, standing by her only son – is he her only son? – in his hour of need?"

"From the way she's vanished," the Commander said, "it sounds as if she expects us – somebody, anyway – to be looking for her and an explanation of that letter. And we're a bit stuck, there: we can't ask the French to help because they'd ask why... No, for the moment, we stick to finding out whether we *need* to find her. Now, do we have anything else? Well, I have: we're going to have to tell the Palace." That brought a sudden silence. "It risks secrecy, but it's pure self-preservation: if they find out for themselves that we're investigating His Majesty, that'll be the end of the Bureau."

"I say," breathed Jay, "are we going to ask if the King really was once roger-the-lodgering this female?"

The Commander ignored him. "I think he's back from Windsor by now, but anyway, I'll fix a meeting with one of his secretaries. You'll come too, Ranklin."

"Aren't I supposed to be back at Bow Street?"

"This takes precedence, but it all depends on what time we can fix a meeting at the Palace."

Ranklin nodded unenthusiastically and Jay, perhaps trying to make amends for his levity, said: "I suppose we have noticed that the King's going on an official visit to Paris next week?"

They hadn't, of course: The King's movements didn't usually concern the Bureau. So, they sat and thought about it for a while. At last the Commander said: "Is there any reason to suppose that isn't pure coincidence?"

Except that, professionally, they didn't like coincidences, nobody could think of one. Jay said: "The British papers won't touch a story about the King having a bastard son. But the Continental and American papers would lap it up. Particularly with the Paris visit putting him in the news for once." He shrugged. "But that still doesn't make it anything but coincidence."

Ranklin said: "If the royal visit's a goodwill thing, it may make us less willing to undo that goodwill by refusing to extradite Langhorn. But again, that doesn't mean it's anything but coincidence, either."

The Commander shook his head slowly and sighed. "But he *is* such a dull king."

* * *

WHEN RANKLIN GOT BACK from the Hotel *Dieudonné,* O'Gilroy had obviously just got in. There was an unopened Gladstone bag in the middle of the floor, a cap and coat thrown on to a chair, and O'Gilroy himself in another with a cigarette and large glass of whisky. He was lanky and loose-limbed with dark hair and he looked like an intellectual buccaneer such as schoolgirls dream about and don't exist. However, if they did, they too would come from Ireland. He was in his early thirties.

"Did you have a good crossing?" Ranklin asked cheerfully.

"Terrible." But O'Gilroy could find breaking waves on a

skating rink. "Most jest the fuss of it. Cab in Paris and then train and boat and train and London cab, with tickets and papers and two sorts of money all the way... Ye never get time to settle. Ah, I'm getting old and soft. Thank God." He reached inside his jacket and handed over a wad of notepaper. "That's yer...report, like—"

"Résumé."

"—of what ye wanted. Made quite a fuss, it did. Say 'anarchist' in Paris and the rozzers, *Préfecture* and *Sûreté* both, they throw a fit. They want this feller Langhorn serious. Can ye tell me why we're interested?"

Ranklin had been careful not to ask the Commander if he could – the answer must have been "No" – so one might say he hadn't been told not to. "I can drop a few hints, but if you haven't eaten, call down and get something sent up. And the same for me." He sat down to riffle through the notes. After a year in Paris, O'Gilroy's spoken French was still "picturesque", to put it politely, and his knowledge of French literature nil, but he read their journalistic jargon fluently.

Passing a bookshop, Ranklin had picked up a copy of *Our Sailor King*, a biographical work for those of a reading age to cope with pictures; he'd been hoping to pinpoint some dates in the King's career. It now lay on a table near the voice-pipe and O'Gilroy picked it up. "Jayzus – are ye studying for a promotion exam?"

OVER SUPPER – it turned out that what O'Gilroy had been missing was mulligatawny soup and game pie – Ranklin explained what was going on. When he reached the allegation about the King, O'Gilroy reacted as he had feared: gave a sardonic cackle and observed: "Ah well, kings will be kings."

"Damn it, the thing's far from *proved*—"

"And 'tis our job to see it never is, right? Funny job for a secret service, with all the trouble there is in the world, but..." His shrug was quite as expressive as his laugh.

Ranklin's voice was tightly controlled. "You're jumping to an assumption just because he's the King. With anyone else you'd wait for some facts. As for the Bureau's involvement, that was originally because Corinna wished it on us – and because the good name of the King is part of our national..." Did he mean "fabric" or "constitution" or what? He waved a hand irritably. "Anyway, what would happen if somebody claimed to be the bastard son of the French President?"

"Be told to get to the back of the queue," O'Gilroy said promptly.

"All right, let's say the Kaiser, then?"

"Ah, there," O'Gilroy acknowledged, "probly be in jail if'n he wasn't lynched first. Ye made yer point. But are we looking to find out if it's true?"

"We need to know if it's possible, then if it's likely. But whether anything could be proved after twenty-three years... Still, that could work as much against us as for us."

"What's Mrs Finn think of it all?"

"She doesn't know the whole story and, please God, never will. She's already blackmailing us for some concession for her bank."

This time, O'Gilroy's laugh was genuine amusement. "Ah, never gives up, she doesn't." He thought for a while. "But jest suppose ye find it could be true, do ye fiddle the books to get the lad off at his trial here? And after that, how d'ye keep him quiet?"

Ranklin sighed. He had been so busy watching where he put his feet in the hour-by-hour investigation that he hadn't looked ahead to the big questions. "I don't really know... What the lad himself says is just hearsay. In the long run, it's what his mother says that matters."

"She wrote the letter ye told me 'bout, didn't she?"

Ranklin nodded but said nothing. He had the pages of the résumé spread beside his plate and had been skimming through

O'Gilroy's schoolroom copperplate script. There was no doubt about the excitement the fire had triggered. Whether the police originally took their tone from the journals or vice versa, they were now feeding off each other in spiralling hysteria. Anarchist outrages obviously sold newspapers this season.

The only calming note came from the *Sûreté Générale,* but one editorial suggested this was just sour grapes. In effect, although presumably not intention, Paris had two competing police forces: the *Préfecture* and the *Sûreté,* and when it came to catching anarchists, real or alleged, alive or dead, the competition was no-holds-barred.

"Did you form an opinion on the case?" he asked.

"Jest from the newspapers. And guessing, mebbe."

"We're not lawyers; let's have it."

"Then sure enough the boy could've done it – and he could've shot the President and cabinet jest as easy. I mean he's a real anarchist, drunk on the stuff like he's never tasted that bottle before. Left a good job on an ocean liner—" Ranklin hadn't noticed that that detail, so carefully kept out of the Bow Street court by Noah Quinton, was available to any Parisian reader. The law, he reflected, was like a fixed telescope: it magnified what it saw, but it missed an awful lot; "—to work in a stinking shebeen. I mean a real hell's kitchen of a place."

"You've seen this *Deux Chevaliers* café? Been into it?"

"Went down there this lunchtime. But not in. Yer not paying me enough to get meself knifed for a police spy." He sounded offended to have found a place too disreputable even for himself; after all, among the toffs of the Bureau, his forte was knowing the underside of life.

"Did you look at the police station where—?"

"I did."

Ranklin thought. Then he gathered together O'Gilroy's notes and handed them back. "Here, you make a report to the

Commander tomorrow. Give him the full *à la carte* and he should invite you to join our charmed circle and we can do this properly."

O'Gilroy put on his lopsided smile that, once you knew him, could have so many variants; this time it was rueful cynicism. "Nice of ye to say so... Only I wisht it was a real job and not hauling the King's wild oats out of a fire."

CHAPTER FIVE

Major Alfred St Claire looked *correct*, but also as if he hadn't been born that way. You could well imagine his stocky, broad-shouldered figure leaning on a farm gate and being knowledgeable about turnips. Instead, a service career and then the Royal Household had smoothed him. His dark hair was now sleek, his long face pink and shiny, even his wide cavalry moustache (he hadn't actually been in the cavalry; he was nominally a Marine) looked sleekly dashing.

And by now he had a courtier's or woman's ability to wear anything and make it seem natural. On him, a frock coat wasn't awkward or old-fashioned; indeed, it made Ranklin in his severe dark lounge suit feel like a tradesman. Perhaps he should have worn uniform, like the Commander, only that wouldn't have been correct because he had thankfully got rid of the regulation moustache which, on him, refused to grow to more than a schoolboy wisp. And the Palace was, after all, the fountain-head of correctness.

With old-fashioned courtesy, St Claire did his best to make them feel at home, coming out from behind his writing-desk and joining them in the elegantly uncomfortable chairs crowded around the tiny fireplace. The room was small, with a view over the inside courtyard, and true to the Palace's reputation, cold even when it was unseasonably warm outside.

When the Commander had been given permission to smoke and stuck his pipe in his mouth, he began: "There's a lad, an American citizen, now in Brixton jail because the French want us to extradite him for setting fire to a police station in Paris."

He paused, and St Claire said: "Yes, I read about the case in this morning's papers. He's an anarchist, isn't he?"

Ranklin said: "Yes, but it's legally important to keep that out of court – according to the lad's lawyer."

The Commander resumed: "It appears that if he is extradited, he'll claim publicly that he's the son of the King."

Perhaps Ranklin was disappointed when St Claire merely nodded.

"His mother was an English girl called Enid Bowman. She wrote the American consulate here a letter that can be read as endorsing the boy's claim. We think she's in Paris – France, anyway – and probably in hiding."

When the Commander didn't go on, St Claire asked: "Is that all you can tell me, Commander?"

"We know more about the crime itself, but what seems to matter most is what the mother may claim. Even if we could go direct to her, it might be a mistake to do so – but an indirect approach is difficult and slow to do secretly. For example, we don't want to involve the police."

"How far have you gone with investigating this?"

"Hardly anywhere. We only heard the exact nature of the threat yesterday evening. I thought it best to come to you before going any further."

St Claire tried to put his coffee cup down on a small table already overloaded with the tray, then put it on the floor instead. "Do you expect me to ask His Majesty if there could be any truth in this?"

The Commander took it evenly. "It would short-cut our investigations. And however careful we are, just asking questions endangers secrecy."

St Claire shifted in his seat. "You do remember that We are going to Paris next week?" There was a definite capital letter on that "We".

The Commander nodded.

"Is this just a coincidence?"

"With what little we know, we simply can't tell," the Commander said blandly.

St Claire gazed out of the window, stroked his moustache, and then, staring at the merely smouldering fire in the grate, began to speak. "His father would simply have brazened this out; sworn it couldn't be true in the highest court and on any bible you cared to hand him. On the grounds that the honour of a British king was far more important than any truth – possibly more important than perjuring his immortal soul. But at least that would have been a matter between him and his God, and not involved us of the Household." He sighed. "I suppose that the upbringing of royal children must always be a problem, but I doubt the answer is to shunt them off into the Navy at the age of twelve. Whatever is said about Queen Victoria not letting Prince Edward see state papers and the like, at least he was *around.* He met people, knew who was who in Europe. Whereas chugging around the Cannibal Isles shaking hands...hardly the best preparation for the subtleties of a modern state. The one thing one can say about His Majesty is that he sets an example to us all as a husband and family man..." His voice dwindled into silent thought. Then he said, almost to himself: "I certainly find it difficult to accept that a British king is for no more than *that...* Nevertheless, it is virtually the only strong card in his hand."

"And you'd like to keep it that way," the Commander nodded. "I quite understand that. But if His Majesty would say if this *could* be true—"

"Forgive me, but you may have missed my point. His Majesty is *learning* what being King of Great Britain means. That said, if he were now told that he might have fathered a bastard, he may well, given his inexperience except in the naval tradition of accepting personal responsibility, admit it openly. And where would we all be then?"

The Commander and Ranklin looked at each other. After a while, the Commander said: "So it may be a matter of saving the King from himself?"

"I don't need to tell you that the British monarchy is going through a difficult patch. In his first four years on the throne, the King has faced the Prime Minister's blackmail – it was nothing less – about reforming the Lords, radicalism, socialism, republicanism, women's suffrage – and now the Irish Home Rule Bill and the likelihood of civil war in either North or South. A successful visit to Paris could make all the difference. It happens to be of particular political importance: the French loved the late King Edward and were rather annoyed that King George chose to visit Germany first – although it was, for a family wedding, quite unavoidable.

"Now you tell me that the visit is threatened by prospective headlines trumpeting a Paris anarchist as the true heir to the throne. Oh, I know he can't be, but that won't stop the French press. This really couldn't have come at a worse moment. So, I ask again: are you sure this is pure coincidence?"

In a marginally controlled voice the Commander said: "And I repeat what I said a few minutes ago, since I haven't learnt anything new since then: I've no bloody idea."

Quite unoffended, St Claire leant forward and gave the fire a poke. Ranklin was coming to an odd – and almost reluctant – conclusion about him: he didn't despise them. The normal reaction for anyone suspecting he was a spy was distaste, with at most some sympathy of the "I suppose someone has to do it" sort. But St Claire was treating them as brother officers who'd been handed a tricky task, that was all. Ranklin couldn't help warming to the man.

Now St Claire was saying: "We seem to be talking about a time well before I joined the Household..."

"Around February 1890," Ranklin said. "When Prince George was a naval lieutenant doing a gunnery course at HMS *Excellent* at Portsmouth." Nanny's scrapbook had given him that much.

"And that is the...the relevant time? Thank you, Captain... I should have asked this before: does anyone in the government know anything about this?"

The Commander said firmly: "Not from us. And I've no reason to believe they'd know from any other source."

"Hm. Thank goodness for rather large mercies. So it wasn't they who passed the problem to you?"

"It came to us," the Commander said, "by a rather round-about route. I don't know if you have the time...?"

"I think I'd better have."

* * *

WHEN THE COMMANDER HAD FINISHED, St Claire fetched a notepad from his table and scribbled. The Commander winced at seeing things committed to paper but said nothing.

St Claire looked up. "And how many are aware of this claim? So far, I've got the boy himself, his mother, this girl from Paris, yourself and Captain Ranklin. How many more in your Bureau?"

The Commander hesitated, then said: "I think I have to say, 'As many as I choose to tell'. If we're to go on investigating, I need to pick the right man for each aspect of it. They wouldn't be in the Bureau if they weren't trustworthy."

The old bastard does stick by us, Ranklin thought. Though, mind you, to say anything else would reflect badly on himself. Still, it does bypass the problem of explaining O'Gilroy.

"Very well. You say the boy's lawyer doesn't want to know? I assumed *Mr* Noah Quinton—" the emphasis showed that Quinton's reputation had got as far as the Palace "—wanted to know everything, but I suppose he must have a strong instinct for self-preservation. And so far, no politicians. What about this American vice-consul and Miss...Mrs Finn? Is she that daughter of Reynard Sherring?"

"She is. They know that a secret – an *alleged* secret – is involved, but not what it is. I doubt the vice-consul wants to know more, he's already concealing things from his superiors, but Mrs Finn..." And he looked hard at Ranklin.

"Not from me. But she does talk to people. More importantly, people talk to her."

"So, she remains," St Claire said, "a weak link."

"If we're looking for weak links," Ranklin said evenly, "we've got the boy himself, his mother and the girl Berenice Collomb. God knows what they're going to do."

"But in the short term," St Claire said, "that seems to depend on the outcome of the case. It was going on this morning, wasn't it?" He glanced towards his table and sighed. "I'm sure the world thinks that all I have to do is lift that telephone and I'm immediately in touch with the wisdom of Solomon. Whereas most of the time I daren't even suggest the Palace wants to know something without starting a riot of speculation."

"Let Ranklin call our office," the Commander said promptly. "We've got a man in court and they should be breaking for lunch about now."

So Ranklin found himself speaking to first the Palace switchboard lady and then the Bureau's, both chosen for well-bred reticence rather than technical skill.

Behind him, St Claire was saying: "If it comes down to it, at least the current Home Secretary is a lawyer. And in my experience, lawyers seldom see the law as something rigid. More like a palette from which they can select the right colours for any situation. I'm sure that if he had a word with the Lord Chancellor – if that's the right person – Bow Street would quickly get the idea that a verdict *against* extradition would be preferred. Even better if the verdict seems to hang in the balance, as you say."

You can't do that, Ranklin thought instinctively. But why not? He himself broke or ignored laws all the time, usually other countries' but sometimes Britain's as well; that was now his job. How was this different? Were there any lines to be drawn? And why was he drawing one at someone seated beside the fountain-head of justice itself proposing to rape the law and then pretend it was still *virgo intacta?*

"It might get the French up in arms," the Commander observed. "There's an appeals procedure, I understand, which could spin it out another two weeks or more."

"Hm. I'll think about that... How am I to keep in touch with you, by the way?"

"I've decided to revive the old Steam Submarine Committee. Good practice to cloak a new purpose in an existing body and I think I'm still chairman of it, though it hasn't met for ten years. Not since we decided that steam-powered submarines were pure balls, in fact. Ranklin here is the new secretary."

Still muddled by his own emotions, Ranklin barely registered that he'd got a new job he hadn't been told about. Then Jay came on the other end of the telephone.

"So," the Commander went on, "if you mention the Committee in any telephone call or message, we'll know exactly what you're talking about."

"And vice versa. Excellent," St Claire murmured.

Ranklin put down the telephone and said tonelessly: "The case was adjourned for another day. The meat porter, Guillet, has gone missing."

* * *

SITTING in a rocking corner of the express to Portsmouth, Ranklin watched the gentle Hampshire countryside unreeling past and thought of what he should have said to avoid being sent on this futile jaunt. Too late now, of course. And he couldn't even alter the minutes of the meeting to make the injustice plain, because the Bureau kept no minutes. Good for secrecy, bad for clarity. People unconsciously developed what had been said until they were convinced that it *had* been said, or agreed, or decided. Good minute-keeping prevented that.

Once, he'd been good at minutes himself. Of mess meetings, staff pow-wows and the like. Could he still do it?

The Steam Submarine Committee met in Whitehall Court at approximately 12 noon on April 16, 1914.

In the chair: Commander C

In attendance: Capt R, Secty; Lieut Jay; Mr O'G

A selection of cold comestibles and beverages was provided by the ground-floor restaurant. Lieut Jay commented unfavourably on the quality of the sausage rolls.

The minutes of the last meeting, held some ten years previously, having been presumed lost, the Chairman opened the proceedings by inviting Lieut Jay to report on events at Bow St Police Court that morning. Jay said that the witness Guillet had failed to appear for his resumed cross-examination. The barrister representing the Crown apologised for the witness's absence and said he had been assured that every effort was being made by the police to find him. Broad hints were then dropped by Mr Noah Quinton that he had been about to expose said witness as a perjurer and this might not be unconnected with his disappearance. The magistrate then adjourned the hearing for twenty-four hours.

The Chairman said he had been told by Captain R that he had seen the deceased witness on the previous night but been assured that he had not brought about the witness's decease, although he was sure that Captain R had been justified in doing so if he had, in fact, done so. When Captain R could get a word in edgeways, he said that he had neither killed nor interfered with said witness, merely listened to him in a nearby public house. He might have pointed out that the witness's testimony could result in a perjury charge, but had come to the conclusion that the witness was more frightened of some unnamed person or persons than he was of such a charge,

Discussion ensued concerning the possible identity of the above-mentioned person (s), the Paris Préfecture of police being mentioned.

Mr O'G opined that he did not think the Préfecture was guilty of such conduct, nor that it really intended to put Grover Langhorn on trial in France. In his view, its intention was to establish a hold over him and compel him to give evidence incriminating others at the Café des Deux Chevaliers. The police would rather convict such others than an American youth.

He further opined that little distinction was drawn by the Paris police between anarchists who robbed banks etc. as "expropriation" and criminals who just robbed banks etc. Lieut Jay said that casual discussions at Bow St had led him to believe that London policemen thought the same way.

The Chairman asked Mr O'G if he thought Grover Langhorn was a sincere anarchist. O'G said that he had received that impression from Paris newspapers which had interviewed Mme Berenice Collomb. She had been represented as saying that Langhorn wanted to slaughter every capitalist in the world but would not, on the other hand, hurt a fly. Capt R commented that such a remark seemed to him consistent with Mme Collomb's mode of thought.

Some pointless discussion then ensued. The Chairman called the meeting to order and asked Lieut Jay what he had discovered at Somerset House. Jay reported that he had uncovered a marriage certificate showing that Ethan James Langhorn and Enid Elizabeth Bowman were married at St Jude's church in Southsea, Portsmouth, on May 9, 1890. The Chairman calculated that the bride had then been nearly three months pregnant and commented favourably on her skill in acquiring a husband in that time.

Continuing, Jay said that the certificate revealed the bride to have

*been aged 25, the groom a boatswain aged 42, his address being a
seamen's hostel in Southampton. The bride's address was given as 15
Abercromby Road, Southsea. No parents were among the witnesses. Of
these, three were female and assumed to be friends of the bride; the
fourth, George Pavlides, might have been a shipmate of the groom.*

*It was then decided by the Chairman that Capt R and Mr O'G
would proceed immediately to Portsmouth to see if they could acquire
any additional information, despite the passage of some twenty-three
years. There being no objections to this except from Capt R and Mr O'G,
the meeting was declared closed at approximately 1.30 pm.*

He must have been moving his lips, because O'Gilroy said:
"Talking to yeself again? Bad sign, that."

"Had a nice refreshing sleep?"

"Wasn't sleeping, jest thinking." O'Gilroy found and lit a
cigarette. "That marriage, with the American sailor, it went
wrong. Or mebbe the feller died a while gone."

Ranklin raised his eyebrows.

"Why else would ye tell yer son his father wasn't really his
father? Either ye've come to hate the feller or he's been long
anough dead it don't matter, and ye reckon ye can tell the truth –
and mebbe make a bob or two out of it."

Ranklin thought this over and accepted it. The trouble with
high-flown meetings around big tables was forgetting that behind
all the national implications lay very simple human emotions.
"You should have said that at the meeting."

But O'Gilroy just grunted. He said as little as possible at such
meetings. Perhaps it had been his years in the ranks, perhaps the
more dangerous years in the ranks of those plotting for a free
Ireland, but the result was that he was the most secretive and
distrusting of them all.

If O'Gilroy got on a tram in a strange city, he already knew
which door to use, how one paid, generally what to do next.
Nobody had told him, he'd just watched how others did it. He

simply hated being conspicuous, of giving away his ignorance or next move by asking – as Ranklin would instinctively have done. So, while Ranklin's protection was that he seemed a simple, open-faced English gentleman, O'Gilroy's was in not being noticed at all. Neither was right nor wrong, except for himself, and essentially, they were complementary. As Ranklin had once put it, they might add up to one competent spy. The hope was that nobody would expect a spy to come in two halves.

Beyond the train's window, a fuzz of bright green, brought out by the last few days of sunshine, was blurring the skeleton hands of the winter trees beside the track. The world was waking again, and Ranklin had felt safer when it was asleep.

CHAPTER SIX

From Portsmouth town station they took a motor-taxi, dropping Ranklin at St Jude's Church and taking O'Gilroy on to Abercromby Road. Ranklin hadn't hoped to find anything more from the parish register – a marriage certificate is simply copied from that – but the vicar might still be the one whose name was on the certificate and remember more.

After twenty-four years he wasn't the same, of course, and his predecessor was dead. Nor was the current incumbent, who'd had a properly busy Easter, in any rush to help. His congregation included too many senior naval officers – St Jude's was quite fashionable, by Portsmouth standards – for him to be impressed with self-important civilians.

Ranklin's only consolation was thinking that, if they'd swapped jobs, O'Gilroy might have ended up in custody for striking a "stupid heathen Protestant".

However, Ranklin kept his temper and finally the vicar commented: "Odd, this interest in that wedding. I had the lady's sister asking earlier this week."

"Really? Does she live locally?"

"No, she said she was staying at the Queen's – a Mrs Simmons, I think."

Ranklin, who'd had no idea there *was* a sister, was afire to be off, but now the vicar had melted to his politeness and held him for a five-minute lecture on the care of the vicarage lawn.

* * *

O'GILROY WAS LOITERING on the pavement, wearing a rather papist expression.

"Nothing on the wedding," Ranklin said, "except that Enid Langhorn's sister was asking about it a day or two back."

"Mrs Simmons? She was asking at Abercromby Road, too. Staying at the Queen's Hotel."

"Right, then…" He looked at his watch. "No, time's getting on. You get round to the Town Hall and see if there's any trace of the women witnesses."

"Enjoy yer tea," O'Gilroy said sourly.

"If she's left, I'll see you at the Town Hall."

* * *

BUT LUCKILY, she hadn't. She sent down a message that she'd join him in the lounge in fifteen minutes. The Queen's was clearly one of the top hotels in town, so Mrs Simmons had done better in life than Enid with her last-known La Villette address. Ranklin waited among the inevitable potted palms and gazed out across Southsea Common to the sea, sparkling in the afternoon sun but dotted with the grey industrial shapes of the Navy coming and going. Why do they say "steaming" when they're so obviously smoking?

"Mrs Simmons?" She was short, with a cottage-loaf figure and dressed a few years behind fashion in layers of cream muslin –

probably – for a skirt, a tightly corseted waist, a lace stock and a wide hat. A year ago, before he had met Corinna, Ranklin wouldn't even have noticed this much about her; he wouldn't have been sure it was proper to.

He introduced himself under the well-worn alias of James Spencer and tried to regularise the position by explaining: "I was asked by Mr Noah Quinton, the solicitor who's defending your nephew at Bow Street –I assume you've heard about that? – to see if I could trace your sister."

"Yes." She smiled a little wanly. "That's what I'm trying to do myself."

They sat down, Mrs Simmons – or her corset – keeping her back rigid. But the face peeking out from under the hat was snub-nosed and perky, a young expression betrayed by the creases of age. She offered to pour her own tea, but Ranklin said he might as well carry on. It gave him something to do, because he was baffled about what to say next.

Mrs Simmons said: "I know she was in Paris, but I didn't get any answer to my letters, so I came here just on an off chance. She lived in Abercromby Road for several years, you know." Her voice was clear, but somehow studied and careful. Perhaps a sign that marriage had taken her a step up in the world.

"Yes. We got that address from her marriage certificate." But how did he broach the question of what she had been doing in Abercromby Road? Let alone with whom. "Mr Quinton very much wants her to appear as a character witness for young Grover."

"I'm sure he does. I really can't understand why she hasn't been in touch with him." Then a thought seemed to flit across her neat, round face. "Unless it was…well, it was something May told me, though—"

"May? I thought her name was Enid?"

"Oh, May was her stage name. Didn't you know she was an

actress? She wasn't one of the lucky ones, but she had a few small parts at the Theatre Royal. Of course, that caused a terrible row with our parents, Pa in particular; he didn't want any daughter of his going on the stage. That's why she left home, of course."

"Was this in Portsmouth?"

"Oh no, we come from Northumberland."

Ranklin offered more tea. "You were saying that your sister told you something...?"

"Yes." She paused. "She said...well, as I say, I think she was having trouble making ends meet as an actress and she did have a lot of evenings free and...well, a girl has to live, doesn't she? She began to...well, *entertain* gentlemen. I do hope I'm not shocking you, Mr Spencer."

"Not at all. Please go on."

"So – she told me – one day a gentleman came to see her, and he said that someone very important had seen her on the stage and would like to meet her and, if it went well, then perhaps they could come to an *arrangement*. He meant an arrangement about money, that she wouldn't entertain any other gentlemen except this very important gentleman. And May said she'd meet this very important gentleman and see how it went and, well...you'll never guess who this gentleman was. It was Prince George who's now King George. There! I said you wouldn't believe it."

For a moment, Ranklin didn't know what expression to put on: shock? disbelief? certainly not ready acceptance. He quickly settled for saying: "I see," in an impressed tone.

"So, this went on for about a year, I think, but you know what a naval officer's life is like: off to sea and coming back at odd times and feeling frisky right there and then and...well, one of them made a mistake and she found herself in pig. Pregnant," she explained quickly. "Naturally, she wasn't saying anything to him, and he was off to command a gunboat at Chatham by the time she was sure, and then he went to the North American Squadron for a year and she married a bosun from the American Line and went to live in America.

"So, you see, Grover's really the son of the King and I suppose that makes him the next king, doesn't it?"

"Oh Lord, no," Ranklin said instinctively, and was then surprised at her startled expression. Had she really been thinking of a luxurious future for herself as a royal aunt? "That is," he went on, "I'm no lawyer myself, but I'm sure that only the legitimate son of the King could accede. And even if it were possible, it would be your sister's word against all the ranks of..." he'd been going to say "Tuscany" but she wouldn't recognise the quotation; "...the Royal family, the courts, the government... And against the evidence of his birth certificate, I dare say. You don't happen to know if she pretended to her husband that he was the real father?"

"I suppose she must have done," she said, with her thoughts elsewhere; she really must have dreamt of a courtly life.

"So, if we can get your sister to see Mr Quinton, I don't think it would help Grover if she repeated what she told you."

"Not even if she could prove it better? I mean there's others who must've seen George visiting, she had a maid – she told me – at the time, if I could find her—"

"Mrs Simmons, I'm quite sure there's no power on this earth that can make young Grover the next king."

"No, I suppose not, with *them* out to stop it." She sounded surprisingly vicious.

"And I think she's got a more urgent problem with Grover at the moment."

"How's that going?"

"I understand from Mr Quinton that the chief witness for the French police turned out to be very unreliable in court, but now he's vanished with his evidence unfinished. I don't think anybody knows what's going to happen next. Do you have your sister's last address in Paris?"

She fiddled inside her handbag and then said: "I thought I had it here, but perhaps I can remember: 18 Rue Castelnaudry..." That was the same address they'd got already, but Ranklin noted it down.

"And are you coming to London to see Grover? I'm sure Mr Quinton could arrange it."

She hesitated. "I don't hardly know him, what with him being born and brought up in America. I thought perhaps I'd go to Paris and see if I can find May myself."

"It's a bit city – and the area they were living in, La Villette, is a pretty rough neighbourhood. Be prepared for that."

She smiled. "I've been in some rough neighbourhoods in my life, Mr Spencer. I'll get by."

"Let me give you Noah Quinton's address. I hope you'll let him know if you find anything."

He wrote it on the back of a James Spencer calling-card. She looked at both sides. "And you said you worked for Mr Quinton?"

"I undertake research for the legal profession. *Not* a private detective." He'd thought up that statement, with its proud disclaimer, on the train but the vicar hadn't even asked.

"Not the government?"

He blinked. "No. I have done work for government departments, but this is strictly for Mr Quinton. And really for Grover, of course."

"You haven't asked me to keep it secret that I've talked to you."

"Why should I?" If she wanted to follow up James Spencer she'd eventually run into a brick wall – but before that, he should have heard she was looking. Still, he'd best warn Quinton that a Mr Spencer had been working for him.

She made a fluttery gesture. "Oh, I just thought lawyers..."

* * *

HE WAS FEELING QUITE CHIPPER when he met O'Gilroy at the town station. Mrs Simmons wasn't quite the horse's mouth but finding the horse's sister was far more than he'd expected.

O'Gilroy wasn't so chirpy. "One of 'em, jest the one. Married and settled and don't hardly remember the wedding at all, jest she was on the theatre with Enid Bowman – I found she'd been an actress, calling herself May, not much good of a one – and didn't know a thing abut Enid's private life but wouldn't be surprised at anything. I didn't say what I was asking about, of course. How'd ye go yerself?"

Ranklin told him – tactfully omitting that he'd learned about the stage, too. O'Gilroy lit a cigarette and frowned with thought. "Drew an ace, then, did ye? Where's that leave us?"

"It confirms that the story could be true..." But now he thought about it, that was just about all. There was no proof, but they weren't in the legal-proof business, and this was a story that simply wasn't susceptible of proof anyway.

"We've done better than anyone expected," he pronounced firmly. They had ten minutes before the next train back to London and he went to find an evening paper.

A down page headline read:

BODY FOUND IN THAMES
COULD BE MISSING WITNESS

* * *

A HOSPITAL MORTUARY is not about death. Whether you believe in oblivion or the hereafter, death can still be something awesome, as both light and shadow may be awesome. There was no awe about this chilly, shabby windowless room, with a line of unlit bulbs dangling over a row of what looked like wooden butcher's tables. It was business-like and workaday, summed up by a mop and bucket propped in one corner. The business of the room was being conducted by three men under a lit bulb over one of the tables; two others sat on a bench in the shadows, talking quietly, waiting their turn. The business was not death, but the living consequences of dying and it had a smell like a butcher's shop spiced with formalin.

As a soldier, Ranklin had seen corpses before, but they had looked less formal than this naked one stretched on the table top. It had the yellow-white colour of fat on raw meat, and was torn, with ragged purple cuts. It had lost a foot, an arm to the elbow, and most of the face was gone. Just torn pale flesh like veal and patches of white skull showing through. There was no blood and the body looked oddly clean; the filthy river had seen to that.

A man Ranklin assumed was a police surgeon, with shirt cuffs removed and jacket sleeves hooked back, was taking measurements and entering them in a notebook. Standing back across the table from him, and guarding a smaller table covered with jars and metal bowls, was a younger man in a long white apron. Ranklin came up beside him and whispered – whispers seemed appropriate: "Was that how he went into the river?"

The surgeon's assistant barely glanced at him. "I doubt it. It's scraping along the barges that does it. And it looks like he got caught in a propeller, too. It's pretty usual with one who's been in the river a day or more."

"Can you tell if he drowned?"

"If there's enough river water in his lungs."

"And were any of the injuries on him before he went into the water?"

The assistant turned to take a proper look at him. "Are you with the police?"

But then two men came in, both without topcoats so they had probably been around the hospital for some time. Inspectors McDaniel and Lacoste, seemingly professionally united. Both gave him a non-committal but thorough police stare.

He stepped forward and held out a hand. "Captain Ranklin, War Office." It was time to be moderately honest.

McDaniel introduced himself and Lacoste. "Didn't know you were concerned."

"Oh, you know, anarchism, international matters and all that – if it's Guillet. Is it?"

"Had you seen him before?"

"Only in court," Ranklin said more moderately than honestly.

"Would you care to identify him?"

Ranklin smiled lightly and shook his head.

"Nor *Inspecteur* Laroste." McDaniel gave a reasonable stab at a French pronunciation. "And he knew him from Paris."

"Then how will you…?"

"The clothes are French and cheap, and I've sent some lads round to his hotel to see what size he wore and if the cleaners have left any of his fingerprints there." He glanced at the body. "Left hand, I hope."

The youngish man in the apron said: "You're lucky. After a few days the skin on the fingers can peel right off."

"I know," McDaniel said evenly.

Ranklin asked: "Was he floating?"

"Must've been, for the river police to spot him."

That probably meant he was dead when he went into the river; in drowning, you swallow enough water to sink, and only surface again a couple of days later when putrefaction gases build up.

But nothing was certain, as the young assistant pointed out: "The shock of hitting the cold water could have killed him, then there'll be very little river water in the lungs. So, it could be suicide."

Almost in unison, McDaniel and Lacoste shook their heads.

"You never know," the assistant insisted.

"That's right," McDaniel agreed. But his expression didn't.

The surgeon stepped back. He was a placid, late-middle-aged

man with smooth white hair. "Do you want to take fingerprints before I start cutting, Inspector?"

"If you please, doctor." McDaniel waved and the two men from the shadows came forward with their equipment.

The surgeon lit a large cigar, which slightly surprised Ranklin but certainly improved the immediate neighbourhood. "I can't give you much at this stage, Inspector." He consulted his notebook. "He was five foot ten tall, and his live weight would be around eleven stone. Ummm, say seventy kilograms," he converted for Lacoste. "Does that fit your missing witness?"

The two inspectors conferred by look, and McDaniel nodded. "Could well be. I know it's tricky, but can you suggest any time of death?"

The surgeon shook his head firmly. "After this time and the water, temperature's no help. I'll probably end up saying between twelve and twenty-four hours ago."

McDaniel hadn't hoped for enough to be disappointed. "Anything yet on cause of death?"

"If he drowned, I *may* be ready to testify to that. That apart, I don't see any obvious bullet or stab wounds, but there's thirteen separate cuts on the body, not counting the ones that took off his arm, foot and face. I think they all happened after he was dead, but I may change my mind when I've had a look inside. Now, is there anything special you want me to look for?"

"Apart from identification, he's not my case. But we don't think he went into the river on his own accord." A small nod from Lacoste backed this up. "We don't think he's the type for suicide."

Ranklin had to stop himself nodding as well.

The surgeon said: "People often fall into the river drunk."

McDaniel looked to Lacoste; this time he got a shrug. Ranklin might have helped here: when he last saw Guillet the man hadn't been drunk and hadn't been drinking in that direction. Still, that wasn't evidence anyway.

"And when a man falls," the surgeon went on, "he just falls. He often hits something before the water, like the wall or a moored boat. So, there might well be broken bones, or a fractured skull, even with a genuine accident."

"You mean you might not be able to tell even if he'd been hit over the head first?"

"I'll do my best, but quite possibly not, unless it were well before."

McDaniel nodded heavily. "Like I say, not my case even if there is a case."

The surgeon smiled sympathetically. "Can I get back to him now?"

"Please do, sir." McDaniel went for a word with the fingerprint men, who were packing up their equipment.

He came back looking satisfied. "We should know in a couple of hours. And have a medical preliminary by midnight. No point in hanging around here."

Lacoste said: "I think we should return to Mam'selle Collomb now."

McDaniel turned to Ranklin: "Now you know everything we do, sir. I'm sure your people can get any of our reports through Special Branch at the Yard. So, if there's nothing more we can do for you..."

"No, no. Thank you." But Ranklin's mind was churning. They had picked up Berenice Collomb, then. Perhaps the hotel had recalled her coming round the night before the trial opened – had she been fool enough to try the next night, too? In fact, had she succeeded in getting to Guillet and...

He took a last glance at the cold, mostly shadowed room with its little group bending to their jobs in the one pool of light. And I'm here for the honour of the King, he reminded himself. Then he followed McDaniel and Lacoste out.

* * *

It was quiet both outside and inside Whitehall Court. This part of London was mostly government offices by now, closed since five o'clock, and nobody could afford a flat in this building until they were past the age of noisy parties. The outer door to the Bureau's offices was locked but that was usual enough. Ranklin let himself in and walked through the dark, deserted outer office to the agents' room. That was dark too, but the door to the Commander's office was open and spilling a little light.

"Ranklin?"

"Sir." He called the Commander "sir" the first time they met each day, but otherwise only when he was tired and instincts for rank took over. There was a solitary green-glass-shaded lamp alight on the Commander's writing table; Ranklin flopped into the most comfortable chair and fumbled for his pipe.

"Was it the meat porter?" the Commander asked.

"Probably. But badly cut up by barges and tugs and things."

"Was he pushed?"

"Again probably, but they may never find evidence." They spoke softly and without hurry.

"Hm. It would be nice if it were a proper murder. It would be a *fact* and excuse all sorts of interest. Unless, of course, you did it yourself."

"Bloody hell."

"It would be quite understandable. The chap wouldn't talk, you lost your temper, one shove—"

"The river's half a mile away from—"

"The Bureau will have to stand by you – in spirit, anyway. I can easily find a couple of chaps to say you were dining with them at a club at the time. Absolutely honest, unimpeachable men convince any court in the land. You haven't got a thing to worry about."

"The man was younger, heavier...a meat porter, for God's sake."

"Ah, but you're cleverer. Well, remember you've got witnesses if you need them."

Ranklin glowered. "And the police have got the Collomb girl for questioning about it."

"Have they?" The Commander thought about this. "You don't find that embarrassing? Good man. What will she tell them?"

"At a guess, nothing. Police are just the sheepdogs of capitalism to her." He had a feeling he'd improved that phrase somehow. "And she doesn't speak any English; that should help."

"Could she get round to her lover's alleged parentage?"

Ranklin shrugged. How could he know?

The Commander was fretting. "But if you didn't do it, could she have done?"

Ranklin rested his head back and closed his eyes. "Same objections as for me. She's just a slip of a girl. Tough as nails, I'm sure, but no match for Guillet. And the river's just as far for her as for me – if she knew where it is."

The Commander would be glaring at him, but he couldn't be bothered to open his eyes and confirm this.

But there was a glare in the Commander's voice. "But *you* know where it is."

"Yes. Too bloody far."

The Commander switched back to Berenice. "I suppose there's no reason for her to mention the other thing."

"I don't see why the police should ask her. From their point of view the story's complete without it. She loves Langhorn, Guillet was bearing witness against him, she killed Guillet. Simplicity begets convictions. You should hear O'Gilroy on the subject."

"Yes, yes, I'm sure... I just hate doing nothing."

That made Ranklin, who felt he had actually done a day's work, open his eyes. "D'you really want to save her from the jaws of the capitalist sheepdogs?"

"Can you do it?"

"I can try, if I can involve an outsider."

"Involve anybody except us."

"Are any of your telephones switched on?"

The Commander had four on his table; the agents had one between them all. "This one's still alive."

Ranklin called Corinna's number. She took a long time to answer and then said a sleepy: "Hello?"

"Is that the beautiful Corinna Finn?" Ranklin asked.

"God Almighty, you."

"Me. How's your fund?"

"Jesus... Not a word for days, then you ring up in the middle of the night to ask, 'How's my fund?'. D'you mean of goodwill? At zero and falling, is what."

"Sorry, I've been busy and it's all your fault really. I mean the fund for hauling destitute Americans out of trouble. Does it apply to their girlfriends too?"

"What? *What* girlfriend?"

"A French lass called Berenice Collomb. She's a bit of a gutter-snipe, but Grover Langhorn loves her. At least she does him. And the police are questioning her about a missing witness who was hauled out of the Thames this afternoon, very deceased."

There was a long silence. "This witness...was he testifying against young Grover?"

"That's right. Not very well, I'd say, but Noah Quinton should tell it better."

"Quinton? Who said anything about Quinton?"

"Sorry."

Another long silence. Then she said "All right. Get off the damn line so I can call him—Oh, where've they got her?"

"Scotland Yard, or the little police station next to it, probably. I'll call you tomorrow. And thanks." Ranklin hooked the earpiece on again. "That's the best I can do."

The Commander, who had been unashamedly eavesdropping, grinned with satisfaction. "I don't think we could have done better. You can sleep with a clear conscience, even if you did kill that porter."

Ranklin ignored that but, as he turned to go, hesitated. And after a time, he said: "Just suppose, by the grace of God, that we bring all this off. Suppose we stuff the skeletons back into the cupboards; that's going to leave us knowing what skeletons and which cupboards."

"You know, that thought never occurred to me," the Commander said, looking as if that were true.

CHAPTER SEVEN

Ranklin was waiting in Noah Quinton's outer office when the solicitor bustled in at a quarter past nine the next morning. He stopped abruptly when he saw Ranklin, then said: "Yes, you'd better come in," and bustled on through.

As Ranklin had half expected, Quinton's office was not just grand, but self-consciously so. There was nothing in it that a long-established and successful solicitor might not have in the way of antique desk, Turkish carpet, silver ashtrays and client chairs covered in dark green plush, but they should have been stained and worn, as if the owner didn't think or care about them. Quinton obviously cared, and you didn't want to be the first to spill coffee or drop cigar ash.

"I suppose," Quinton said, unpacking papers from a briefcase on to his desk, "that I have you to thank for a new client. I'm getting a little too old to be hauled from my bed in the early hours, but the Mrs Finn connection is...welcome, shall we say?"

Ranklin, sitting uneasily in an easy chair, just smiled.

"I suppose you want to know what happened." Quinton sat down and automatically shifted his chair by fractions of an inch to just how he liked it. "Well, it's not privileged... The police haven't charged Mam'selle Collomb with anything, they'd only detained her but were clearly going to hang on to her for as long as they could. I got her released on bail, put up by Mrs Finn, who's now looking after her."

Ranklin frowned; he hadn't expected that, and Corinna wouldn't have, either. He was going to hear more about it. Considerably more.

"The police objected to Mam'selle Collomb going back to her Bloomsbury address. They made it out to be a *community—*" a very suspect word, that, "—of intellectual depravity. My own brief impression of Mam'selle Collomb is that she could teach any Bloomsbury intellectual more about depravity than he could stomach – but that's neither here nor there. So, she's now officially in the care of Mrs Finn."

"Did Mam'selle Collomb say anything interesting?" Ranklin asked casually. "Or tell the police anything?"

Quinton looked at him warily, but Ranklin was all boyish innocence. So Quinton said: "I wouldn't say so… The police didn't even seem certain that Guillet's death was murder."

"They can't be," Ranklin said. "Death was due to a mixture of asphyxia and shock. Not enough water in the lungs and stomach for drowning. There had been a heavy blow to the head, above the right ear, some time before death, but it'll take more time to work out if it was long enough to suggest he'd been deliberately whacked. It might have been him hitting a moored boat or river steps – they don't even know where he went into the water. He hadn't got enough alcohol in him to have been drunk."

After a time, Quinton said: "I suppose I hadn't better ask you where you got such remarkably exact information."

"Take it as some small recompense for having to get up so early." And for what was to come.

Quinton nodded, quickly, birdlike. "So, it may be that the police can persuade the coroner to write it off as an accident if they can't induce anyone to confess to it. Or does your behind-the-scenes knowledge give you a different opinion?"

"We have professionally suspicious minds," Ranklin said, "so naturally we incline to murder. But I suppose accidents do happen, even to important witnesses in the middle of a case. And concerning that, what's going to happen now Guillet's dead?"

Mention of the case made Quinton look at his watch; there was a clock on the wall, but it looked too expensively antique to be trusted. "That's up to the magistrate. The French will fight tooth and nail to keep Langhorn in custody until they can come up with something, and I shall fight just as hard to have the matter wound up. Knowing this magistrate, I think he'll adjourn until Monday now, and hope for divine guidance over the sabbath.

"But remember, even if Langhorn's freed, he won't have been declared innocent. Extradition isn't about guilt or innocence, so there's no double jeopardy involved. The French could ask for him to be re-arrested on new evidence – if they can find it."

"And if they can find him," Ranklin mused. "I'd think he'd be off home to America like a shot from a gun."

Quinton nodded. "And America won't extradite one of its own citizens."

But did the Bureau want young Grover – and presumably his mother – landing in America stony-broke and looking to raise cash from the American scandal sheets? Incautiously, he said: "I'm not sure we'd like that, either."

"I'm sorry if that displeases you," Quinton said, dryly sarcastic. "Does that mean that you've been investigating further, and found there was something to investigate?"

But it had to come to this anyway, and this was one of the reasons Ranklin had come, though it still wasn't going to be easy. "I was down in Portsmouth yesterday looking for traces of Mrs Langhorn, the boy's mother. There was a Portsmouth address on the marriage certificate. I had to have some sort of excuse so I, er, said I was working for you."

"Did you?" Quinton considered this. "And did you learn anything?"

"Nothing of relevance to Grover Langhorn's case."

"Oh? I think I might be the better judge of that."

Ranklin said nothing. Quinton leant forward, chin on hands, elbows on desk, expression stern. "Let me see if I've got this right: without my permission, you posed as an investigator working for me, but you won't tell me what you found out – is that correct?"

No, it was *not* going to be easy. Ranklin did his best at a disarming smile; at least his features ran to that. "Well, more or less, but—"

"Captain Ranklin—" Quinton threw himself back in his chair "—when we first met, I assumed you must be Palace officials or liaison between them and the Prime Minister. I'm sure such people exist, and it seemed quite reasonable that, moving in the circles she does, Mrs Finn should know them. It seems I underestimated the width of her acquaintance; judging from your behaviour, I do believe that you and your precious Commander are from the *Secret Service*."

It was said with such contempt that Ranklin recoiled. He knew that the Bureau and spying generally weren't held in high regard, but what right had a Jewish lawyer to sneer at him? Then he recoiled again, only inwardly this time, and took a hasty glance at his own prejudices. He hadn't (he told himself) been despising Quinton for being...well, what he was. But perhaps he had been secretly hoping the man would do or say something so that he could despise him anyway.

"Or, at the very least," Quinton added, "take it that your conduct leads me to that conclusion."

Ranklin squeezed out a smile. "If we were what you suggest, then obviously we'd deny it. But whoever we are, you must have known we'd have to follow this up in a rather surreptitious manner. And I thought you were happy to remain ignorant of that and concentrate on the legal end."

"True. But I then believed, rashly it seems, that you could do such following *without* pretending that I was behind it. So, in effect, you've been spreading the idea that I sought and have now got knowledge that I didn't seek and haven't, in fact, got. What sort of position does that leave me in?"

"I don't think there's anything to worry about."

"I wish I had a penny for every time someone has told me, in this very office, that there was 'nothing to worry about' or so-and-so 'wouldn't do that' and so on. My whole professional life is worrying about such things. Trying to make legally sure of things my clients are certain about already. Believe me, they shriek loud enough when I fail. So, unless you tell me exactly what you've learnt, I'm sure you'll understand that I reserve my position on this."

Sounding pained and almost offended, Ranklin said: "I am working for the government."

"And I'm working for my client, Grover Langhorn."

After that, Ranklin decided not to ask for a lift to Bow Street in Quinton's motorcar.

* * *

WHEN RANKLIN ARRIVED by taxi at Bow Street's wide pavement, it looked like old home week. Quinton's Lanchester was parked at the kerb again and he had presumably already gone in. Corinna's father's Daimler, similarly Pullman-bodied, was parked just behind and Corinna herself was chatting to Lieutenant Jay. In the background, wearing a shabby tweed suit and cap, O'Gilroy was leaning against a wall.

You had to admire how he did that. He wasn't skulking or trying to look invisible. He just leant there, smoking an interminable stub of a hand-rolled cigarette, half-wrapped in his own concerns, half conscious of the world around, and wholly ready to tell it to bugger off and mind its own business.

It was a good day for leaning on walls: fine and bright and perhaps a shade warmer than the day before.

Jay asked: "D'you want me to go in, or are you?"

"You go." And Jay darted inside.

Corinna said: "Good morning," in a tone that suggested Ranklin was to do the rest of the talking and had better make it *good*.

"I'm most frightfully sorry that you had to take over Berenice. I had no idea... But I'm very grateful. Er – where is she, by the way?"

Corinna jerked her head, almost dislodging her matador hat. "In there, watching the boyfriend come up – or go down – for the umpteenth time. Is anything going to happen?"

"Quinton doubts it. Umm... I imagine you had a rather busy night?"

"I imagine I had a *totally* loused-up night. Getting up and flogging down to Scotland Yard just to be ignored by pompous policemen and given cups of what they think is *tea*... I'll say this for Noah Quinton, he knows how to handle those bastards. They don't like him, but they run scared of him... And then having to speak French to that...that—God Almighty, the girl is a complete *slut.* And d'you think she has a word of thanks for it all? She despises me! Thinks I'm the 'idle rich' – idle! After a night of running around promising God knows what for her on top of a busy day...

"It'll take more than Professor Higgins to make a duchess out of *that* squashed cabbage leaf." Shaw's *Pygmalion* had just opened at His Majesty's and its characters had already passed into the language.

"Well," Ranklin said, "I can't say how grateful—"

"You can try!"

"Er – are you stuck with her indefinitely?"

"It seems like it – until your wonderful police say different.

We're going round to Bloomsbury when this is over to collect her things."

Ranklin was a bit surprised to hear that Berenice actually had any "things". But perhaps even the inhabitants of La Villette might own more than they could wear at one time.

"D'you want to take O'Gilroy with you?" he offered. "Just on general grounds."

"No, Bloomsbury isn't the East End. It sounds like a bunch of half-assed artists being anarchists on money from home." It was the wrong morning for anyone to expect the benefit of the doubt from Corinna.

Then there was an eruption at the court door and several obvious journalists rushed off towards Fleet Street. It hadn't taken long, but clearly something had happened. Ranklin had already guessed what when Jay came out to report: "Adjourned. The police say they're treating the meat porter's death as murder."

Ranklin had instinctively stepped away from Corinna to listen to him; now, they both watched as Berenice Collomb shuffled up to Corinna. Her very pace was sullen, as if she were going from one funeral to another. Ranklin saw Corinna's face set into a wide, false smile.

"So that's Paris's answer to Eliza Doolittle?" Jay observed. Trust him to have seen the latest play. "I saw her around yesterday."

"You didn't see—" Ranklin began, then saw him for himself. Gorkin, wearing the same check suit and foreign-looking hat, came out, smiled at Ranklin, then vanished round the corner into Broad Court. Ranklin thought about nodding O'Gilroy to follow, but that would just be make-work; he had Gorkin's address anyway.

Corinna was ushering Berenice into the car, relaying instructions to the chauffeur, driving off.

"What d'you want me to do now?" Jay asked.

"Did the police say anything more about Guillet than just murder?"

"Pursuing various lines of enquiry, that's all."

"See what else you can dig up. Here or through the Yard. Try and be in the office around lunchtime."

Jay, looking like a playboy who has unaccountably got up before noon, moved off to deploy his rakish charm. That left Ranklin, who wanted a word with Quinton, and the unacknowledged O'Gilroy. Since Ranklin hadn't the Irishman's talent for loitering, it was lucky that, after almost a week of sunshine, other Londoners had finally decided they could risk simply standing around in the open air.

It was twenty minutes before Quinton came out, and Ranklin intercepted him. The solicitor seemed quite ready to speak to him, smiling in a somewhat interrogatory way, and letting Ranklin lead off.

"I gather that the police now have Guillet chalked up as murder?"

"They must have got a new pathologist's report."

"Is that good or bad for Mam'selle Collomb?"

Quinton shrugged. "I believe he was struck a quite heavy blow – for but an iron bar would do that by itself, you wouldn't need much strength. If they knew this happened some distance from the river, that would imply a slip of a girl dragging a heavy man that distance – which is unlikely. But if it happened at the top of some landing steps, all she'd need do is roll him down them."

"D'you think they'll ever find out where?"

"It seems highly unlikely now, after two days. Unless they find a witness, which would add a whole new dimension anyway."

For a moment, Ranklin thought of producing such a witness, and wasn't even shocked at himself. But that would call for very careful scripting – certainly better than Guillet himself had got. "And for how long does Mrs Finn have to nursemaid her?"

"Until the police have lost interest in her, I'm afraid. Or changed the terms of her bail."

"Are they likely to call her in for more questioning?"

"Not until they've got far more to go on, now they know they've got me to deal with." Which was perfectly reasonable but could have been said more humbly.

Ranklin nodded vaguely. There didn't seem much more to say.

But Quinton went on: "I had a little talk with my client." He paused, smiling. "Aren't you going to ask me what he said?"

Ranklin just nodded but felt lead in his stomach.

"He told me about his putative father. I can now see, I confess, why your people have been acting as you have. But that does *not*, to my mind, excuse your interference in the legal process."

Ranklin thought quickly back. As far as he could recall, the legal process was about the one thing they *hadn't* interfered with. Yet. "Sorry, but I don't follow."

Quinton adopted a foursquare stance in front of him, a bit like an outraged bantam. Oddly, Ranklin only now noticed they were much the same height. Usually he was very conscious of men's heights.

"Word has seeped out," Quinton said, "that if this case goes to the King's Bench on a writ of *habeas corpus,* it is to be heard by judges who are *sympathetic* to the boy's plight – for or at least the King's."

The Palace. The damned Palace.

Ranklin shook his head slowly. "Not our doing, I'm afraid. We simply don't have that sort of influence."

Quinton eyed him closely. "I'm certainly glad to hear that – and on balance, I'm inclined to believe you. I suppose," he mused, "you'd have to tell someone closer to the King that...yes, I think I see what would have happened. But Captain, I believe I am doing a good job of representing my client and have a reasonable chance of getting the case against him dismissed on grounds that even the French authorities will accept. I can manage very well without string-pulling in high places, and especially the implication that I need that. Perhaps you can find a way of passing that on."

"If the opportunity arises, yes."

"And in regard to what I learnt from my client, I can assure you that I am not breaking any confidences." Quinton seemed anxious to prove his own legal virginity. "He spoke out because he's concerned that nothing seemed to be happening in that area. I said that I was sure steps were being taken."

"Did he have a view about Guillet's death?"

"Oh yes. He believes that was punishment for Guillet failing to tell his lies properly. And that the capitalist sheepdogs at the *Préfecture* must be rehearsing a new witness to take his place.

"Single-minded little bugger, isn't he?" But Ranklin's vehemence was aimed at more than just Langhorn.

Quinton smiled coldly. "You might tell your Commander *Smith* that I'll be in my chambers the rest of the day, if he wishes to speak to me." He got into his limousine.

Ranklin watched it go, saying several un-bright-spring-day things under his breath. Trying to stifle this scandal was like trying to stop ripples on water... And they couldn't even be sure whether it was true, dammit.

He was about to nod O'Gilroy off duty when Corinna's Daimler rushed back down the street, stopped with a jerk, and she jumped out long before the chauffeur could get round to the door.

"That bloody little tramp! She's shut herself in a room there and won't come back with me! Can I let the police have her back? Never mind the bail, I just want *shot* of her."

Ranklin made soothing noises whilst thinking quickly. There wasn't time to check with the Commander, he had to act himself.

He pointed up the street, as if giving her directions, and muttered: "This isn't for your benefit, I'm trying to instruct O'Gilroy. Ah, he's got it."

The shabby figure was moving away at a slouching amble.

"Right, get the motorcar turned round, we'll pick him up further along."

In the dingier and less public surroundings of Endell Street, Ranklin swung the door open, O'Gilroy stepped in, and they zoomed off. Well, not zoomed, in a Daimler, but definitely hurried – through the wide tangle of traffic near the top of Shaftesbury Avenue, across New Oxford Street and up Blooms-bury Street. By then O'Gilroy knew as much or as little as there was to tell.

"What's the address of this place?" Ranklin asked.

"14 Bloomsbury Gardens." He knew that address and checked with a card in his wallet: it was the one Gorkin had given him.

He hadn't time to work out what that meant. "Are you armed?" he asked O'Gilroy and got a nod. That meant a .38 semi-automatic Browning: O'Gilroy was a modernist in these matters.

"Good. But keep it out of sight until I say so."

* * *

IT WAS a middle-middle class area which the young of the upper class regarded as daringly slummy. Most of it was squares like this: rows of tall, narrow terraced houses that had been built of yellow brick now black with London's soot (like the rest of London), around a private but communal garden across the road. There were no front gardens, just a handful of steps leading up from the pavement to the front door, which had a fanlight above to align it with the tall windows.

Ranklin pressed the bell. After a while the door was opened by a tall young woman. It took a moment for Ranklin to decide that anarchists wouldn't have maidservants, so she couldn't be one. She had long, very definite pre-Raphaelite features and gingery hair drawn back into a bun. She wore a pale violet garment like a smock that went straight from ankle to throat without being visibly distracted.

She looked past Ranklin at the Daimler. "And who would you be?" Her voice was light, pleasant, educated.

"We've come to collect Mam'selle Collomb."

"She doesn't want to go."

Ranklin nodded. "The problem is, the police released her from custody to Mrs Finn. They think they've got first call on her. So, if Mrs Finn doesn't get her, the police will."

"That will be an example of police oppression."

"Did you want an example?"

That hadn't been the expected answer. She frowned.

Ranklin went on: "You do know that it's a death they're questioning her about?"

A slight, cool smile. "I'm afraid you're wrong. They have no evidence—"

"They seem to have now; I've just come from the court. It's murder, now. And a rather embarrassing one, a French witness. So, the police feel a bit on their mettle. They'd rather like a Frenchwoman to have done it – keeps the British out of it, one might say. And an unworldly little girl from La Villette...by the time they've finished, she'll have confessed to everything and the Jack the Ripper murders as well."

She frowned again. "Do you really believe that?"

"Don't you?"

She licked her thin lips. "You're just saying that."

"I asked you if you believed it."

"Well, yes. I certainly believe the police are..." She wasn't quite sure what.

"Capitalist sheepdogs?" Ranklin suggested cheerfully. "I think they're actually more complicated than that, but it still leaves the question of how you're going to protect Mam'selle Collomb from them."

"They'd never dare come tromping in here."

"Ah, that's what you really believe, isn't it? That they're nice friendly men in uniform who tell you the way when you're lost, just like nanny said. Well, probably they are to people who live in houses this size, but not to Berenice Collomb. And I think it would be rather sad for you to learn that by putting her on the gallows. Still, it'll be a good chapter for your memoirs, so maybe you think it's cheap at the price."

She jerked the front door wide. "You'd better come in."

A few steps down the narrow hallway was Gorkin, who had obviously been hearing every word.

"Hello, Dr Gorkin," Ranklin called. "Sorry I haven't had time for you to convert me but been rather busy. Still am, as a matter of fact."

"You have come to return Berenice to the rich Mrs Finn?"

"I have. Mrs Finn doesn't like it either but seems ready to go along with it on behalf of a fellow human being." He turned back to the woman. "Can you fetch Mam'selle Collomb?"

"You'd better come up and talk to her yourself."

They went up to the second floor. The house was sparsely furnished, mostly with rather rigid, elongated Art Nouveau pieces, oriental pottery and a lot of paintings in bold primary colours. And William Morris wallpaper, of course: the silly bastard had once proclaimed himself an anarchist, hadn't he?

The woman rapped on a door and said: "Berenice?"

"Ils sont retournés?"

"Oui," Ranklin called. *"Avec moi – James Spencer. Vous avez un choix: venir avec moi et Madame Finn, ou avec les flics."*

She told him, in colloquial French, to go and fuck himself. Ranklin grinned at the woman. "You'd better talk to her. I'll let Dr Gorkin show me the error of my ways." He wanted to get Gorkin out of the conversation to come. He had nothing against the man except for his tendency to be present, watching and listening. For example, he had followed them up the stairs.

So Ranklin took him by the arm, led him aside and launched straight in: "One thing that bothers me about anarchism, especially when it depends on a revolution, is the transition period from the *ancien régime* to a perfect anarchist state. Can you get people to give up their old dog-eat-dog ways overnight, without a period of education? – and what happens during that period?"

"People – working people – are oppressed, not corrupted. You see it everywhere in working communities, the help they give each other. It is the *bourgeoisie* who put up fences and have secrets."

Thinking of Aunt Maud's house, Ranklin couldn't but agree. "You could be right – but there's getting to be an awful lot of the middle class: are they all going to perish in the revolution?"

"They can choose." Gorkin was looking over Ranklin's shoulder, trying to hear what the woman was saying to the still-locked door.

"You're talking to me," Ranklin reminded him. "So, the middle class can make a quick choice: either join the revolution or off to *Madame la Guillotine?*"

"Once the revolution has happened, there will be no need for guillotines. It will be secure – in science, a stable state, if you understand that."

"The only truly stable explosive is one that's exploded already? Yes, I think – ah."

He had heard the click of the door behind him. Berenice came out, carrying a small, tattered shopping basket. She gave Ranklin a look of sullen dislike, and he smiled back and gestured politely at the stairs. The woman had got things this far; let her stay in charge. He followed them down, keeping Gorkin well separated.

Outside, O'Gilroy was standing by the open rear door of the Daimler. He let Berenice in, then went to sit by the driver.

The woman had stopped at the foot of the steps and Ranklin paused to ask: "One thing: was Berenice out on Wednesday night? – the night before last?"

"Yes." Cautiously.

"What time did she get in?"

"About ten o'clock."

"Was it only you who saw her then?"

"Oh no. There were several of us." She half-turned towards Gorkin, watching from the doorway. "Including Dr Gorkin."

"Have the police asked you about this?"

"No."

"If they get really serious, they will. Tell them the truth. It helps her. Thank you, Miss, er…"

"Venetia Sackfield."

They shook hands, hello and goodbye, and Ranklin got into the back seat of the Daimler and they headed for the Sherring flat in Clarges Street.

"How in hell did you pull that off?" Corinna growled.

"All done by kindness. And threats, of course."

CHAPTER EIGHT

Ranklin left O'Gilroy at Clarges Street with instructions not to use his pistol and not even much muscle if Berenice looked like fleeing the nest again. He half hoped that she would warm to the Irishman's cynicism, since he suspected that O'Gilroy was something of a natural anarchist himself. He might want to end British rule in Ireland, but the moment the place had its own government, he would be deriding and undermining it.

Ranklin only hoped the citizens of La Villette weren't as fastidious as most French about hearing their beloved language mangled.

He reached Whitehall Court at about midday and reported the morning's activities to the Commander, who nodded approvingly. "Sounds as if you handled that quite smoothly – the way you tell it, anyway. Where's young Jay?"

"I sent him to find what the police are up to. I've got a bit of bad news: young Langhorn's told Quinton who he thinks his father is."

The Commander chewed an unlit pipe quietly for a time. Then he sighed. "I suppose it could have happened at any time... How did Quinton react?"

"I think he's quite intrigued, and with the extradition business seemingly petering out on him, he's not being so upright about legal confidences. *But—*" And he repeated what Quinton had said about high-level legal string-pulling.

"The bloody Palace!" The Commander jumped to the same conclusion. "And now I suppose every lawyer in the land is asking why the Palace is interested in this gutter arsonist. God save the King from his well-meaning friends." At least the Bureau, Ranklin reflected, was not well-meaning: it was trying to strengthen its position by doing the King a favour. Good, honest self-interest, and if the King didn't know about the favour, the Commander would likely find ways of telling him.

However, there wasn't much to be done about that right now, so he asked: "Is there any way of keeping Quinton quiet?"

"As a lawyer he should be able to keep a secret. But how do you make sure, with a man who likes to be thought a gentleman?" And after a time, a slow, self-satisfied smile spread around his pipe-stem. Ranklin knew the signs: The Commander was going to be devious.

* * *

HAVING missed lunch the previous day, Ranklin arrived at Clarges Street just in time to miss it again. "And a very tasty one, too," O'Gilroy assured him. "Can I pour ye a cup of coffee?"

He and Corinna were sitting alone at the dining table, he with an expression of contented innocence, Corinna with a smug, cat-got-the-cream look. Ranklin knew this meant, for him, Bad News.

She said: "Conall, could you nip along to the kitchen and ask them to whip up more coffee? – if they can fit it in before cutting our throats (Berenice is there trying to stir up the menials to revolt). I want a word with Matt."

O'Gilroy stood up. "Ye know what she's got in there? – a bottle of absinthe."

Corinna nodded. "She made me send out for it. She was surprised I didn't have it around."

"And a third drunk already. That girl's not going to see thirty, this rate."

"A child of her age and place," Corinna said sententiously. "Shut the door behind you."

It was a big flat, almost divided in two: Reynard Sherring's set of rooms and Corinna's. If you got lost, a glance at the decor put you right. Sherring favoured rich, dark clutter, Corinna liked clean-cut brightness – except for her bedroom, which had a rather soggy feminine luxury, as if she wanted somewhere to slump away from her good taste.

They moved to Corinna's drawing room, and she began: "I've been having some fascinating talks with Berenice. I won't say she's not so bad when you get to know her, because I think she's worse. She's got the makings of intelligence – she came of a reasonable lower-middle-class family in Cherbourg, I guess that ties up with Grover in his Atlantic liner days – anyhow, she knows just enough to think she knows everything, and I'm corrupt and old – *old!* – I don't mind being corrupt... And incidentally she told me about who Grover says his father was."

Ranklin had half seen this coming, but there had still been a spark of hope that it wasn't. He nodded resignedly.

"You poor little bunny," she said, suddenly maternal. "Running around wiping up after your King when you should be deciding the Fate of Nations."

"Look, nothing about this is *proven.*"

"It seems odd that a prince – he was, then, wasn't he? – didn't take proper precautions... But I suppose things weren't as advanced in those days."

Ranklin, who didn't think things were very advanced now, repeated: "I tell you: nothing is *proven.*"

"I'd still advise against letting journalists get hold of it, particularly French ones. By the way, I'm supposed to be in Paris for the

Visit myself next week. Pop's got seats for some royal concert thing they're putting on at *l'Opéra* and if I don't go he'll take one of his whores."

Ranklin smiled and she said sharply: "It's not your King I'm thinking of, it's Pop's reputation. Not that it sounds as if your King should be too offended... Is there enough to show Mother Langhorn could have known him twenty-whatever years ago?"

Ranklin nodded reluctantly.

"The Plaything of a Prince and he Cast Her Aside Like a Soiled Glove. I've often wondered: Why gloves? *I* have them cleaned and if you start casting, you end up with just one of a pair. What does she want? – just getting Grover off this extradition charge?"

"Perhaps, but we don't know. We haven't heard from her beyond that letter you gave us."

"And you've been snooping about asking if it could be true... That must have been delicate work, I do wish I'd seen it... Hey, you didn't ask the *King* if it could be true?"

Ranklin shook his head.

"And then what?" she asked. "Pulling legal strings to make sure Grover gets off?"

"No," Ranklin said grimly, "but somebody closer to the King has been."

"Of course, you'd have to tell them... Is it working?"

"I hope not."

She looked surprised. "Why so scrupulous? Does it shake your faith in Great British Justice? I don't think your judges are as crooked as some we get in the States, but they can be as pig-headed and biased as anyone."

"Yes, but that's individual. Even taking bribes is. But if I thought they were taking orders from the top, then the whole system... We'd have slipped back three or four hundred years."

"Doesn't being monarchy mean – in the end – taking orders from the top?"

"No, I don't think so."

She hesitated a moment, then asked: "What *do* you think of the monarchy? I know you don't worship the King or think he can do no wrong, but what do you actually *think?*"

"I think…" he said, and then was silent for some time. Finally, he said: "Perhaps 'think' is the wrong word. The monarchy just *is.* It shapes our whole society – society without the capital S. The still centre of the wheel, and on the whole, the stiller the better. But if we want to be a monarchy, have a king and protect his honour, that's our business. Specifically, it's mine as an Army man. I'm not supposed to defend freedom or civilisation or anything like that, just this country."

"You mean that at least your intentions are honourable. More than his were, back then."

"Perhaps… But whether sacrificing our ideas of law to save the King's good name is particularly honourable…"

She waited a moment, then asked gently: "And what would happen if the whole story came out? – let justice be done 'though the skies fall'?"

He sighed and shook his head. "It's a nice idea – in theory. But whoever said that thought the skies were pretty firmly nailed in place, at least in his own vicinity. The King's a special case. He's not a real man; he stopped being one the moment he put on the crown, and it goes on until he dies. If he starts acting like a real man, pretty soon we'll be a republic like you and France and Switzerland – and this time it'll stick. Meantime, I dare say there are compensations—"

"Hah!"

"—one of which is having people like me papering over any cracks in your past. Mind you," he added thoughtfully, "there are diplomatic aspects as well. If the French press prints nasty things about our King, there could be an anti-French revulsion in this country. And what price the Anglo–French alliance then? – just when we need it to stop Germany doing something stupid."

"But that just derives from having a king in the first place."

Ranklin shrugged. "Suppose they started printing nasty things about your President? – wouldn't that come to the same thing?"

"It would not," she said with the firmness of someone who isn't quite sure. "You English will think we think of the President as our king. We don't: he's just an elected politician, like your Prime Minister. He can be impeached, even, it's all there in the Constitution. And that's what our military people swear an oath of loyalty to, the Constitution. And when we want a bit of reverence and show, we've got the flag."

"Yes, I must say I've never understood the fuss you—"

She cut him off sharply. "You want to know one big advantage of a flag? – it doesn't go around fucking the wrong people."

* * *

O'GILROY CAME BACK with the maid bringing a tray of fresh coffee. The staff here, who didn't know what the two men did (really didn't know; Ranklin was sure Corinna hadn't been that stupid) had the idea that O'Gilroy was a sort of valet to Ranklin but, since they'd met in the Army, which was true, it was all rather informal.

"Where's Berenice?" Corinna asked.

"Went to the toilet. Thank ye, I'll take another cup." At least you never had to ask O'Gilroy if he'd eaten or drunk. An Irish childhood and his years in the Army had convinced him that the next meal was a matter of luck, so be sure of the one at hand.

Ranklin asked: "And did Berenice tell you any more?"

"Mostly I should get a proper job and 'twas me own fault me being yer servant. I told her ye'd saved me life oncest, and I was beholden to ye. Don't worry, she wasn't impressed, not at all."

"Haven't I saved your life?"

"Not near so often as ye've made the need of it. One thing: she's terrible taken with this feller Gorkin. D'ye know him?"

"He was at Bow Street this morning. You saw him: beard, foreign hat, check suit. How d'you mean, 'taken with him'?"

"Thinks he's God with a three-speed gearbox. As an anarchist. Big thoughts, has the answer to everything. She says everyone at the Bloomsbury house thinks so, too. Sounds to me he's missing a great career peddling pills."

"I thought he was a reporter for that Paris anarchist paper."

O'Gilroy gave him a superior look. "Ye don't have reporters on papers like that. It's got no news, jest tells ye what to think about it. He writes pamphlets, books, lectures. Big man." Ranklin realised he should have wondered more about that doctorate of Gorkin's; not many reporters would have any sort of degree.

Then Berenice came in. Ranklin and O'Gilroy stood up; she looked at them in listless surprise. *"Vous êtes en départ?"*

Corinna switched into French. "No, no. Sit down and have some coffee."

Berenice dumped herself into a chair and took her coffee with a muttered *"Merci"*.

O'Gilroy stayed standing. "Fact, I'm going. Thank ye for the lunch, delicious. *Et bonjour, mam'selle.*" He bowed formally to Berenice and went.

Berenice watched him go with perhaps a glimmer in her usually dead-fish eyes, then asked Ranklin: "Is that man your servant?"

It was debatable whether she would appreciate a spy more than a manservant, but it wasn't up for debate anyway. "I think of him more as a friend."

That brought leaden disbelief, but she let it drop.

Ranklin said: "I talked to *Maître* Quinton again this morning."

"Do you know now what will happen to Grover?"

"No. I'm sorry, but the death of Guillet has delayed matters."

Corinna sat back in her chair, a slow but definite movement, withdrawing from the conversation.

In a gentle voice, Ranklin said: "May I ask a question? – do you believe we're trying to help you?"

All he got was a sullen glower. She wore a shapeless dress of faded green over holed black stockings and sprawled back with all the elegance of damp washing, smelling of absinthe and poverty.

"Then put it another way: would you rather be in the hands of the police?" He waited for a while, then said, still gently: "I do want an answer to this. You're not in prison here, it is not possible to stop you walking out. It would be more convenient for Mrs Finn if you did. But if you do, the police will take you back."

"The police are—"

"Possibly. But if they're what you believe, do you think you can undergo hour after hour of questions without them tricking you into a confession?" Now Quinton was involved, that was pretty unlikely, but let her think of that for herself.

"I did not kill him!"

"I don't think you did. But the police believe you went to try and see Guillet again at the *Dieudonné* that night. Did you?"

A nod.

"What time?"

A shrug and gesture: obviously, she had no watch.

Ranklin shook his head in patient refusal. "If you have no watch, you must be used to looking for clocks and London's full of them. So, what time?"

"I quit the hotel at half-past nine."

"And how long had you been there?"

A shrug, then reluctantly: "About an hour."

"Did they let you sit in the hotel all that time?"

"They didn't let me sit in the hotel a fucking *minute*. I waited outside."

A girl just standing around in the street after dark... "Didn't men—?"

"Naturally they did. I'm used to it."

Ranklin sat back to think. Guillet's bed hadn't been slept in. "Somebody could have been killing him while you were waiting."

Despite herself, a shaft of interest lit her face. "Not at that time. The streets were too busy. And I have seen the river, there is too much light there."

"The river moves. He didn't have to be pushed in where he was pulled out. He could have gone in higher up. In fact, it's more likely." Mind, the Thames at London was tidal: the natural flow might even reverse with a flooding tide. A body could be pushed back and forth, banging into moored barges... well, that had certainly happened.

But on balance, it should have travelled downstream – perhaps from the quieter, less lit areas of Chelsea or across the river in Battersea. "A long way to walk first," he said to himself, then translated for her.

"An auto," she said.

"He wouldn't have got into an auto except with someone he knew."

"And the only person he knew in London is *Inspecteur* Lacoste." There was a little triumphant smile on her shabby face: *ergo,* Lacoste had killed him. Hadn't she said it was the *flics* all along?

Ranklin thought that unlikely. Whatever one's view of the *Préfecture,* being let down by a witness must happen fairly often to a detective, and he couldn't kill them all; it might cause comment. But he didn't fancy trying to argue that to Berenice.

So he said: "Did you know Guillet in La Villette?"

"I saw him a couple of times when he came into the *Deux Chevaliers.* He did not belong there, *he* was not an anarchist. But he had some business with the *patron.*"

"*The patron?*"

She regretted having mentioned him, but it could hardly be a secret. "M'sieur Kaminsky."

Ranklin would have liked to learn more about the man running the *Café des Deux Chevaliers,* but he didn't see how it was relevant to the shenanigans in London. He swung the conversation back towards home. "The lady in Bloomsbury – Venetia Sackfield – she agrees that you came home at about ten o'clock. Were there others there?"

Shrug. "Some women, men – they're just a bunch of children. But also, Dr Gorkin."

Tempting her, Ranklin was dismissive. "Oh, *him*."

It was too easy. "He is a great man! A true champion of the workers, a real thinker. Did you read what he wrote about the Dreyfus case? No, of course you didn't. And he is also a healer, not a fashionable two-hundred-franc doctor but a man who *cares*. He treats the poor who have the pox, when the nuns would just say it was the wrath of God for their *wickedness!*"

Corinna couldn't help butting in. "But does he know anything about medicine?"

"Of course, he does. He studied for years, but he also worked for the Cause and the Russians drove him out."

"Fine, fine. I just asked."

Berenice stood up. "I am going back to the workers."

"She means—" Corinna reverted to English as the door banged "—the kitchen and the absinthe. Have you met this great thinker and healer?"

"Had a drink with him, the first day at Bow Street. We talked about anarchism – he's quite a good debater."

She considered, then smiled. "You really couldn't be further apart. In the red corner, the prophet of anarchism, in the blue corner the devoted officer battling to save the King from his youthful Dark Secret. I'm sorry: *alleged* Dark Secret."

Ranklin scowled. But it always amused her, seeing his face attempt that expression.

She went on: "But you must admit a few minutes of royal romping more than twenty years ago is causing you and a lot of people a whole heap of trouble today, however honourable your intentions are." She began moving about the room, tidying in a purposeless way.

Ranklin said: "You'd better not meet Dr Gorkin: it sounds as if you're ripe for the plucking."

"I doubt it, and I've had young Berenice softening me up all morning. But anarchism, communism, socialism, they all seem much the same as Christianity: fair shares, feeding the poor, loving your neighbours—"

"It also seems to be about upping the pace on such matters."

"—but without Christianity's saving grace, which is seeing that mankind is fallible. Very practical, that. I hate as much as anybody listening to a preacher telling me we're all poor sinners – what does that bastard know? But in the end, he's right. We *aren't* trustworthy, we do need laws and leaders – preferably elected leaders, so we can throw them out when they get too fallible. You try telling that to an anarchist: they don't even believe in democracy, just *agreement.* They say you've got no faith in your fellow men, you've been corrupted. They've done away with God and they're stuck with believing mankind's perfectable – practically perfect already. All it needs is a revolution and you and me under the guillotine."

"Well, you, anyway. *I'm* not rich."

"See what I mean about the fallibility of man?" She stood above him, running a finger through his silky fair hair. "Are you let off the hook this evening?"

"With Berenice around?"

"She isn't sharing my *room*. And it would be rather nice to have a man around. Then if someone rings up in the middle of the night with some smart-ass scheme, *you* can handle it."

But then the telephone rang. Corinna answered it, smiled, and said: "Hello, Conall. You want the great man himself. He's here."

She tactfully faded away as Ranklin took the earpiece. O'Gilroy said: "Ye'd best be getting back. Things has happened in

Paris. And did ye see a dark red Simplex landau parked outside there?"

"No."

"Ye should've done. Coupla fellers in it. Anyways, I'm sending young P over to take yer place. He'll keep the cab."

Ranklin hung up and Corinna came across, her expression querying his worried look. This time, she had a right to know. "O'Gilroy says there's a couple of men watching from a motorcar outside."

She took it well – if a resigned sigh is well. "He's usually right about these things."

Ranklin peered through the lace curtains without disturbing them. He thought he could identify the car, but it was just a closed car like several others in the street. "Anyway, he's sending over Lieutenant P – youngish chap, you haven't met him – to stand guard. I've got to get back. Oh, and P doesn't know about all this – yet – so I'd be grateful if you didn't—"

The idea of herself hiding a Shocking National Secret from a Secret Service agent tickled Corinna. Still, for that reason alone, she'd do it.

Ranklin smiled ruefully. "I know: tomorrow the world, but until then…"

CHAPTER NINE

"Jay's over at Scotland Yard," the Commander said, "and he was on the telephone just now saying someone's put advertisements in the Paris afternoon papers asking Enid Bowman to present herself to the British consulate, where she'll hear something very much to her advantage."

"The Palace again?"

"Who else could it be? We should never have told those stupid buggers." Quite overlooking that it had been he who had insisted on it. He added grudgingly: "Though at least they had the sense to use her maiden name. Would've had French journalists swarming all over them at the mention of 'Langhorn'."

"Probably offering her a bribe to keep quiet," Ranklin guessed.

"What they're actually doing is getting the Paris police frothing at the mouth. The *Préfecture* cabled that French rozzer over here the moment they saw it, and he's round at the Yard asking what the hell the perfidious English are up to. First killing their witness, now trying to bribe the mother of that anarchist fire-raiser. Naturally, *he* thinks it must be us – the Bureau – playing silly games. And he's got the Yard, at least Special Branch, half believing it, too. And how can I tell them it was really those morons on the steps of the throne?"

"What d'you want me to do?"

But it seemed the Commander just wanted someone to complain to while he waited for things to get worse. So Ranklin went ahead and made it so: "Mrs Finn's got the story out of Mam'selle Collomb."

"May as well shout the whole thing from the rooftops," the Commander said bitterly. "Do you know what the devil is going on?"

Ranklin shook his head. "No idea at all, except that it's more than we thought. You know about the watchers in Clarges Street? If this all adds up to some anarchist conspiracy, it's something to get our teeth into."

The Commander grunted something unintelligible. Ranklin took out his pipe, knocked out some encrusted old ash, reamed out some more with his penknife, then filled it carefully. After a while, the Commander started to do the same to the pipes in a little rack on his table.

About twenty minutes later, a telephone rang and the Commander gestured Ranklin to answer it. It was Jay at Scotland Yard. "It is respectfully requested that someone more senior than myself get himself over here and do some explaining." His voice dropped. "Or bluffing."

Ranklin relayed this to the Commander, who whispered raspingly: "If it's to see Sir Basil, I'll go. Anyone more junior and it's your job. And I want you back by five: meeting of the Steam Submarine Committee, including Noah Quinton."

Ranklin gave him a puzzled frown. The Commander had perked up a little and was now smiling deviously. "How d'you get a man to keep a secret? – you tell him more. Take him into your confidence. Always works with the middle classes."

Strictly interpreted, that should put Corinna on the Committee, too, but Ranklin chose not to suggest it. Anyway, the telephone was squawking plaintively: "Hello? Hello? Have we been disconnected?"

Ranklin answered: "No, still here. Who wants us?" And when he knew: "Tell him the deputy chief is on his way – oh, and what name are you using?"

* * *

SCOTLAND YARD WAS BARELY FIVE MINUTES' walk to the Westminster Bridge end of Whitehall. There, Ranklin was shown up a long flight of stone steps and abruptly from high-ceilinged space into a small cubby-hole of a waiting room with a uniformed constable sitting behind a table and the walls hung with photographs of uniformed policemen seated in stern moustachioed rows. And Lieutenant Jay, apparently known to the police as "Mr Hopkins".

"Captain Ranklin, Deputy Chief of the Secret Service Bureau," Ranklin reported briskly to the constable. It sounded odd, said out loud like that, a bit like releasing a bat in daylight. He turned aside and fell into muttered conversation with Jay.

"Tell me about this advertisement," Ranklin demanded, and Jay did better: he'd copied it (presumably from Lacoste's cable) into a notebook. But it was just as the Commander had said, except that it had been published in both French and English. That was a point that nobody had brought up: how long Mrs Langhorn had been in France and how good her French was.

Ranklin read it twice without learning any more, then murmured: "You know who probably placed this?"

Jay nodded. "Will they tell us if she appears?"

"Not they. They obviously think they can handle this by themselves, and if she turns up it'll convince them they're right." He pondered this. "And maybe they are, and we can go back to our proper job. But I somehow doubt it."

"Could we find out through the consulate?"

"O'Gilroy might be able to." He frowned at a thought. "The

Palace must have sent their own man over, they wouldn't trust this to consuls."

"Fine, no skin off our nose."

"There *oughtn't* to be." But if something went wrong, it was unlikely that the Palace would volunteer to take the blame.

Then a buzzer sounded, and the constable said that Superintendent Mockford would see them now.

"Just like a dentist," Jay said cheerily, and Ranklin gave him a warning look.

As his experience with Whitehall grew, Ranklin was developing a theory that went along the lines of: Rooms where the inhabitant and his furniture really belong are devoted solely to comfortable time-serving. The real work is done in rooms where everything is mismatched and looks temporary.

If there were anything to Ranklin's Law, Mockford was a worker. His room was long but half of it had just a table and chairs and looked unused. At the far end, a big desk backed on to a window and a rolltop one stood against the opposite wall, with a dusty, cold fireplace in between. There were cases of law-books and piles of papers, and the walls were painted light green up to a hip-high dado rail and shiny cream above. Ghastly, but normal.

There were three people in the room: presumably Mockford himself behind the desk, *Inspecteur* Lacoste in a chair near the fireplace, and Inspector McDaniel swinging gently in the swivel chair by the rolltop.

Mockford stood up to shake hands. He was stout, stout all over, his eyes made lazy by pouches of flesh and with a full set of double chins. The only non-stout thing about him, appropriately for a detective, was his lean, sharp nose. Long strands of dark hair sprawled untidily across from his right ear without hiding the pink beneath. It looked as if he didn't mind going bald, but his wife had told him to do *something,* for Heaven's sake.

"I think you know Inspectors McDaniel and Lacoste." Ranklin got a friendly nod from McDaniel and a stony look from Lacoste, who was dressed as before only more rumpled. He must have brought just one suit, while the one-day hearing had already dragged on for three. "Pull up chairs. Now: can you tell us what's going on?"

Mockford's manner was polite but he didn't waste time on pointless courtesy.

"Before we start," Rankin said, hauling a stiff dining chair towards the grate, "I wonder if you can track down a motorcar for me. A dark red Simplex landau with a London number." He sat down and read out the number.

Mockford said: "Naturally we want to help, but this sort of request usually comes from Major Kell's Bureau and through Special Branch."

It was a polite reminder that the Secret Service was supposed to ply its trade abroad. Ranklin took a decision. "It's been parked in Clarges Street with two men in it, most likely watching the address where Mam'selle Collomb is staying."

"Give it to McDaniel, he'll try. Now, can we go back to my question?"

"I'm afraid the answer to that is No. Half we just don't know, the other half we can't mention without a specific direction from our masters. And frankly, I doubt you'd get that, even going through the Home Secretary."

"Hm." Mockford leant back in his chair, producing a distinct creak. "Then was it your Bureau put the advertisement in the Paris papers?"

"We did not. As our title implies, we prefer more secretive methods. And this must have involved the consulate, who wouldn't touch it without permission from the Foreign Office, who don't love us."

"Yes, I tried to explain that to *Inspecteur* Lacoste. He's bothered that we might be interfering in a purely French case of arson."

"I quite understand, and I wish it hadn't happened," Ranklin said for Lacoste's benefit, and then expanded it. "The FO thinks we intrude on their God-given right to collect foreign intelligence and get in their way. Just occasionally they may be right, as when we stir up a local fuss and they have to apologise for us – since we, I'm sure you understand, don't exist." This might confirm Lacoste's worst beliefs about British perfidy, but perhaps intrigue him as well. The way things were heading, Ranklin didn't want to add the Paris police to their enemies. "So, if we wanted the FO to help us, it would go to Cabinet level, take at least a week and the answer would still probably be No."

McDaniel, who was using a telephone on the open rolltop desk, suddenly popped his safety valve: "I dinna give a hoot how short-handed ye are, Superintendent Mockford *wants that name!*" It seemed that anger brought out the native Scot in him.

Mockford ignored the outburst. "Then to find who placed that advertisement, we have to think of who could order the Foreign Office around. Hm." He looked at Lacoste, who gave a neutral shrug. So, he looked back at Ranklin. "The King is visiting Paris next week, had you remembered?"

"I believe he is," Ranklin said, matching Lacoste for stony-facedness.

"So, there'll be no thanks for stirring up trouble between our nations right now."

"We regard that as primarily a matter for the Palace." There was, he recalled, an Irish phrase O'Gilroy sometimes used: "Mind ye, I've said nothing."

"I see," Mockford said and looked at Lacoste to see if he saw.

This time, Lacoste looked resigned.

McDaniel pivoted round from the rolltop desk. "The motorcar belongs to a Mr Rupert Peverell—"

"A *fact!*" Mockford said with rich satisfaction. "A nice uncomplicated *fact*. Now I do hope your Bureau isn't going to complicate it for us."

"It's not *much* of a fact," Ranklin objected. "The only thing you've got against that motorcar is that I've told you it's been watching the flat where Berenice Collomb now is."

"Not much, I agree, but we're grateful for any straw to clutch at. And I'll tell you why we're so interested in any motorcar that might be involved. It's because we've been thinking and studying tide tables and the like and, while this isn't useable evidence, we think Guillet was pushed into the river some way upstream. But we don't think he walked up there, nor took a bus or cab – but he might have gone for a ride in a closed motorcar, where nobody would see him getting conked on the head and rolled out on a quiet stretch of bank."

So Mockford had paralleled – only more scientifically – Ranklin's own thinking. However, he'd also gone further: "And there might be signs in that motorcar, human blood spots and so on, that nobody's yet cleaned out. Now I'd like you to explain why we should give them time to clean it out."

"I quite understand," Ranklin said, "albeit, as you say, tenuous. What d'you know of this Rupert Peverell?"

"Nothing. Do you?"

"Not me, but—" Ranklin turned to Lieutenant Jay.

"He's the second son of General Sir Caspar Peverell of Downshire Hall, and just come down from Cambridge where he acquired some rather extreme political views and a taste for free love."

"You know him well?"

"Never met him," Jay smiled.

Taken aback, Mockford blinked and paused, impressed by Jay's encyclopaedic knowledge of upper class gossip – but perhaps not just by that. Rupert Peverell sounded like somebody who didn't get jumped on by policemen.

Ramming it home, McDaniel said reproachfully: "I did try to say, sir: the address given is in Belgrave Square."

Jay said cheerily: "Yes, that's the family's London place."

You didn't go kicking down doors in Belgrave Square, either. Not unless you were a good friend of the family.

There was a long silence. Mockford clasped his hands at his chins and thought. McDaniel swung gently on his pivoting chair. Lacoste went on being stony-faced, only now gloomy with it.

At last Mockford raised his head. "I could have a beat bobby ask the men in the motorcar what they're doing."

"We know what they're doing," Ranklin said. "They're keeping an eye on Mam'selle Collomb. He'd just frighten them off."

"Is your Bureau proposing to do anything about it?"

"We're interested," Ranklin said cautiously.

"When there's any policing to be done in this town, the police are going to do it," Mockford warned. Then he seemed to come to a decision. He hauled himself to his feet and suddenly became fawningly polite. "Thank you so much for taking the trouble to drop in on us, Captain Ranklin. And you too, Mr Hopkins. I do hope we'll meet again soon." It was as false as a half-crown gold watch and intended to seem so. Except for the bit about meeting again soon, perhaps.

On the way out, Jay said: "He's going to put watchers on that motor."

"I think so. But you heard him: it's his beat, not ours."

"And they won't be as good as O'Gilroy, so they'll probably be spotted."

"Let's hope the two in the car aren't as good, either."

* * *

RANKLIN WAS BACK WELL before five, but O'Gilroy had already been deputed to get the flat ready, which meant little more than putting decanters on the sideboard and ashtrays on the vast table. Jay had gone up to brief the Commander; they both came down soon after, and everyone sat down to wait for the voice-pipe to announce Quinton. Pedantically, he arrived on the dot of five.

Ranklin met him at the lift, explaining misleadingly: "This is just a quiet place we maintain. It's right across from the War Office, so..." Implying that that was where their real offices were.

In the big, gloomy dining room Quinton carefully placed his topcoat and hat on a chair and looked around. "I imagine this is a good place for extracting confessions."

The Commander chuckled. "Not our business. And we took this as is when the previous tenant died."

Quinton sat down. "I see he liked William Morris wallpaper."

"Possibly better even than Morris did," Ranklin said with feeling. "Can I get you a drink while the Commander does the introductions?"

So Ranklin was mixing a brandy and soda at the sideboard as the Commander reminded Quinton that he already knew Ranklin, and the others were "Lieutenant Jay" and "Mr Gorman from Paris". The Commander might not remember to stick to those aliases; he was just spreading an aura of professional secrecy to make Quinton feel he was being allowed to stay up for dinner with the adults.

The table itself was too big for handshakes, so there were distant smiles and nods and Quinton carefully positioned his chair and briefcase to colonise his few square feet. Ranklin put his drink on the table and Quinton positioned that, too.

The Commander said: "Very well, the Steam Submarine Committee is in session again. We welcome Mr Noah Quinton to our humble table."

"May I second that, chairman?" Jay said smoothly. "We're well aware of Mr Quinton's distinguished record in the law and honoured to have him join us." This was obviously pre-planned: Jay didn't normally say things like that. "And if I may presume to call on Mr Quinton's extensive knowledge of the law, could he explain why young Grover Langhorn can never lawfully become king? – assuming, of course, that he *is* the King's eldest son. Is it the Settlement Act of 1700-odd?"

"Not that one," Quinton said briskly. "That's mostly concerned with putting the House of Hanover on the throne and keeping Roman Catholics off it. No, it must go back earlier than that, but this isn't a question that crops up every day, you know. I'd need to look up a few things."

Since this was all a ploy to make Quinton feel important, Ranklin tried to keep him going by saying: "As I recall from my schooldays, when the Tudors were feuding about religion, both Mary and Elizabeth were declaring each other illegitimate and having Parliament re-legitimise themselves."

Quinton nodded. "The very point being that illegitimacy would have kept them off the throne – so we have to look back even further than the Tudors. We'll probably end up in common law."

"Surely not *common* law?" Jay said, reverting to his usual self and getting a sharp look from the Commander.

"The common law of England," Quinton said firmly, "is a sight more sensible and reliable than many of the half-baked measures dreamed up by Parliament these days."

The Commander could agree on that. "Self-serving tradesmen," he said in a cloud of pipe-smoke.

"And under common law principles of inheritance, neither property nor titles of honour can pass down an illegitimate line. Perhaps monarchy comes under 'titles of honour'."

The Commander sniffed loudly. "Let's assume it does. After all, history's full of royal bastards and none of them acceded to the throne. Now—"

But now Quinton had got the taste for exposition. "You know, this has interesting echoes of the Mylius case three years ago."

From his expression, the Commander could have managed without Mylius, but said politely: "Do tell us."

"It was a criminal libel case. I believe the Palace wanted to ignore the whole thing, but the Home Secretary – then Winston Churchill – took a more aggressive line. Mylius – he was writing in an English-language paper published in Paris but distributed over here – claimed the King had secretly married a daughter of Admiral Culme-Seymour in Malta in eighteen-ninety. What he was really attacking was the supposed doctrine that the monarch can do no wrong."

He paused and Ranklin asked: "Does that still hold?" He got a look from the Commander for encouraging the man.

"What Mylius wrote, and I quote—" he had even brought a paper to quote from "—was: 'The King is above the law and can do no wrong. He may commit murder, rape, arson or any other crime, yet the law cannot try him.' Of course, he could have pointed out that any diplomatist enjoys as much immunity, possibly more. However, the doctrine that the King can do no wrong is thought to obtain, for a constitutional monarch, only so long as the King does not act except upon the advice of his ministers. So, unless one can envisage a minister *advising* the King to commit murder, rape or arson—"

"Lloyd George?" Jay suggested.

The chuckles threw Quinton off his stride and the Commander took the opportunity to say: "Most instructive. Now can—"

"Mylius got a year in jail," Quinton muttered.

"Richly deserved. But if we can get back to the present day… We haven't established that this anarchist puppy *is* the King's son—"

"Probably impossible to do so." Quinton bounced back fast; probably lawyers had to. "Presumably his birth certificate – have you dug that up yet?"

"He may have been born in America," the Commander said. "What weight does a birth certificate have in court?"

"It's accepted as proof unless it's challenged. And even then, you can only show that the father named couldn't be the real one – by reason of impotence, say, or that he was discovering the North Pole at the required time. But that tells us nothing of who the real father is. So, assuming that the birth certificate says the father is Langhorn senior, I'd say the King was not liable in law. But have you found out whether he did...ah, *know* the boy's mother?"

"Dammit, *of course* he was poking her," the Commander growled. "Every lieutenant who could afford it had a loose woman in Portsmouth. Place was stuffed with them. That's not the point. It's what the foreign newspapers will make of the lad's claim to be a royal bastard if they get to hear of it. Now: is there any legal way of stopping that?"

"You – or rather, the Palace – could take out an injunction. That can be done secretly – but in the end, all it could do is bring the wrath of the law on Langhorn's head if he spoke out. And if he wants to shout it out the next time he's in court...well, I've advised him not to, but in the end, I can't stop him. And what he says in court is privileged and could be reported even here."

O'Gilroy said: "If he ups and says he's the next king, surely everybody'll laugh and say why not Julius Caesar or Napoleon?"

The Commander nodded firmly. "Yes, we should be concentrating on what the mother may say about the King – the Prince, in those days."

Quinton asked: "Did he write her any letters?"

It was as if a sudden ice age had struck the room. Everybody held their breath and went quite still. Then it passed, leaving only shivers behind.

"God, I hope not," the Commander said fervently.

In an even, reasonable voice, O'Gilroy said: "She didn't pick this road until jest recent. She could've started causing this ruckus twenty-four years ago, when she found she was going to have a baby. But she didn't. She married the American feller and started a new life in America. If she had any letters and such, probly she burned them then. Never thought she'd want to look back."

"Thank you for that touch of common sense, O'G—Gorman," the Commander said. "I just hope you're right."

Quietly, Ranklin got up, fetched the whisky decanter, and refilled the Commander's glass. O'Gilroy and Jay shook their heads, and Quinton had taken only a couple of sips at his brandy.

"Do we know," Quinton asked, "what the mother wants out of all this?"

"We haven't had a peep out of her since that letter you saw," the Commander grumbled. "But it seems to have been assumed by...certain others, that she'll settle for a pension. They've put an advertisement in this afternoon's Paris papers asking her to come in and get some good news from our consulate, which we take to mean money. Naturally enough, this has got the French police up in arms."

"You know," Ranklin said thoughtfully, "I don't think we should necessarily assume that the woman *will* settle for a pension. She might just be taking this my-son's-the-next-king stuff seriously and sees herself as the Queen Mother."

Quinton said: "I've explained—"

"Not to her."

"Well, I certainly have trouble envisaging Mam'selle Collomb as our next queen."

Ranklin shut his eyes and shuddered.

The Commander, who hadn't met Berenice, smiled automatically. O'Gilroy looked disapproving on behalf of all fairy-tale milkmaids who reach the throne.

The telephone rang in the drawing room and Ranklin got up to answer it. Behind him, Quinton was saying: "I'm sure Mrs Langhorn's position will be explained to her..."

"I have a call from a Mrs Finn," the office switchboard girl told Ranklin. "She says it's very urgent. Should I connect her?"

"Please do," and he listened as she wrestled with the "instant" communication that was going to change the world.

At last a very distant Corinna came on: "Matt? Matt? Get over here, Berenice has been kidnapped."

CHAPTER TEN

Rolls-Royces might not zoom, either, but this one certainly *surged* when the Commander put his foot down. Ranklin felt the clenching of mechanical muscle like a horse preparing to leap, then the release as it soared off. But unlike a horse, it soared on and on as the Commander kept accelerator and horn depressed. Ranklin got the (fleeting) impression that other motorists turned angrily to see what frightful bounder was making that din, saw two tons of speeding Rolls-Royce behind, and chose to live long enough to write to *The Times* about it.

Looked at coolly, it was an odd way for the Secret Service Bureau to cross London, but by now Ranklin was praying that the Commander was at least looking, never mind coolly. They were all armed: Ranklin and O'Gilroy with their own pistols, Jay and the Commander with weapons grabbed from his collection in the inner office.

The steel-on-steel brakes screeched like escaping steam as they swung out of the Mall and up past St James's Palace, barged into the traffic of Pall Mall, up St James's, swerved into Piccadilly, and finally up Clarges Street. Corinna was waving energetically from the pavement.

"That Sackfield bitch from Bloomsbury Gardens called," she panted, "and wanted to take Berenice for a walk and I couldn't exactly stop them, but I could go along, and your young guy following *incognito*. And near Hyde Park Corner an automobile pulled over and they shouted for Berenice to jump in and she did, and the Sackfield woman stopped me interfering but I stopped *her* getting in and her eye won't be the same in *weeks*, and your guy came running but the automobile got away, and I think he may have got a taxi round in Constitution Hill, but I got one back here to telephone you."

"What motorcar?" Ranklin asked.

"Dark red and a landau body." The Yard might have felt inhibited about offending that car's owner, but not so the Bureau.

"Go up and telephone the office," the Commander told Ranklin. "See if P's called in."

Ranklin bounded up the stairs, leaving Corinna and her skirt plodding after. He had already rung the bell, rushed in and grabbed the telephone by the time she caught up.

"What happened to the Sackfield woman?" he asked.

"God knows. I wanted to get back here."

"And you obviously didn't have your pistol with you."

Corinna travelled with an outdated but still handy Colt Pocket Pistol in her "purse" but: "In daylight in Mayfair?"

Then the office switchboard answered: yes, Lieutenant P had just called, he'd lost the red Simplex, but it had been going up Shaftesbury Avenue and he'd called from the post office there. *Damn* – P wasn't properly briefed, he didn't know the Bloomsbury Gardens address.

"If he calls again," Ranklin said, "tell him to get back to the office to act as co-ordinator." Then he ran.

"What do I do?" Corinna yelled after him.

"Guard the telephone."

"Don't you want another automobile?"

Ranklin stopped.

* * *

IN THE STREET, the Commander was talking to two men, one in a sober suit and bowler hat, the other a derelict loafer – obviously Superintendent Mockford's men.

O'Gilroy intercepted him and confirmed: "Coppers. Was watching the motor, but scared it off, more like. Drove away an hour and more ago. And of course, the coppers didn't have their own motor to follow in."

Ranklin nodded and pushed straight into the Commander's conversation. "He lost it heading north-east, it could have gone to Bloomsbury Gardens."

The Commander abandoned the policemen in mid-sentence. "Right, all aboard!"

The more respectable looking one said: "I think I'd better come along, too, sir."

"Sorry, no room." The Rolls-Royce, an open tourer, could have carried a platoon. And a policeman could add legitimacy to what might otherwise be an outright brawl.

"Mrs Finn's having her own motorcar brought round," Ranklin said. "O'Gilroy and I could go in that. Then we can split up if Berenice isn't at Bloomsbury Gardens."

The Sherring Daimler appeared at the end of the street at the same time that Corinna shot out of the apartment house.

The Commander waved a hand impatiently. "Oh, all right. Get in the back, Inspector or Sergeant or whatever you are."

By the time the Rolls-Royce surged away, Corinna had talked the chauffeur out and taken his place. Whatever she promised or threatened, Ranklin didn't hear, but they left the man looking pretty bewildered.

"Bloomsbury Gardens?"

"Please. But if it looks like getting at all rough, you stay in the motorcar. And if anybody starts shooting, get out and hide behind the engine... That's at the front."

"I know where the *engine* is!"

"It's solid enough to stop anything."

She turned her head to look at him. "Why this sudden concern? You've had me loading *artillery* guns for you."

"That just happened. I don't want your luck running out —*Please* watch the road!"

* * *

THE SIMPLEX WASN'T PARKED outside 14 Bloomsbury Gardens, nor anywhere else in the square or within a hundred yards down any of the streets off it. By the time the Daimler had finished its reconnaissance, the others were inside the house. The Commander was only just inside; he'd found a chair and was letting things develop around him.

Venetia Sackfield, with a rip down the front of her pale violet dress and a wet towel held to her left eye, was in full protest: "You've got no right at all to come charging into this house! This is sheer oppression!"

The bowler-hatted policeman said: "A complaint has been made, madam, that—"

Corinna pointed melodramatically: "I want that woman arrested for assault and kidnapping!"

"Berenice got into that car willingly!"

"Do you agree, madam, that you were present—?"

"Are you saying you didn't assault—?"

"Berenice is within her rights—"

Ranklin and O'Gilroy left them to it and went to help Jay search the house. A kidnapping charge might even make that legal, though the Bureau wasn't too expert on legality.

They met Jay coming downstairs escorting a young man in shirt-sleeves who looked pale, just woken, and hungover. "Meet Rupert Peverell," Jay said cheerfully. "The owner of a dark red Simplex landau."

"Ah, the chap the police say helped murder the French meat porter," Ranklin said loudly.

Peverell got several degrees more sober. "They say… I didn't… *What?*"

"'T was yer motor they used," O'Gilroy said. "That makes it for yeself to prove yer innocence." His law was as twisted as his grin, but the grin was indisputable. It possibly reminded Peverell of a shark halfway through a good meal.

"I-I-I lent it t-to some chaps," he stuttered.

"Names?" Ranklin snapped.

"J-just some friends o-of Feodor's."

"Gorkin's?" Ranklin glanced at Jay, who shook his head: no one else in the house. "Look the place over for clothes and luggage." Back to Peverell. "Where is Gorkin?"

"I-I d-don't know. I-I've been as-sleep. G-got a bit tiddly. Sorry." He sat down abruptly on the stairs, leaned slowly over and was sick.

Ranklin went back to the policeman standing just inside the front room with Corinna and Venetia Sackfield. "I've got the owner of the Simplex for you. But he's no idea where it is."

"Good. The Super very much wants a word with him. It seems there isn't a telephone here, so—"

"Telephone wire going into the place two doors down," O'Gilroy told him.

"Oh, splendid. I've informed this lady she's under arrest, so if you'd watch her for me? If she tries to escape, please do not use violence, just follow her."

"I'm not trying to escape, you nincompoop!" Venetia flared. "I *live* here."

When the policeman had gone, Ranklin nodded Corinna after him.

"Now hold on, I—"

"Out." Ranklin jerked his thumb. She flounced: but flounced out. He turned to Venetia and made his voice quiet and reasonable. "We are genuinely worried about the fate of Berenice. It isn't a question of the police this time, it's some unknown men that Mr Peverell lent his motorcar to. The police think Guillet, the murdered Frenchman, *may* have got into that motorcar just before he was killed. So, I hope you understand our worry about Berenice definitely getting into it. I want you – please – to tell us anything you know about those men and where they've taken Berenice."

"She's going back to France, of her own free will. That's all."

"Too late for a boat today," O'Gilroy said.

"Of her own free will."

"One last appeal," Ranklin said. "Please?" After a moment, he turned to O'Gilroy. "She's obviously in it with them. Maybe two murders, and I doubt the police'll be able to prove it. Hardly seems just, that."

He walked over and snapped the bolt on the door.

O'Gilroy took out his pistol, examined it – then thrust it at Venetia's face.

Ranklin walked back. "She suddenly produced a firearm – this one." He took out his revolver. "From under that cushion there. You had no choice."

"We need her fingerprints on it," O'Gilroy said, his gun quite steady.

Ranklin seized Venetia's hand and squeezed it round the revolver. She pulled free and Ranklin shrugged. "I'll get better ones when she's dead. Nobody can tell."

"And mebbe a touch of gun oil on the cushion underside?"

"Good point." He smiled at Venetia. "You see? It's the little things that give conviction." He put the revolver down and his fingers in his ears. "In your own time, Mr Gorman."

"I don't *know* their names!" Venetia wailed.

Ranklin shook his head irritably. "Get it over with, man." He replaced his fingers.

Venetia collapsed into a chair and spoke in one panting rush.

"Dr Gorkin met them at the Jubilee Street anarchists' club. I don't know their names, honestly. They come from around there, they mentioned a Tarling Street. It's in the East End, you go down Whitechapel High Street and just after it becomes the Mile End Road—"

By then Ranklin was unbolting the door. Unbelieving, Venetia stared at him. Then she rounded on O'Gilroy, who was calmly uncocking his pistol. "You aren't police! I'm going to *tell* the police!"

"What'll ye tell 'em? That ye helped two fellers ye knew was from the anarchist club kidnap her?" He turned away and, when he had turned, swallowed hard. He honestly hadn't been sure what would have happened next, what was *supposed* to happen next. Ranklin had been so convincing about wanting the woman killed...

Well, she had been convinced, and that was all that mattered.

When he got outside, Ranklin and Corinna were standing on the pavement, with her pointing out that it was *her* automobile, God damn it.

"It'll be the East End, and if we catch up with these men, I don't want to have to worry about you."

"But I'll be driving, leaving you free to—"

"O'Gilroy can drive – and when we get there, I'd like him guarding my back, not staying behind with you."

That was a low blow and the fury on her face showed it. But it ended the fight: she stood aside, looking daggers. Nasty Eastern curly ones.

The bowler-hatted policeman appeared again. "Superintendent Mockford's on his way. He wants you to—"

"Save your breath," Corinna advised, as the Daimler pulled away behind the Commander's Rolls-Royce. "No women or policemen allowed."

* * *

Perhaps traffic was lighter in the City, but the roads there were narrower. Then suddenly they were out on the broad highway of Whitechapel High Street and though neither the Commander nor O'Gilroy knew this territory, all they had to do was follow the tram lines and scatter the queues coming out to board a tram.

By now the Daimler was leading, Ranklin in the front seat and reading from a London map. Having located Tarling Street, he directed O'Gilroy down the Commercial Road.

"Are we looking for this club place?"

"No, they'd tell us nothing. Also, I forgot to ask whereabouts in Jubilee Street it is and it's nearly half a mile long. We'll try Tarling Street; it's shorter."

He had O'Gilroy turn down Sutton Street East and stop, then walked back to the Rolls-Royce. "Tarling Street's the second on the right," he told the Commander. "D'you want to give any orders?"

"You carry on, you're doing fine."

Ranklin nodded. "Our one hope is finding that Simplex. We've got no proper address, no description, nothing but that motorcar. And it may not be parked outside the right house. Down here…" He gestured: down here, a private motor would stand out like a lighthouse; the locals had as much chance of owning one as they did a holiday home on the moon.

"So, if you spot it, knock on doors and ask questions." And Jay, who would be sent to do the knocking and asking, nodded unenthusiastically.

"You take the next right and work your way down," Ranklin told the Commander. "We'll go down to the railway—" it crossed Sutton Street on arches two hundred yards ahead "—and work our way up."

Already the sight of two big shiny motorcars had brought an audience to the nearer doorsteps. The women all wore aprons and kept their arms folded except when they were cuffing their children. Ranklin felt like an explorer meeting an alien tribe and wasn't sure how they'd answer if he tried speaking to them.

The whole area was alien, dreary, shabby and above all featureless. Just rows of terraced houses, as small as they could be and packed as tight as they could be. These streets lacked even the small, starved shops and sad little pubs of the Commercial Road. Here and there a scrubbed doorstep and shining-clean windows stood out, but such signs of determined hope were rare. And if Ranklin had thought brickwork was just brickwork, he learnt that here it wasn't: it could be unskilled and careless, with rotting mortar.

And it was so *small,* everything so Lilliputian – except in area. They had passed miles of such streets and he knew there were more miles all around.

They trundled slowly down Sutton Street: there were no side streets on the left, and nothing parked anywhere on the cobbles except for an occasional hand-cart and a couple of horses and carts delivering things. They turned right alongside the railway and there was a motor by Shadwell station, but it was the wrong make and colour and had someone in it obviously waiting for a train passenger.

Right again up Watney Street, which would bring them past the other end of Tarling Street. But first there was a Congregational Church on the corner of a small cross street, and outside was parked the Simplex. It was empty.

O'Gilroy stopped in front of it and they got out and, for want of something to do, peered into the motor. A couple of small boys, in trousers chopped off around the knees, sidled from an alleyway opposite and walked quickly towards the corner, glancing across at them furtively.

O'Gilroy was the one to catch on. He waited until the boys were out of sight, then ran. Bemused but trusting, Ranklin followed. At the corner of the church O'Gilroy stopped, crouched and peered from an unexpected height.

"What are we doing?" Ranklin asked.

"They'd paid those kids to guard the motor, of course. And warn 'em when the likes of us arrived." And the kids, lacking the Bureau's deductive reasoning, were instead leading them to the right address. Simple. Except that Ranklin would have missed it.

O'Gilroy hurried across the road. Ranklin saw the Rolls-Royce and waved it towards him. O'Gilroy was peeking round into Tarling Street. Then he ran around the corner.

As the Rolls-Royce came up and turned, Ranklin jumped on the running-board, and they accelerated after O'Gilroy. The two boys scattered from a front door halfway down a terrace of two-storey houses. A man stuck his head out, saw the might of the Secret Service Bureau at full charge, and slammed the door in O'Gilroy's face.

He didn't bother with it. He tried the front door next along – it wasn't even locked – and plunged in. Ranklin reached the shut front door just ahead of Lieutenant Jay. He tried one push, fired his revolver twice into the lock, then stab-kicked the door. It tore open – and he hesitated before barging into the dark hallway ahead.

From next door came a wave of outraged yells and children's screams charting O'Gilroy's route through to the back yard. Ranklin said: "Oh, bugger it. Cover me," and charged ahead in a crouch. He must remember he had only three shots left.

He threw open a door on his right, got no reaction, and saw it was dim but empty. Jay had rushed past, holding some long cowboy pistol from the Commander's collection. Suddenly there was uproar from a closed door at the end of the hallway, perhaps including Berenice's voice.

Jay kicked in the door and ducked. Past him, Ranklin saw a man dragging Berenice out into the back yard. Then, from next door's back yard, O'Gilroy shouted: "Yer surrounded!" The man part-loosed his grip on Berenice to raise an odd-shaped pistol at O'Gilroy's voice. Berenice wrenched free and went sprawling.

Four guns went off in a mixture of cracks, bangs and the boom of Jay's cowboy weapon. The man staggered, tried to correct his balance, and died trying. He fell like a puppet with its strings cut.

Thinking back afterwards, Ranklin wondered if, after days of tiptoeing around with legalisms and delicate questions, there hadn't been a subconscious desire to *do* something.

CHAPTER ELEVEN

The average policeman looked very big in that small, low, narrow house, and this many looked like a Derby Day crowd. By the time Superintendent Mockford arrived, Ranklin had tidied matters up a bit. A second man had been found hiding under a bed upstairs, with a jammed pistol nearby. Questioning him had been delegated to Jay and O'Gilroy. Meanwhile the Commander had been persuaded (it hadn't taken much effort) to go away.

And Ranklin had talked to Berenice. She was badly shaken, shivering and pale under her grubbiness, but he had found a man's topcoat to wrap around her while she told of being taken "to see Dr Gorkin", which hadn't happened, and gradually coming to the conclusion that she was going to be killed.

"Oh, you were, you were," Ranklin said as convincingly as possible. The last thing he wanted was her saying she'd been having a wonderful time until the Bureau arrived.

* * *

AND NOW IT was just after sunset and Mockford and the three

agents were standing in the little paved area by the corpse, watching a police doctor decide he was dead and a photographer set up his camera and tripod.

The doctor stood up and washed his hands under the tap against the house wall. "He's got at least five bullet holes in him – I wouldn't be surprised to find more when I get him stripped down – and very little bleeding. I think you can say death was instantaneous, if that's of any help."

Mockford asked: "And where do you think his one shot went?"

O'Gilroy waved his hand towards the chest high garden wall to the right. "Somewheres over there."

Mockford looked at the darkening eastern sky and grunted. "You can have him when the photographer's through, doctor," and turned back into the house.

It was full of policemen, making laborious lists of things found and wrapping some of them in brown paper for fingerprint tests later. In the hallway two constables were waiting with a well-worn coffin to remove the deceased, and they had to ease their way past them to reach the front room. Another constable came through the broken front door with a billycan, a handful of enamel mugs and enough sense to offer tea to the Super first.

Ranklin had never seen a police investigation in action before and was struck by how slow, how mills-of-God it seemed, in contrast with the few seconds of action that had caused it. Like gravediggers on a battlefield, perhaps.

"Have you found anything?" Mockford demanded of a searcher in the front room.

"Nothing much, sir, but—"

"Then probably there's nothing here. Try again later." He took a spindly chair, shook the heaviest dust off it, and sat down. They all found places to sit, and the four of them filled the room nicely. So, then they had to have a fifth, a sergeant with a notebook who looked carefully at the wall before leaning on it.

The single gas lamp had been lit and curtains, only thick enough to blur the vision, pulled shut.

"First, sir, can you tell me why you didn't just watch this house and the motorcar, and send word for us?"

"Not that easy," Ranklin said. "We didn't know which house except by following the kids who were to tip them off that we'd arrived. Then we either had to charge in at once or lose surprise. Basic military tactics."

"This was not a military exercise – sir."

"I don't know...it might be best if it somehow was. You're going to meet a lot of pressure not to say who we really are."

"Don't write that down, sergeant," Mockford said quickly, then sighed. He was used to being told "your superiors won't like this", but not to its being true. And certainly not to Ranklin's sympathetic tone, as if the whole thing had been just an incident that was nobody's fault. "You could still have just set a watch on the house – sir. Even if they knew you were out there."

"Again, I can't agree. They'd either have sat tight and you'd have had the Siege of Sidney Street all over again or they'd have broken out – they were armed, but didn't know that we were – and what then? A shooting match in the middle of the street? Either way, you'd have had more people killed, probably including Mam'selle Collomb."

Privately, Mockford might well have agreed but even a siege, with dozens of police, hundreds of soldiers, thousands of pounds worth of damage and several more deaths, could have been somehow made normal. Coroners' verdicts, court cases, committees and commissions would have chosen heroes and villains and fitted the whole thing into the British way of life. Instead, one man had been killed by the wrong people in the wrong way and it didn't fit at all.

A man didn't have to be thinking of his pension to think like that. He need only think of what he had devoted his life to: law *and order,* a proper way of doing things. Without that, you had the jungle – whatever Dr Gorkin might say.

Mockford grunted and wriggled on the undersized and rickety chair. "Let's look at what these two villains intended, then. One's dead so we can't question him, the other seems very reluctant to talk to us – did he say anything to you? You can take notes, sergeant."

Jay said: "He didn't want to say anything but we...we persuaded him."

"*Don't* note that, sergeant," Mockford said wearily.

"I had to speak German to him, although I think he's Russian or Latvian or something. I don't think O'...Mr Gorman could follow it all, but he gave excellent moral support."

Ranklin could imagine O'Gilroy smiling his smile and clicking the Browning and sighting it occasionally at various parts of the man's body.

"What it amounts to," Jay continued, "is that they were going to drug the girl, wait until dark, then take her away in the motor and dispose of her. Of course, once he knew his colleague was dead, it was he who'd done everything, planned it all, been in charge. I imagine that's an old story to you, Superintendent."

The sergeant, by now thoroughly confused, looked at Mockford. He nodded, and then they waited in silence for the notebook to catch up. Not true silence: the cardboard-thin door and walls passed on every movement in the house and a garbled mutter from every conversation.

At last Mockford asked: "And who got them to do all this?"

"He described a man who could have been your—" Jay nodded to Ranklin "—Feodor Gorkin. But I hadn't, as one might say, completed my inquiries when your chaps arrived."

Mockford grunted. "I should think he was very glad to see my chaps arriving." He got up, threaded his way to the door and bellowed: "Inspector McDaniel? Do you know anything about a Feodor Gorkin?"

From somewhere at the back of the house McDaniel called: "I think the French inspector does, sir."

Mockford looked back to Ranklin, who said: "I first thought he was just an anarchist journalist and pamphleteer, but he's beginning to look more and more the ringmaster. Only I don't know of what circus. He was staying at the Bloomsbury Gardens house."

"But there weren't any clothes or luggage that might have been his," Jay said. "So, we rather fancy he's gone."

Mockford seemed about to give an order, and Ranklin said quickly: "Our Chief was going to ask Special Branch to keep watch at the ports for him. I meant to ask Miss Sackfield just when Gorkin left, but we had to hurry on here."

"Did you?" Mockford asked pointedly. When Ranklin said nothing, the Superintendent went back to his chair and sat down carefully. "Now, did anybody mention the murder of Guillet?"

"I *knew* I'd forgotten something," Jay said sunnily. "I said to our chap: 'You murdered Guillet,' and he looked blank and Mr Gorman made a...a gesture—" putting a loaded pistol to the man's head, probably "—and it suddenly came back to him: the other chap had murdered him, he'd only watched."

"Jesus Christ," Mockford said heavily. "Yes, I see – but I wonder if you do? Your heavy-handed and quite illegal questioning of this man, which defence counsel will bring out at a trial, may make it impossible to convict him of either murder or kidnapping – do you realise that? He may actually go free."

Jay looked contrite. "I'm most frightfully sorry. Perhaps we should have shot both of them."

That hadn't been the right answer. Mockford looked at Jay without expression for a moment, then turned to Ranklin. "I suppose I'm still not allowed to know just what it is you're doing or looking for?"

"I'm afraid not."

"Then will you answer me this, sir: is it more important than solving a murder?"

Ranklin felt Jay and O'Gilroy looking at him and felt also that he shouldn't be answering for them. But really, he had no choice; he was the senior, his answer would be theirs, and his first duty was to protect them.

He temporised. "But you've solved your murder. We know it was those two thugs and they used the Simplex."

"No!" It was a sudden bark. "To us, just knowing is *not* solving it at all. Every bobby on the beat knows who's done what. The hard part is catching and convicting them and that's what we have laws for. Not so we'll know, but so we can do something about it. And be seen to do something. A murder isn't solved until someone's been hung for it, all nice and legal.

"So, I'll ask you again, sir: is whatever you're doing more important than us solving a kidnapping and murder?"

Ranklin didn't answer immediately. He was remembering how shocked he'd been at the idea of the law being manipulated to bring the "right" result to Langhorn's extradition. Hadn't he said something about it setting us back three or four hundred years? Yet now he was blithely assuming that laws would be twisted to protect the Bureau.

But if there were any excuse, that was it: The Bureau. They hadn't come dashing down here as individuals, but as agents of the Bureau. O'Gilroy and Jay were owed the protection of the Bureau, and it was up to him to see that they got it.

"Do you believe in patriotism, Superintendent?"

Mockford looked wary but said: "Of course I do."

"And yet patriotism sometimes requires men to go out and kill others, destroy property, do all sorts of things which are against the laws of any country you care to name."

"Then are you claiming that you've been behaving patriotically?"

"Indeed I am. It's not just the best excuse we've got, it's the only one."

* * *

PERHAPS MOCKFORD WOULD HAVE FOUND a reply to that, but there was a hideous scraping noise from the hallway. He yanked open the door to see the laden coffin being dragged towards the front door.

One of the constables straightened up and panted: "Too heavy for the two of us, sir, and not room enough to get more."

As they reached the battered front door, Noah Quinton appeared outside. Seeing the coffin, he took off his hat and let it go by. Then he came in.

"Good evening, Superintendent."

"Evening, Mr Quinton. Who are you representing this time?"

"Mrs Finn said that Mam'selle Collomb was in trouble again. Is she here?"

Mockford turned away, mouthing "damned vulture" once he got his back turned.

Quinton followed him into the front room, peered through the dim gaslight until he recognised everybody who mattered, and put his briefcase down on the table. It sagged, and he had to stop the case falling off. "Good evening, Mr...er..." He didn't know who Ranklin was being in this context and didn't mind his uncertainty showing.

"Berenice Collomb is next door or somewhere," Ranklin said shortly. "I think we've just about reached an understanding here—"

"*Have* we?" Mockford asked.

"Well, perhaps an impasse, then. You're obviously going to talk to Sir Basil and he'll talk to the Home Secretary or my Chief, probably both, and..." He spread his hands.

Quinton looked from one to the other. "Am I allowed to know what happened here?"

Ranklin said: "Berenice Collomb had been kidnapped, we

tracked her down to here, a man trying to drag her away took a shot at Mr Gorman, so we shot him."

There was a short silence. Then Quinton murmured: "Most succinct. However, I can't say that I would have advised you to say anything like that…"

"Never mind that. Whatever gets said at a coroner's inquest is going to be arranged at a much higher level than this. It might help if you had a talk to Berenice. She's got an anarchist view of the police —"

"Not only them," Quinton reminded him.

"—and the last time she met them, they suspected her of murder. So, if the Superintendent could now say that she is no longer under suspicion, she might tell us something useful."

Quinton looked at Mockford, who shook his head. "I can't do that, sir. Not until I know more about the whole matter." Being kept in the dark as he was, he was sticking doggedly to the rules. Ranklin could hardly blame him but did.

"Talk to her anyway and see what she says about being kidnapped. We'll think about the rest later."

Quinton took his briefcase away to the back room. Mockford waited until he was sure both doors were shut, but even then, kept his voice low. "It seems to me, sir, that Mr Quinton knows more about this affair than I do."

"Possibly." Ranklin adopted a soothing tone. "He's been involved in it since before we were: extradition, anarchism… God knows what." Then he added: "And perhaps only God."

Mollified or not, Mockford changed the subject. "Before you go, sir, I'd like to take signed statements – just to show my superiors, no question of them being used in court."

Ranklin shook his head. "Sorry, Superintendent, but what isn't written down can't be misplaced."

"You may be called to give an account of your actions to Sir Basil Thomson."

"That's happened before."

Mockford was still digesting that when Quinton came back. "Mam'selle Collomb will only say anything if Mrs Finn's present."

Odd how sudden and strong the bonds of womanhood – the word "femininity" didn't spring to mind around Berenice – could become. Ranklin stood up.

Jay said: "Ho for Clarges Street, then." It seemed that a little of the East End went a long way with Jay.

* * *

BY NOW, the street outside was full of people and rumour, clustered at doorways and under the rare gas lamps hung from the house walls. The local women were now wrapped in shawls – but still with their arms folded – and supplemented by men home from work. And journalists who flocked around whoever came out of the house, asking urgent questions.

"Just smile and shake your head," Ranklin briefed his crew, "and tell them to ask the police. And don't do or say anything to make yourself memorable." He was speaking more to Jay than O'Gilroy there.

Probably Tarling Street hadn't seen so much traffic in its life: several taxis retained by journalists, Quinton's Lanchester, the Sherring Daimler and a more modest vehicle from Scotland Yard. Quinton took Berenice and O'Gilroy, Mockford and a sergeant driver followed in the police motor, while Ranklin took Jay to report to the Commander at Whitehall Court and then try to find and charm *Inspecteur* Lacoste *in re* the matter of Dr Feodor Gorkin. Then he drove the Daimler back to Clarges Street.

The others had got there ahead of him. Corinna opened the door – the staff didn't live in and had gone off duty – and greeted him with a heavy outward breath. "Well…you're back in one piece. I've got garbled accounts of what happened and I'm not sure whether I'd have done better to come with you—"

"You wouldn't. If they'd had a few more seconds' warning, it could have been very different."

"Anyway, you rescued Berenice. I felt bad about her, though I won't pretend I'm wild about having her here again. In fact, I'm not wild about having a class reunion here."

"I could do with a drink."

"In the drawing room. And I've telephoned the Ritz and they're sending round something to eat."

Ranklin couldn't remember eating in days. He followed her into the drawing room and O'Gilroy, who had taken charge of the drinks (had he ever been a barman? Probably; he'd been most other things at some time) gave him a whisky and soda.

Quinton allowed Ranklin one mouthful before looking very obviously at his watch and saying: "I'd like to get on..."

Ranklin took another gulp. "Let me try and put the position to Berenice first. It may help."

So O'Gilroy took Mockford into the kitchen and the other four settled in the drawing room. Ranklin paused to change mental gear into French, then began: "Probably now you understand that all this is more complicated than any of us thought."

Berenice nodded cautiously.

"May I first ask you one thing? – was coming to London all your own idea?"

"Naturally. I used my own savings and did not tell anyone. Who should I tell?"

"How did you come to stay at the house in Bloomsbury Gardens?"

"I went to the court of Bow Street to ask about the trial and there I met Dr Gorkin who saw I did not speak English, so he helped me. Then he took me to his friends at Bloomsbury Gardens. But," she frowned, "I do not understand. Why did Mam'selle Sackfield help to have those men take me?"

"I don't think that some of the people you thought were friends really were." But Berenice wouldn't believe him if he started denouncing Gorkin. She'd have to work that out for herself.

In English, Quinton asked: "Are you trying to establish that she wasn't part of anything that's been going on?"

"*Parlez Français!*" Ranklin snapped. Already Berenice's suspicious look had returned. "Mam'selle Collomb was no part of any plan. So, her being in London was a danger to the plan, but not much until she came away from Bloomsbury Gardens and they didn't know who she might talk to and what she might say. Then they decided she'd have to be killed."

Corinna interrupted: "But *what* might she say?"

Ranklin shrugged and looked at Berenice. "I don't know. Perhaps you'd care to think about that. And who might have wanted to blame Grover Langhorn for the fire and who forced Guillet to go to the police and offer false testimony against him. However, what happened in Paris isn't a matter for the British police. If you just tell the Superintendent about the kidnapping, we can get rid of him and then think about Paris."

Berenice frowned over this, then looked to Corinna, who nodded and said gravely: "I think that is best." She jerked her head at Ranklin. "I trust this man. He may not look much, but he's good at these things. And of course, his intentions are as honourable as hell."

A compliment is where you find it. Ranklin went along to the kitchen and told Mockford: "She's all yours."

CHAPTER TWELVE

A couple of men from the Ritz turned up with trays and baskets of, among other things, a mousse de foie gras, ham in aspic and a chicken mayonnaise. Ranklin and O'Gilroy filled plates and backed off to the drawing room, leaving the other five (now including the police sergeant-chauffeur as note-taker) seated around the kitchen table. Berenice seemed more at ease there, and probably Corinna was happy to confine the smell of absinthe to one room.

There was apparently no question of anybody using Reynard Sherring's rooms, so no absinthe bottles under Reynard's bed.

For a fair while, Ranklin concentrated on simply eating. Then he put his plate aside, found a cupful of warmish coffee still left in the pot, and lit a cigarette.

"What are we doing now, then?" O'Gilroy asked.

"I just don't know." There seemed no obvious step he could take. "Do you know anyone in the consulate in Paris?"

"Coupla fellers."

"Do they know who you are?"

"They've mebbe got an idea; I've told 'em one or two things, jest so's they owe me something. I reckoned—"

Ranklin waved aside explanations: it was the sensible thing to have done. "Then when we get back to the office, I want you to try and raise one of them on the telephone. You know about the Palace advertising for Mrs Langhorn? I'd like to know if there's been any response."

"She'd never turn up for that. Aren't ye thinking same as me? – that someone's organising this whole thing and's got her pretty much locked up?"

"Nevertheless, I think it's worth asking."

* * *

IN THE KITCHEN, the police sergeant-chauffeur was stacking dirty plates half-heartedly, and Corinna was, as he had obviously hoped, telling him not to bother. Quinton was feeding papers back into his briefcase, and Berenice was slumped in a chair, sucking on a cigarette and not even bothering to seem interested in the buzz of English going on round her.

And Mockford was saying: "We may make a charge of kidnapping work out. I've no doubt she was kidnapped but – thanks to you – things may get very delicate when the question of how she was rescued comes up. So, I'd prefer to concentrate on the murder of Guillet: at least that was over and done with before you decided to lend a hand. But it all depends on what evidence we find in the motor."

Ranklin asked: "Are you satisfied that Berenice Collomb is innocent?"

Corinna began: "'Innocent' is *not* a word I'd apply to that young..." then had to smile hastily at Berenice, who had looked half-interested at the sound of her own name. "Not guilty of a particular act, perhaps."

Despite himself, Mockford smiled. "I do see what you mean, madam. I think you and Mr Quinton may take it that she is no longer under suspicion. But we'd obviously need her as a witness at any trial on the kidnapping charge."

There was a thoughtful silence before Mockford added: "Yes, that's another reason why we'd prefer to stick to the murder charge." He picked up his overcoat and wriggled ponderously into it, took his bowler hat, and went out into the hall. All except Quinton and Berenice followed.

"Does this mean," Corinna asked in a low but clear voice, "that I'm no longer responsible for Berenice? And if so, may I say 'Yippee'?"

"You can certainly regard her as no longer on bail," Mockford said, straight-faced.

"But what about tonight?" Ranklin asked. "She can hardly go back to Bloomsbury Gardens, and I don't fancy hawking her round the hotels until I find one that'll take her in. I suppose I *might* put her up at the flat—"

"Ye could not!" O'Gilroy said, his propriety outraged.

Corinna looked dubious about that, too. She turned inquiringly to Mockford.

He shrugged his big shoulders. "We might get her taken in for a night by one of the Protection Societies or the Young Women's Christian Association…"

"And I suppose," Corinna said bitterly, "you'll explain the absinthe as a sentimental childhood toy. All right, she can spend one more night here. But only one. Tomorrow she's on a boat or on the street and I don't mind which."

And Mockford went his way. The rest of them drifted back into the kitchen.

* * *

"WELL," Corinna said, "it seems like you've got your international conspiracy after all. Certainly, it sounds as if you've shed your inhibitions about the use of firearms."

"They'd murdered one man and were planning to do the same to Berenice: we stopped them. It's only the Super who'd rather we'd had a grand siege with more dead and damage because that's what the law allows for."

"And quite right, too," Quinton suddenly burst out.

Startled, Corinna instinctively switched her stance to defend Ranklin. "And what else should they have done? – they saved Berenice's life, didn't they?"

"And me own, like enough," O'Gilroy said mildly. "The bastard was popping off at me with one of them damn great ten-shot Mausers."

"You being illegally on enclosed premises at the time," Quinton pointed out. "As indeed you all were. I wouldn't say this in front of Superintendent Mockford, but I'll say it now: I've stood by and watched you over the past few days – and been dragged into your deliberations, too, just to flatter me – and your whole attitude that you and your Bureau are above the law is far more destructive of the law than any burglar or murderer who commits his offence and runs away. And mark you, I'm not talking about justice, about crusades and big earth-shaking decisions: that's for eminent judges and KCs to babble about in after-dinner speeches. Probably I get involved in *justice* for a tenth of my time, if that much. No. I've given my life to the *law*. Simply a code of behaviour that lets men sleep soundly in their beds and eat breakfasts that don't poison them and go to work without being run down in the street and know they'll be paid for the day's work. And shall I tell you why? Because people are obeying the law without even thinking about it. *That's* civilisation, far more than motorcars and telephones and aeroplanes and rubbish like that and I hate – yes, I *hate* – to see it trampled underfoot by you and your kind."

Ranklin dragged himself up towards the surface of his tiredness. "Your law isn't God-given. It's created by the same government that set up our Bureau, so—"

"Next, you'll be telling me you're just doing your job, and

you're not employed to think," Quinton said contemptuously. "I expect to hear that argument from the gun, not from the man wielding it."

The accusation cut through Ranklin's fog of weariness like a sword. This was a new Quinton – no, it was the real Quinton that Ranklin had been too careless to see. All he'd noticed had been the humble origins and *nouveau riche* knick-knacks, missing that the man had never been simply sailing with the tide of his profession, believing what it believed and saying what it said. He must have thought about every step of his life, because for most of the time the tide had been trying to strand him somewhere out of the way.

"We're dealing with an accusation against the King—"

"Ah, the King. Yes, I wondered how soon we'd get around to that. Are you going to argue that the King needs you and your Bureau because he can't answer back for himself? You know that's nonsense. You just get on the wrong side of the monarchy in this country and you'll very soon find yourself answered. You can say goodbye to promotion and your friends in your profession for a start. You'd be an outcast and you know it."

And he stared at Ranklin until he nodded and said: "All right, I won't argue that, then."

"But don't get me wrong, Captain. I'd take on the defence of the King myself and guard his secrets with every law I know because he's as much right to his secrets as any beggar in the streets. As much but no more."

Ranklin nodded again. "But the trouble is that a beggar disgraced is just that, but the King brought low affects us all. The whole country. Like it or not, that's what being a monarchy means. And whether it's accidental or deliberate, if this country's being put at risk, that's where we come in. Not you, perhaps; you're privileged."

"Privileged?" Quinton both bridled and showed suspicion, getting a lot into a single word.

"Let me put to you a hypothetical question. Suppose you had a client who lied to you, lied *about* you, changed his story…in every way seemed likely to ruin you. What would you do?"

"I'd have to drop him."

"In my profession," Ranklin said mildly, "we call that desertion in the face of the enemy."

After a silence, Ranklin went on: "Could we just take it that there are some problems you can't touch? – but we have to? I'm not saying we're the perfect solution. I'm Army and we're never the perfect solution, only the last resort."

Quinton looked at him for a long time, then nodded and sighed. "If we'd spent a hundredth – a *thousandth* – of our time and money trying to build international laws instead of guns and battleships… All right: I accept you – grudgingly – as a last resort and thank God our civilisation isn't a fragile thing. It can swallow a bit of law-breaking by men like you without it poisoning the whole system. But only so much, only so many, and God help us all if you ever become the *first* resort. Too many secret men doing secret things can pull a nation apart, as is happening in Russia. It could happen here. Anywhere," he added, glancing pointedly at Corinna.

She bridled at having the United States suddenly bracketed with the other nations. "We don't have a king and we certainly don't have a bureau of…whatnot."

"You have battleships," Quinton pointed out.

"Anyhow," she said, sweeping the US Navy aside, "have you found out whether this rumour's *true?*"

She looked from Ranklin to O'Gilroy, who was looking at Ranklin, who was looking abstractedly at the floor. Did someone, he was wondering, really murder a man to disgrace a king? And kidnap and plan to murder a young girl for that? Then he half woke up and said absently: "What? Oh, that, yes. I met the woman's sister when I was down in Portsmouth and she—"

"You did what?" Quinton asked.

"When I was looking for traces of Mrs Langhorn, I found her sister who was also looking."

"Mrs Langhorn has no sister," Quinton said flatly.

Ranklin woke up some more.

Quinton said: "When I took on Grover Langhorn as a client, I went rather carefully into what relatives he might have in this country – people who could visit him in jail or give evidence as to his character. I've had his grandparents traced – they're all dead – and his mother's two brothers, who emigrated together to South Africa. She never had a sister."

Ranklin said slowly: "This was a Mrs Simmons who seemed to know quite a bit about Mrs Langhorn's life – when she was Enid Bowman – in Portsmouth. Personal things you'd only tell a sister."

"Nevertheless, I can assure you—"

"Ye met Mrs Langhorn herself," O'Gilroy said.

* * *

IN THE BACK of the taxi, Ranklin was trying to recall all he could of "Mrs Simmons". "She was talking of Enid Bowman as a young actress and she said she'd been 'unlucky'. She didn't say 'untalented' or 'not much good'. You wouldn't say that about yourself, would you? You'd say 'unlucky'. Oh *blast*!"

O'Gilroy said: "I should've worried more, with her turning up like that to answer jest the questions we was looking to be answered. And leaving her hotel address everywhere we was looking so's we'd be blind not to fall over her."

"I should have taken you with me to meet her."

"I'd never have seen a thing. 'Twas all there in jest the finding of her, and I should've thought of it then."

Ranklin glanced suspiciously at him, but O'Gilroy wasn't giving him an oblique lecture, he really did blame himself as much as Ranklin. It was a comfort, but a bleak one. He'd had Mrs Langhorn, probably the key to the whole thing, in his grasp and let her slip away.

Could she have planned the deception all by herself? How could he know? He'd come away feeling he knew *something*, however little, about the woman he'd met – but now he knew she'd fooled him, he obviously hadn't understood a thing. So, she could have done anything. Except, of course, pay for it all: the crossing to England, several nights at the Queen's Hotel (she couldn't be sure when she'd be found) plus a decent outfit and luggage. All that certainly hadn't come from the purse of a woman living in La Villette.

It was a slightly less bleak comfort that he'd been duped by a conspiracy, not just one middle-aged woman.

"What'd ye have done if ye'd known 'twas her?"

Ranklin was still thinking back to Portsmouth. "Something else she was saying…not actually any one thing, more just the way she seemed to be thinking. As if Grover really had a right to the throne…" But had that, too, been part of the deception? Or the dream that made each new day in La Villette bearable? Aunt to the King hadn't sounded like much, but *mother…* And mothers could certainly assume glittering futures for their sons; his own had once been sure he was a future Field Marshal.

"I asked ye: what'd ye have done if ye'd known who she was?" O'Gilroy persisted.

Ranklin shook his head. "God knows…"

* * *

BACK AT THE OFFICE, the Commander had got impatient with keeping a lonely vigil in his own sanctum and was slumped in the most comfortable chair in the agents' room. Jay, who had bought the chair, was sitting on a hard one at the telephone. He called off hurriedly as Ranklin came in. O'Gilroy had stopped off at the switchboard to start his round of calls to Paris.

"Well?" the Commander demanded.

Ranklin said to Jay: "Get on to the Queen's Hotel at Portsmouth and see if Mrs Simmons is still there – and anything they can tell us." He flopped into a chair. "What's the position at the Yard?"

"They're fuming about the usual things," the Commander said. "Have you got anything new?"

"The last straw – the last one I found out about – is that I was probably talking to Mrs Langhorn herself at Portsmouth. Pretending to be her non-existent sister. I *had* her – and I let her walk away."

"Hmm." The Commander thought about this. "Well, just having her wouldn't have solved our problems in the long run."

Ranklin said nothing.

"Then is that all?" the Commander asked.

"We're definitely up against a conspiracy."

The Commander snorted. "Even I can see that. Murder, kidnapping, motorcars... All that isn't the work of one retired loose woman and her son – who's in jail anyway. But who *is* it the work of? – this Gorkin fellow?"

"I'm convinced he's been running things in London, but I don't think he's been doing it all in Paris. Particularly when he wasn't there. There's a man, Kaminsky, who runs their café, the *Deux Chevaliers,* and probably an anarchist, too... But have you heard anything of Gorkin?"

"No, but he could have got away on the afternoon boat. The alarm wasn't sounded until after that had sailed, and the Yard doesn't have enough to ask the French police to hold him, so..." He heaved his wide shoulders in a shrug.

"Anyway," Jay said from the telephone, "he's an *intellectuel.*"

"What d'you mean?" Ranklin demanded.

The Commander took over the explanation: "Jay got it from that French copper. You know how the French respect brains? – intelligence, education, that sort of thing? It seems the French police have an unwritten law about going easy on..." the word stuck in his throat, but he finally coughed it out: *"intellectuels."*

Jay added: "So we'll need a doubly cast-iron case before we'll get them to help us nail him down."

Ranklin said: "Oh," and left it at that because there didn't seem anything more to say. Then Jay got his telephone connection and started being charming.

The Commander lowered his voice a trifle. "Well, what do we do now?"

"I've got O'Gilroy trying to find out if anybody's turned up at the Paris consulate. But I don't know what we'll do even if anyone has. By now, it may not matter so much who did what; we may have a runaway train and be looking for ways of stopping that."

They were both throwing quick glances at Jay, who was charming in top gear, but scribbling as well.

"All we want is information," the Commander growled at him. "No need to seduce her as well."

Finally, Jay rang off and became instantly business-like. "Mrs Simmons left yesterday evening, despite having to pay for last night anyway—"

"Right after I saw her," Ranklin said.

Jay nodded and consulted his notes. "And it seems there was a man staying with her – but quite separately, nothing indecorous – name of Kaplan, supposedly French but didn't sound like it. Solidly built, not tall, dark, moustache, smallpox scars – would you believe they remembered that last of all? He left at the same time." He struck a match and lit the paper, as per the Commander's standing orders. "They could easily have caught the overnight boat from Newhaven and been in Paris well before lunch today."

"Everybody getting back to Paris," the Commander said.

"In good time for the Royal Visit," Jay said.

The Commander started to give him a nasty look, then realised this could be the simple truth, and rescinded the look.

O'Gilroy came in from the outer office and Ranklin swung round on him. "Did you get through?"

"He says Mrs Langhorn turned up at the consulate."

"How'd they know it was her?"

O'Gilroy gave the ghost of a smile. "Had all the right papers, knew all the right things."

Ranklin nodded. "What did they tell her?"

"Go and meet a feller at the Ritz tomorrow morning at ten, she'd learn more then."

"Somebody from the Embassy or the Palace?"

"He didn't know. Seems they're being a bit hush-hush."

"They didn't think to have her followed when she left?"

"Be yer age, Captain, this is the *consulate*."

"Hm. Ten to one it's some floozy with Mrs Langhorn's papers."

"Ye was expecting that, wasn't ye?"

But Ranklin had turned back to the Commander. "We've got a chance: they've left a door half open there. Whether it's Mrs Langhorn or not, if we were there and followed her it should prove a link to Gorkin or whoever once and for all... And if I've already met Mrs Langhorn, I ought to know if I'm meeting her again."

O'Gilroy said: "There's nary a boat 'til around eight tomorrow, not now."

The Commander stared at his feet. Then he erupted out of his chair and snatched the telephone away from Jay. "Get me through to the Admiralty. Duty Officer."

CHAPTER THIRTEEN

One thing Ranklin knew about torpedo boat destroyers was that they looked incomplete. A simple hull with funnels, ventilators and guns sprouting directly from the deck as if the naval architect had forgotten the superstructure.

Presumably this was what they were heading for across Dover's dark harbour, the wallowing of the steam pinnace squeezing from O'Gilroy the first of a monologue of moans that would last to Calais. Yet this same man had slept while being driven at sixty mph on dark roads by the Commander, who became deranged behind a steering wheel. Tired as he was, Ranklin hadn't wanted God to catch him asleep.

Then the pinnace thumped against a throbbing steel hull and he scrambled up a few rungs of ladder. He was hauled aboard with a gesture that was half a handshake by a lieutenant ten years younger than himself and passed to a mere schoolboy of an officer while the lieutenant greeted Jay and O'Gilroy, then strode off forward shouting orders. The boy led them aft along the cluttered deck to a hatchway that was round and steel and very final-looking, as if they were being battened down to be shot to the moon. Before they had all got below, the destroyer had shaken itself like a wet dog and started moving.

"Take up as much space as you like," the schoolboy said, looking proudly around a ward room that would have been about the size of a railway compartment but for the bunks on both sides. "We'll have you in Calais in two shakes of a duck's tail."

"How long without the shakes?" O'Gilroy muttered.

"Get into a bunk," Ranklin ordered, "and try and be quiet."

"Can I get you mugs of cocoa?" the boy offered. And when that met dead silence, he added: "I'm sure the Captain wouldn't mind me raiding his coffee if you'd prefer?"

"Two mugs of coffee would be splendid," Ranklin accepted, then his voice turned firm. "My colleague will try to get some sleep." He passed O'Gilroy a silver flask of brandy.

"Do we stay here the whole voyage?" Jay asked, fitting himself into a chair at the narrow table.

"Well, sir, there aren't any passageways on these ships, so you have to go up on deck to get anywhere... And there really isn't anywhere to go."

"The Captain won't expect a courtesy call on the bridge, then?" Ranklin asked.

"I'm afraid there isn't a bridge, sir. He conns the ship from the forward gun platform."

"How splendidly economical," Jay murmured, and when the lad went off to clatter in the pantry next door, added softly: "Did you notice that everybody wears rubber boots? I regard that as a bad sign in ships and country houses both."

Still, one had to admire how the Navy, once it had agreed to something, went full ahead without requiring a dozen documents signed in triplicate. Perhaps they had nothing better to do, there being no wars or pirates in the English Channel, but there was still something about having a private craft over twice as fast as any millionaire's. Ranklin just hoped the Lieutenant-Captain remembered to slow down when they neared France.

As they cleared the harbour mouth the thrumming of the engines increased, the water roared and slapped a few inches away and the destroyer shot forward across the calm sea. But the Channel is never truly calm, and this was no big, ponderous ship that took time to roll and pitch. At barely four hundred tons, this vessel twitched suddenly and unpredictably, and Ranklin couldn't help recalling that destroyers had only a short life before they shook themselves to bits.

On the bunk, O'Gilroy moaned. Jay, by contrast, seemed perfectly at ease, sprawled in his chair with one foot braced against an upright, cradling his swaying coffee in both hands. It seemed unlikely he had ever been in a destroyer before, but you never knew with Jay. It was best to assume he knew everyone and had done everything until proven wrong.

In fact, Jay was feeling both buoyant and overawed at being on his first mission abroad with a truly experienced team. And he positively relished that he didn't understand either of them, let alone their bond. The dark, sardonic Irish ex-ranker and the mild, tubby English officer made an odd team, but their exploits together had become legendary (he didn't yet realise that secret services, wary of records, are great breeding-grounds for legend). In his youthful cynicism, Jay had decided that while all life was a pretence, the Bureau and the two men he was with were worth pretending for.

The truth was that Jay was a secret enthusiast. He had joined the Army an overt enthusiast but found that it, or at least his battalion, had no place for enthusiasm. Not merely was it bad form to show it, you weren't supposed to have it at all. What mattered was correct form. Since Jay could be correct without even trying, he turned to things that needed some effort, like seducing senior officers' wives and rigging horse races. On the brink of disgrace – which had become familiar ground – he had been snapped up by the Commander, who believed "the black sheep of the best families" was what the Bureau needed.

It wasn't, Jay had found, that the Bureau particularly wanted rank and breeding; it valued them, but just as it valued being able to lie convincingly or pick a lock. They were tools, for which the Bureau would find a use.

So here he was, in what felt like a stuffy tin coffin running on square wheels, any thought of seasickness stifled by sheer excitement. Not, of course, that he showed it. He did, however, allow himself an admiring glance at Ranklin, who was sitting smoking and hunched in thought, not caring that most of his coffee had spilled or what his pipe might be doing to O'Gilroy. Not much really, Jay decided, not in an atmosphere that was already thick with the smells of stale food and hot oil.

"What do we do when we get to Paris?" he asked.

Ranklin roused himself. "Get to the Ritz ahead of the supposed Mrs Langhorn. Then you and O'Gilroy follow her to see if she leads us to Gorkin." They had to speak loudly. The cabin seemed to be next to the engine room and a high-speed thudding pulsed steadily through the bulkhead.

"Is she part of this plot?"

"The real her?" Ranklin chewed his pipe and shrugged. "Yes and no, probably. I'm assuming she'd do anything to save her boy and that others are trading on that. Getting her to write that letter, bringing her to England to pretend to be her own sister. Which fooled me completely, I admit. My only excuse is that we'd convinced ourselves she was hiding from us and we weren't thinking of conspiracies at that stage."

"And what about the beautiful Berenice Collomb – was she originally part of it?"

"Wild card," O'Gilroy said.

Ranklin swung clumsily around. "I thought you were asleep."

"Tried that. Didn't work. Now I'm trying to die."

Ranklin nodded. "'Wild card' sounds about right. She just came trailing after her lover. Gorkin hid her away in Bloomsbury

Gardens, but then when we got hold of her, he tried to have her done away with. Like Guillet."

Mustering his courage, Jay asked: "You really didn't kill him yourself?"

"Of course, I didn't," Ranklin said with only a hint of impatience. "D'you think if I'd killed him I wouldn't have got more out of him first? If he'd confessed to being bribed or blackmailed into his evidence we'd have been on to this conspiracy almost two days earlier."

Jay nodded and set out to memorise it all. In his bunk, O'Gilroy moaned, except when he was medicating himself with the brandy flask. And the Captain *did* remember to slow down before running into the Calais quayside, where they were met by a lieutenant-commander posted in to make arrangements for meeting the Royal Yacht four days later. He scurried them through the empty streets in a hired motor to board a train that then crawled its way to Longueau, just past Amiens, where they changed to a faster train coming in from Lille. They arrived at the Gare du Nord just after eight o'clock, among a crowd that looked disgustingly bright, well dressed and, above all, well slept. After a long wait, they got a taxi to O'Gilroy's *pension* to wash, shave and for O'Gilroy to change his clothes. Ranklin was at the reception desk at the Ritz hotel by half-past nine.

* * *

THE LESS YOU knew what you were doing, the more assured you should seem – or so ran Ranklin's experience. However, having the inspiration that Major St Claire himself might be the man upstairs was what did the trick at the desk.

At St Claire's room – actually a suite with a drawing room joining two bedrooms – he was greeted with surprise: "What on earth brings you across?"

"More or less the same as you, I think. We got word that you'd found Mrs Langhorn."

St Claire wasn't happy that words like that had got loose. "You'd better come in... Yes, actually we have. How did you find out?"

"Do you mind me saying that the Bureau has its sources? Best I can offer, I'm afraid. Are you going to appeal to her patriotism to get her to drop the claim, then?"

"Ah...no, not exactly. We're actually going to offer her a pension, payable for just as long as she keeps mum about the whole thing."

"Ah... You don't think that might look like admitting her claim is true?"

At that moment, a tall, well-built man in his fifties hurried out of one of the bedrooms, just finishing the knot of a very dull necktie. He wore a dark grey suit, gold-rimmed glasses and what was left of his hair was very pale. He relaxed but frowned when he saw Ranklin.

St Claire stumbled over the introductions. "Captain Ranklin of the...um, well, let's say the War Office – does that suit you? Mr Harland, the solicitor who's acting for His Majesty in this matter. Don't worry," he reassured Harland, "Ranklin knows as much about this as we do. More, I rather think. Shall we sit down?"

When they were seated, and Harland had started fiddling with his tie again, St Claire went on: "Mr Harland will actually be making the offer of a pension and it will be traceable only as far back as the bank. There will be no connection to be made, I assure you."

Ranklin looked grave. "Hm. I can't help feeling that if news of a pension seeps out, everyone will know it comes from the Palace, no matter what."

Harland cocked his head. "I intend to make it clear to the woman that the pension will continue only so long as news of it does *not* seep out."

"Fair enough – but could we consider the thought that it might not be the real Mrs Langhorn but someone who just wants to find out what you're offering and then reveal it all?"

St Claire stiffened. "The consulate officials checked her papers and questioned her closely. They reported themselves as satisfied she was who she claimed to be… And misbehaviour of that sort sounds well beyond the capabilities of a woman of her class living in that part of Paris."

"Quite. But if it *isn't* Mrs Langhorn, that should suggest there are more devious minds involved, shouldn't it?" And while they were considering this, Ranklin went on: "I may be able to identify Mrs Langhorn myself. So, if I can sit in on the interview, and you would hold off on making the actual offer…"

Harland turned to St Claire. "It's for you to decide, Major, but I understood you wanted the matter settled as quickly as possible."

"We do, we do," St Claire soothed. "But if the lady isn't the right one…" He was still puzzling out the implications of this.

Harland turned back to Ranklin. "Are you planning to challenge the woman's identity?"

It was Ranklin's turn to soothe. "Oh no. Whether she's genuine or not, I don't want her to think we have any doubts."

"Then am I to make this offer or not?"

"May we see how it goes and I'll leave you in no doubt about what to do?"

St Claire nodded, and Harland sighed.

"And one more thing," Ranklin said. "I'd like to ask a Mr Jay – one of our people – up here and pop him in one of your bedrooms for a while. Then he'll come out on some excuse, get a look at the lady, and go downstairs ready to follow her. If she isn't Mrs Langhorn—" he thought for a moment, then added: "—and perhaps even if she is, she might lead us to the man behind this affair."

Harland and St Claire exchanged looks, then Harland asked: "Do you really think there is such an affair and such a man?"

"There's been some remarkable goings-on in London, probably orchestrated by a Dr Gorkin, who we think came back to Paris yesterday... Now I'll just pop down and collect Mr Jay."

Harland said: "I fully appreciate the need for discretion and caution in this matter. I just question whether we need all this... this..." He waved a hand.

"Have you ever had occasion to hire private detectives, Mr Harland?"

"I have. And no," he smiled rather bleakly, "I didn't tell them how to go about their business if that was your next question. I'm just concerned about the number of people getting involved."

"We all are," St Claire growled.

* * *

WHEN HE GOT BACK with Jay, leaving O'Gilroy sitting at the back of the lobby, there was a smartly-dressed, middle-aged lady seated in the corner of the room. This certainly was neither Mrs Langhorn nor someone trying to be, which left Ranklin puzzled until St Claire introduced him to Mrs Winthrop, wife of one of the Embassy staff. "I've invited Mrs Winthrop to sit in as chaperone, just for the look of things."

Gracious, polite, interested but not *too* interested – a lot of the diplomatist had rubbed off on Mrs Winthrop. "I understand I'm not to ask what this is all about and not to guess, either," she said, smiling. "You have my word."

Nice to meet someone who *doesn't* know, Ranklin thought sourly, given that Harland and St Claire do, and Corinna and Quinton and...there may be some hermit in the Hebrides who hasn't heard the story yet, but who else? Oh yes, the King himself was supposed not to know. Ironic, that.

A tray of coffee arrived soon after that, and Jay posted himself beside the bedroom door. They drank coffee, discussed the programme of the Royal Visit, and waited.

At ten-past-ten "Mrs Langhorn" arrived and she certainly wasn't the "Mrs Simmons" Ranklin had met at Portsmouth, although she looked about the same age. Instead of being fair and pert, this woman had a sharp, bony face under mousy-brown hair. She was dressed in a skirt and high-buttoned jacket, both in faded grey-blue. An old fur stole dyed a quite unnatural orange was wrapped around her neck. She certainly looked like La Villette in its Sunday best, and from Harland's forced smile, she had him convinced.

And don't forget she may BE Mrs Langhorn, Ranklin reminded himself. It's only my – and O'Gilroy's – deduction that she shouldn't be. I must keep an open mind.

Harland began in legal fashion: "You are Mrs Enid Langhorn, mother of Grover Langhorn who is now – unfortunately – the subject of an extradition hearing in London?"

"That I am, sir."

"And before your marriage, you lived in Portsmouth?"

"Southsea it was, yes, sir."

"And thereafter in the United States of America?"

"For nigh on twenty-two years, sir. Then me and James parted, and I come over to be with my boy Grover. James, he'd taken to the drink something awful, he had, when he'd retired from the sea, and why should I stay around just to be bashed about? I tell you—"

Her voice was genuinely English, without any strong regional accent or touch of American. Still, some people did cling to their original voices, perhaps the one thing from the Old Country that they could retain.

"Quite so," said Harland, who had probably steered his career well clear of domestic violence cases. "And you now live in La Villette?"

"That's where Grover was working, sir. I don't say it's the best part of Gay Paree, but the lodgings ain't expensive and the folks round there—"

They Jay bustled in from the bedroom carrying a cable form. He smiled an apology at Harland and gave the form – blank – to Ranklin. Ranklin made a show of reading it carefully and nodded to Jay. "Yes, that's fine. Get it sent immediately."

When Jay had gone out into the corridor, he smiled at "Mrs Langhorn". "Sorry about that: I just got in from London this morning," he said rapidly. "The police there have arrested one man – another resisted and was shot dead – for the murder of Guillet, the meat porter who was giving evidence against your son. And foiled an attempt to kidnap and possibly murder Berenice Collomb, and they're looking for an anarchist Dr Gorkin who could have been organising all this, along with a certain Monsieur Kaminsky whom you may have heard of. All very complicated, but it does sound as if a big conspiracy's been going on and you may – quite unwittingly, I'm sure – have been a part of it."

Seated more or less beside Harland and St Claire, he couldn't see their expressions. But he could sense the startled bewilderment radiating from them like sparks from a generator.

He hurried on tonelessly: "So it looks as if all the evidence against Grover was quite false and he should be released any moment now."

There was a long silence when he had finished. And then a wide smile broke across "Mrs Langhorn's" face – but late, far too late. She'd been so busy memorising the details of London's happenings and deductions that she reacted too slowly to the one thing a mother would have cared about: her son was accepted as innocent.

Ranklin looked away quickly and murmured to St Claire: "I should have told you this earlier, but I'll give you the details later." He smiled blandly at Harland. "Please continue."

"This...ah, doesn't alter anything?"

"Oh no. But I do think we should take our time and get this

dead right. We can have lunch sent up here, can't we?" He smiled at "Mrs Langhorn". "You can stay for lunch, I'm sure."

Stay on for another three hours? – of course she couldn't. But she didn't let her act slip. In fact, she traded on it, dabbing a grubby handkerchief at imaginary tears of joy.

"Oh sirs, I'm that shook up with the news of our Grover, I can't think of anything else. Oh dear, I just don't know what to say. I couldn't think of nothing else at this time, I really couldn't." She got to her feet, making a nice floundering motion of it, and clutching at her chair arm for support. The men sprang up, too. "Oh sirs, could I come back another time – this afternoon, maybe? I've just got to go and…my head's in such a whirl…"

She fumbled her way to the door and out.

Harland was open-mouthed, his bewilderment quickly turning to annoyance with Ranklin. "Well, I don't know where that leaves us. We don't know where she's gone, whether she'll be back… I just hope *you're* satisfied."

"Indeed I am. She's hurrying off to report what I told her about the conspiracy being spotted. And with any luck, complete the link with Gorkin."

Also anxious but also baffled, St Claire asked: "Then you don't think she was the real Mrs Langhorn?"

Ranklin was about to explain when Mrs Winthrop said in her well-bred voice: "I've no idea what this is all about, but if that woman is the mother of a boy on trial in London, then I'm Lillie Langtry."

"But how could you tell?" St Claire was honestly puzzled.

She stood up from her chair in a corner and gave him a look. "*Men.*" Then she smiled at Ranklin. "Not including you – in a manner of speaking."

CHAPTER FOURTEEN

Jay, a natural Ritz person, had been wandering about the front of the lobby consulting theatre pamphlets and the like while O'Gilroy sat in a corner reading a newspaper and refusing to take off his long topcoat. When "Mrs Langhorn" came downstairs – sooner than they'd expected – Jay strolled after her. O'Gilroy calmly folded his newspaper and drifted off in their wake, watching to see if Mrs L had any other admirers in tow.

He quickly spotted two: both men in nondescript dark topcoats, bowler hats and heavy moustaches, so similarly anonymous that his instincts told him "police" rather than "criminal". But police followers didn't mean there weren't the other sort as well. Whether or not the lady was the true Mrs Langhorn (which he didn't yet know), she would only be there by order of the villains (whoever *they* were) and they'd be fools not to cover their bet with a watcher or two. It troubled him that he couldn't spot anyone.

Meanwhile, Jay was ahead on the Rue de la Paix, pausing to glance into shop windows, then striding out to keep "Mrs Langhorn" in sight. He wasn't doing a bad job, but to an old hand like O'Gilroy he was concentrating more on not appearing to be a follower than on following. The two *flics* were taking one side of the road each in classical pattern.

At the Place de l'Opéra she vanished down into the Metro and there was an unobtrusive rush to be closer to her when she chose her platform. O'Gilroy hung back, following the last *flic* instead, so perhaps he was the only one to spot that a fifth man had joined the party. She must be taking a prearranged route and this one, dressed in what he probably thought was Grands Boulevards fashion and which made him look like a cheap swell, was there specifically to see if she was followed.

To a Londoner the new Paris Metro had a toytown look, with overlarge tunnels and over-small wooden carriages rattling in with a jaunty air. By the time their train arrived, O'Gilroy had positioned himself to get into the carriage behind. He found a seat at one end with his back to the other passengers and began. First, he sprinkled a matchbox of talcum powder over his good-quality boots so that, at a glance, they looked dusty and thus cheap. He dumped the bowler hat and replaced it with a greasy cloth cap (in Paris, berets were for country yokels). Then he took off the long topcoat and revealed a torn, button-less jacket and out-at-the-knees trousers several sizes too big; the Ritz would have had the vapours to know what he'd been wearing under the coat. Finally, he pocketed his tie and collar, rubbed his hands on the carriage floor and then on to his face.

He simply abandoned the coat and bowler, and never mind the Bureau's accountants. The Bureau just wanted believability, and believability was O'Gilroy's stock in trade: he was radiating it when he shuffled off at the next station and into "Mrs Langhorn's" carriage.

Of course, if they turned out to be heading for some posh suburb, he was sunk. But there, Jay would come into his own again, and the further east they went, the less likely posh suburbs became. And the Metro had its standards, skirting around the nineteenth *arrondissement* to make sure that anyone visiting La

Villette, or trying to escape from it, was doomed to a good long walk. Sure enough, the woman got out at Bolivar station and began the trek down the Rue Armand Carrel.

You might say that this was Paris's equivalent of London's East End, but that had been built on virgin land to cram the new breed of factory workers into a dreary, geometrical pygmy-land. La Villette lay within Paris's walls, so had started as farmhouses and village cottages, the gaps gradually filled in with whatever fitted the space and need, until you had today's above-ground warren of unmatched buildings and rambling alleyways. Even in the sunlight, it had a grey Northern bleakness. The slums of Naples might be worse, but their cracked and scabbed walls seemed to have soaked up colour from the Mediterranean sun. They could look quite charming – in paintings. Nobody bothered to paint La Villette. There was a dead cat in the roadway that had been there, judging by the smell, for days. That was the essence of the place: not just dead cats, but nowhere worse to put them.

If the *flics* hadn't been involved, O'Gilroy would have signalled Jay to drop out: on these streets, he looked like royalty gone slumming. But as the police – almost equally obvious – were soldiering on, he let Jay persist. And the sheer number could be cover for himself: the swell might not have much experience of counting above three. Moreover, the sunshine had brought out modest crowds of locals, running children and odd loafers with the shambling preoccupation that was O'Gilroy's speciality.

Then "Mrs Langhorn" stepped into a shop.

The *flics* instinctively bracketed it: one loitered, one went on past. Jay, now right out of his depth, just looked like royalty who'd taken a wrong turning. But O'Gilroy concentrated on the swell, who had kept going and even speeded up. By now, he reckoned, they were only a quarter of a mile and a few twists and turns from the *Café des Deux Chevaliers* – if that was where they were heading.

It lay, he recalled, halfway along a street whose other side was the arches of a railway that looped through the abattoirs a little further east, and as they got closer, O'Gilroy lagged back. He wouldn't dare go into the place, however he was dressed, and doubly so on an occasion like this. What was the swell *doing?* Certainly not his job of watching "Mrs Langhorn's" back, since he was running ahead of her.

Sure enough, the swell vanished into the café, but came out again less than a minute later with two tough-looking characters dressed much as himself. That answered O'Gilroy's question: Jay and the *flics* had been spotted all right, and these were reinforcements. They hardly glanced at O'Gilroy as they hurried back up the street, but by then he was studying the gutter for cigarette ends.

He resisted the temptation to run after them once they had turned the corner – someone might be watching from the café – and shambled instead. It was obvious they were going back to dissuade "Mrs Langhorn's" followers, but less obvious why. The *flics* must know about the café and could raid the place at any time they had their own reinforcements. Was "Mrs Langhorn" heading elsewhere and preferred to do so unaccompanied?

So, he decided to stay out of any street barney, much as he liked the tactical idea of taking the café thugs from behind. And as he rounded a corner he saw "Mrs Langhorn" come around the one ahead, pass the three toughs with a brief word, then keep going. O'Gilroy paused, apparently watching them as they waited by the corner, and as "Mrs Langhorn" went right ahead past him towards the Avenue d'Allemagne, he followed.

Behind him, there was a shot. Then a burst of several, from at least two guns. "Mrs Langhorn" didn't even glance back.

* * *

THE LONG TRUDGE on those crumbling pavements had scraped away at Jay's temper. He was observant and quick-witted and could have given a good performance as an aimless local ne'er-do-well – but not in the dark suit, topcoat and bowler which had belonged so well in the Ritz. Still, there was nothing he could do about it except plod on, ignoring suspicious and deriding glances, and hating everyone who had got him into this. The big Army revolver in his topcoat pocket – he was a firm believer in the knock-down power of the government .455 bullet – made him feel lopsided and uncomfortable, too.

He had spotted the two *flics* since getting off the Metro and guessed who they were (though who could they think *he* was?), so even apart from the gun, he felt quite safe. Just obvious, pompous, angry and hot. And, when the woman vanished into the shop, quite baffled. There was no other shop window to gaze into, not that he'd have wanted to buy anything for miles around. Or could act as if he might. So, he consulted his watch, then took out a piece of paper and pretended to be searching for an address. When three ruffians came around the corner ahead and confronted him, it was almost a relief. He stepped close to the wall to cover his left side, and smiled pleasantly, feeling suddenly alive and at ease.

The one in the most garish clothes snarled something at him in an incomprehensible patois. Jay said: *"Vous desirez de la monnaie?"* and reached for his pocket. The man pulled out a large Mauser pistol, the twin of the one the man in Stepney had used (could anarchists have done a bulk-purchase deal with the Mauser company?). Jay reacted with exaggerated fright, cowering back a couple of steps and looking aghast.

The *flic* on the other side of the road shouted something and started across. The gunman swung, levelled his aim, and fired. The *flic* staggered. Jay took out his own pistol and shot the gunman twice in the ribs. The impact knocked the man off his feet and sprawled him in the dirty roadway, dead or alive but out of the fight. Then everyone was shouting and more than one firing; Jay crouched against the wall, making himself as small as possible and waiting for a clear shot at someone who looked dangerous.

And suddenly it was over. The other two roughnecks had run, one *flic* was helping the other to the pavement and blowing a whistle furiously, and neighbours were flocking out of doors. Jay went over to the gunman, who was wheezing and trying to sit up but not bleeding too badly and collected the Mauser.

By then the *flic* had sat his colleague, who had only an arm wound, on a doorstep and took time off from blowing his whistle to start asking questions. Jay gave him a visiting card and offered to surrender his pistols.

The *flic* puzzled out the words "attached to the War Office" and asked: "*L'Intelligence?*"

Jay rocked his hand to indicate "you might say something along those lines" and the *flic* nodded. They understand these things so much better in France.

* * *

ONCE THEY HAD CROSSED the Avenue d'Allemagne, the buildings became substantial warehouses and the people more purposeful. Now O'Gilroy was getting suspicious glances not because he was a stranger but because he might be a pilferer. The world had taken a step up from the streets of La Villette.

Then "Mrs Langhorn" turned left along a broad rectangle of water which O'Gilroy realised must be the *bassin* of La Villette, unloading point for the cargoes of grain and whatnot brought in from the countryside along the canal. Nothing much seemed to be happening, which was normal for any port he had seen, but the *bassin* was jammed with long low barges that seemed very wide to British eyes. The cobbled quayside was lined with warehouses, chandleries, shipwrights, a few stubby cranes and occasional crowded dockers' cafés.

Carts and a few lorries gave some cover, and O'Gilroy was

working his way closer around one when "Mrs Langhorn" vanished. He kept his head bent but his eyes flickered all around, and there was a glimpse of her crossing behind the cabin of a moored barge to the one tied up outboard of it. This had to be the end of the line, unless she proposed to swim, and all he needed now was the name of the barge and he'd call it a day.

But that wasn't so easy. Apart from all being "barges" to the layman, the craft were very varied: some were just open metal tanks, some had raised hatches, others had tarpaulins stretched over their holds, and their cabins were of all sorts. What they had in common was the obscurity of their names. Perhaps their very individuality made names superfluous – to other bargees. So, trying to find the name of one that was mostly hidden by the quayside one, while still looking like a passing tramp, in the end defeated O'Gilroy. He memorised a rough description and was shuffling away when a man ran along the quayside behind him and danced his way across to the outer barge. News of the shooting affray?

So, he sat on a bollard almost out of sight for twenty minutes, but nothing more happened.

* * *

THEY HAD DECIDED to meet at the buffet at the Gare du Nord, which was cosmopolitan and roughly halfway towards La Villette anyway. Ranklin hadn't rushed there, but still had to wait through three coffees before seeing a figure looking like the roadside flotsam which had so fascinated him and disgusted his mother when he was a small boy. He nodded at his Inverness cloak, hung on a nearby peg, and O'Gilroy covered his shame with that. It was too small, of course, but its looseness hid a lot.

"Ye've heard nothing of young Jay?" O'Gilroy asked (Jay was about his own age, but newer to the Bureau). "Was a bit've shooting jest after I saw him last, so mebbe he was in that."

Ranklin was startled. "The devil he was! He could be hurt."

"He can take care of hisself. Anyways, was a couple've *flics* following her as well, so mebbe they helped out – *un grand au lait, s'il vous plaît – et une fine,*" to a hovering waiter. "How it went was…" and he told the tale.

"Hm." Ranklin wondered whether to roast O'Gilroy for not going to Jay's help but decided no: the job had been to follow the woman and he'd done that. If Jay couldn't look after himself in a Paris street fight, then he had to be expendable. Such conclusions were inseparable from being in command, but that didn't mean he liked them. He switched thoughts. "So they – whoever they are – could be hiding out on a barge. And the police may not know about it, or at least *they* don't think they know. But you don't know what it's called?"

"I know where it is, and I got a drawing…" He produced a crude sketch, although not much cruder than the way those vessels were built anyway. "'S'got a green cabin and red handle thing to the rudder and—"

But then Jay came smiling past the crowded early-lunch tables and stood a moment looking down at O'Gilroy. "My loyal colleague. Where were *you* when the fun and games started?"

"Listening. And following 'Mrs Langhorn.'"

"Oh well." Jay sat down. "I suppose somebody had to."

"Are you all right?" Ranklin demanded.

"Never better. I actually shot someone under the very eyes of the police and they said, 'Thank you'. There, I bet that's never happened to *you.*" He smiled at O'Gilroy. "Interesting thing, though: they were from the *Sûreté Générale,* not the *Préfecture.* Do I hear the merry clash of competition there?"

"Probably," Ranklin said, wondering if this was good or bad for their cause. Either force might now act hastily, but that itself should distract them from the Bureau's doings.

"They took me down to the Quai des Orfèvres," Jay continued, "and I had to sort-of-explain who I was to excuse following that woman. But mostly, they were wrathy about one of their chaps getting plugged, and I think they're going to use it as an excuse to do something drastic. But they showed me the door before I found out what. Funny people, rozzers: when you don't want to be there they hang on to you, but once you start getting interested, they heave you out. Still, I've got the name of a chap there who might be useful... Should we pool everything we've got?"

Ranklin nodded and said: "First off, the woman *isn't* Mrs Langhorn. I don't know who, perhaps just an Englishwoman of a certain class living over here and down on her luck. But it more or less confirms the gang have the real Mrs Langhorn under control: they wouldn't send a fake unless they knew the real one wouldn't turn up. Anyway, I presume this fake went off to report what I said about their conspiracy coming unravelled in London."

"D'you think it is?" Jay asked.

"It isn't all going as they planned...anyway, O'Gilroy knows where she went."

So O'Gilroy told about the barge. When he had finished, Jay said: "So that's as far as we've got? Are we any closer to stopping this runaway train you spoke of?"

Ranklin shook his head sombrely. "Not that I can see. But I'd like to know where Dr Gorkin is. I think the La Villette end is being run by the café proprietor, Kaminsky, but I still fancy Gorkin as being the brains behind all this."

Jay lounged elegantly back in his chair and tapped the table top with a coffee spoon. Given half a chance, he enjoyed being a boneless dandy. "Are we hypothesising, then, that Gorkin came up with the strategic plan and then relied on the *apaches* from the *Deux Chevaliers* to do the dirty work? And when he was without them in London and things went wrong he rounded up some local thugs, sight unseen, and they turned out to be less competent?"

"Something like that. But sorting that out isn't our concern.

We should he worrying about what Gorkin's going to do with what he knows now."

O'Gilroy said: "If we're really looking for him, there's the office of *Les Temps Nouveaux,* and an intellectual anarchist café on the left bank near the Boul' Mich'."

Ranklin decided: "You two try and trace Gorkin without him knowing. Meanwhile, I promised St Claire I'd report back to him. I shan't tell him anything, but I don't want him having any more clever ideas."

Jay said: "If you can't stop runaway trains, you can always try blowing them up."

"We've only been in Paris about five hours and already shot one man. Let's try and leave it at that." But something Gorkin had said, or he had said to Gorkin, was echoing in his head – only just out of hearing. And it had seemed relevant, in an oblique way...

CHAPTER FIFTEEN

St Claire and Harland were waiting in the lobby of the Ritz, showing signs of having been there for some time and with better things to do.

"Sorry if I'm late," said Ranklin, who didn't think he was and wasn't truly sorry anyway, "but one of our chaps got mixed up in a shooting fracas down in La Villette. No, I don't think we're in any trouble, we may even have made some friends in the police: they credit our chap with saving one of their lives. And yes, the police were following her as well, from right outside here. You haven't been terribly secretive about all this, you know."

St Claire abandoned any lecture he was about to give and said in a subdued voice: "I'm supposed to be over at the Quai d'Orsay approving the arrangement of Their Majesties' apartments. Perhaps you'd care to come along and tell us what's been going on as we do that?"

Again, St Claire was treating him as a brother officer. It wasn't clear that Harland seconded the motion, but it was the Palace in charge. "Fine. Let me go first. I'll take a taxi and wait round the corner in Rue St Honoré. You stroll out in five minutes and jump in with me."

St Claire looked puzzled. Harland, quicker on the uptake now, said sourly: "This is for the Captain's sake, not ours. He assumes that anybody watching the hotel knows us, and he doesn't want to be associated with us. But only in the criminal mind, I'm sure."

* * *

"THEY'VE COMPLETELY REDECORATED and refurnished these rooms," St Claire murmured as they were led up the wide marble stairway of the Ministry of Foreign Affairs, "so what they want is admiration, not fair comment. I *may* manage to get an ashtray moved, but that's about all. But one of the first things royalty learns is to take what they're given. The least hint of criticism brings dismissals, ruin, suicide. Ah me, the problems of monarchy."

The big double doors were too heavy to be flung open: a flunkey leaned hard and got them to swing apart, St Claire stepped inside and immediately went into well-prepared raptures of appreciation. Ranklin fell into place beside Harland, a few paces behind St Claire and the Grand Whoever who was showing it all off.

The décor was apparently Louis Quatorze and the furniture First Empire, and to Ranklin it all looked chokingly lush and crowded. But perhaps he was getting seduced by Corinna's taste, and royalty found this perfectly normal. The air they breathed was almost pure lavender, presumably to mask the smell of paint and wallpaper paste.

"So, the lady in the case was definitely not Mrs Langhorn," Harland muttered.

"No. She did head for La Villette as we expected, but for a different address, not the café they use as an HQ." He had decided not to mention the barge, even to his own allies. "Putting off her followers was where the shooting came in. Luckily one of our

177

chaps does a very good tramp act, and he got through and followed her to earth."

"But the police got involved."

"That does tend to happen with shootings. But they were anyway. Remember, this whole thing started with someone trying to burn down a police station."

"But you said it's now thought that wasn't young Langhorn himself."

"Well, we think not. It may take a little time for Bow Street and the Paris police to catch up." If, that is, the *Préfecture* had ever believed it and weren't just trying to get Langhorn within the jurisdiction of their thumb-screws, as O'Gilroy believed.

They were now in the King's bedroom and staring at the bed: set in an alcove and fashioned like a Roman couch from mahogany, with gilt trimmings.

"Too many things to look at," Ranklin muttered. "And too many eyes looking back," he added, looking at a tapestry of idyllic rural life. "I doubt I'd sleep a wink in this place."

"If you tried, it would probably come under the Treason Act," Harland commented.

The writing table (it looked like a small desk) had apparently been Napoleon's, and the symbolism of putting it in an English King's bedroom could hardly have been accidental. Perhaps His Majesty would carve "Wellington" on it. Alas, probably not.

They trailed back into the "Green Room" between the King's and Queen's bedrooms. This would be where their Majesties met visitors, and St Claire could be more authoritative – though still elaborately polite – about some minor rearrangement. The High Official listened, nodding, and went off to find some furniture-movers, leaving just a flunkey at the door.

St Claire sat down in a thick padded-and-buttoned chair. "Protocol," he sighed. "We could have made the changes ourselves in a couple of minutes. So: I understand you found neither Gorkin nor the real Mrs Langhorn?"

They also sat; the chairs felt as if they were supposed to be comfortable, and Ranklin said: "My chaps are trying to track down Gorkin and we think they've got Mrs Langhorn at a new address in La Villette." When you thought about it, a barge made an excellent prison, easily guarded and short on neighbours. And better still if the police didn't know of it.

"Then what should we do next?"

"I would prefer it if *you* did absolutely nothing."

"Come now, Captain—" was St Claire beginning to pull rank? "—we can still offer Mrs Langhorn a pension if—"

"For God's sake, just *don't make it any worse!*" And rank be damned. "You knew we were following this up, but you went right ahead having ideas of your own without telling us. It's only by the grace of God and the Navy that I got here in time to stop you offering a pension to the wrong woman providing she kept quiet about a liaison with the King. Don't you see that's exactly the sort of thing Gorkin wants?"

St Claire looked huffed but mystified. "What d'you mean?"

"I mean that if he just wanted to publicise the King's affair all those years ago, he'd have done it a dozen times over by now. But he wanted something more up-to-date and befitting the anarchists' cause, and we've given it him. And he'll have the royal bastard heir-to-the-throne story as well."

"A bastard *cannot* be heir to the throne," Harland said firmly.

"What law says so?"

"I'm not exactly sure, perhaps it—"

"But you expect a French newspaper reader to know?"

St Claire said: "What d'you mean *we've* given it him?"

Ranklin took a deep breath. "Just think how we – all of us – have behaved since we knew of this claim: exactly how an anarchist would say we'd behave. They gave us an opportunity to prove what a corrupt society we are, and we've gone right ahead and proved it. We've concealed facts, hobbled the judiciary, shot a man in Stepney, tried to bribe the key witness. All they need do now is get it published, and that should happen at the beginning of next week."

There was a shocked silence.

Harland said: "But the King arrives on Tuesday... They wouldn't, the French are in favour of this visit, the papers wouldn't spoil it..."

But his years at the Palace had taught St Claire something about the ways of newspapers. He shook his head heavily. "They might not want to, but they'll have to – as they see it. Each one'll suspect that another will, and they daren't be left behind. They'll print it... But print exactly what?"

"I can't say precisely, but all that I said and probably try to blame us for Guillet's murder as well."

"*Was* that your people?"

"No. It'll all be one-sided and a lot of it unprovable, but people will believe it."

St Claire said to Harland: "Could we bring a libel suit?"

The solicitor pulled a long face. "In a French court? And we could only do that after it's been published. And we'd have to be specific. We might get them to retract some details – months later, if that's any help."

"Then is there nothing you can do to stop the man?"

Ranklin shrugged. "We might kill off Gorkin, but even if we did, I'm sure he's thought of that himself and arranged that it would do more harm than good."

Another silence, then: "Very well, then, I shall prepare a bulletin we can give to the Press once this appears in print."

Ranklin nodded but sighed as well. "I suppose you have to, but I doubt it'll undo one-tenth of the damage. The French will still believe Grover is the rightful heir to the throne and that the British government and the Palace were prepared to sanction murder to do him out of his rights."

St Claire winced and looked at Harland.

The solicitor looked grave. "I'm afraid the Captain is most

likely right. For better or worse, what the public wants to believe is beyond the reach of the law. Look at Richard III: everybody knows he was a bad hat who murdered the little princes in the Tower. In fact, he didn't, and was quite a good king – probably better than Henry Tudor who rebelled against him and won. But don't ask me how you can change public opinion after this time."

"We're not trying to refute Shakespeare," St Claire said crossly, "just stopping some damned anarchist printing libels about our King – and ourselves. Can't you get an injunction through the French courts?"

Harland steepled his hands in front of his face; a grave lawyer-esque gesture. However, he then spoiled it by looking at his hands, which made him cross-eyed. "I could try, given clear instructions from you. But couldn't such a move be seen as yet another example of the Palace manipulating the law to protect itself?"

Near to boiling over with undirected anger, St Claire got up and strode to the window and stood there, hands clasped behind his back, staring down at the glittering Seine beyond the Quai.

Harland took out a cigar case, then decided that might cause a Diplomatic Incident and put it away again.

It was very quiet in the apartment. The traffic looked busy on the Quai beyond the courtyard and railings, but barely a sound seeped into these high-ceilinged rooms. A good place for a king and queen to get a night's sleep – if it weren't for the eyes of those impossibly happy rustics on the tapestries.

Then St Claire turned from the window and began pacing the room, still with his hands clasped behind his back. His anger had gone, and when he spoke it was in firm and thoughtful tones.

"Incumbents of the British throne have had what one might most kindly describe as very *individual* notions of monarchy. So, it is the duty of us in the royal household to maintain the *ideal* of monarchy, no matter who happens to occupy the throne at the time. If I may offer a very crude analogy, one might say that it is our task as minor actors to behave as if the principal player were giving a perfect performance, but not failing to point out any shortcomings... And we do our best.

"But just whose standards should we be applying? I think you, Ranklin, would say instinctively: your own. And you'd be right. Because you'd be talking of your own people, the yeomen and squirearchy, the very backbone of England. Those who live with and from the land, who run their villages and parishes according to real standards. Not the aristocracy; most of 'em just don't matter. They've got private standards of their own that don't mean a damn to anyone else. At worst they're animals in a perpetual rutting season, at best they're just aping the standards of their social inferiors, the squires and yeomanry. Your people."

Ranklin couldn't help but be flattered. But nowadays, he couldn't help but be wary, too. However, he didn't have to react; it was entirely proper for him to be tongue-tied by such compliments.

"It's your people the monarchy rests on, your standards it should take for its own. Doesn't always, as we know full well. So, by saving the King from his youthful...mishap, shall we say? – you'll be protecting your own standards.

"Now, I think that Mrs Langhorn herself is the key to this whole matter. Whatever young Langhorn himself says has to be hearsay – am I right, Harland?"

Harland nodded cautiously.

"So, it's what his mother says that matters. And if she says nothing, for whatever reason, then the rest is just Gorkin's vapouring. The views of a man with a known anti-monarchist, anti-authority stance. We tried to settle the matter with money – as you said, to buy her silence. We may well have been misguided. But now, if we're to leave this in your hands, I hope you'll bear in mind that it is her silence that we want above all... Now, is there anything you want me to do?"

Ranklin just sat. After a time, he shook his head slowly. "Noth-ing. And I do mean nothing. When you get back to the hotel, stay there. Just sit in your room and work on that bulletin – oh, and don't throw any first drafts into the wastebasket, either. Burn them and keep the only copy in a safe inside pocket."

St Claire widened his eyes, then nodded. Ranklin went on sitting there. The man might not despise him, but he certainly wasn't above manipulating him. However, that might just be habit. You couldn't order kings around, so you learned manipulation. For example, he had just been inviting Ranklin to kill off Mrs Langhorn. Perhaps Ranklin was a little surprised at St Claire, but certainly not at the idea. That had occurred to him long ago.

CHAPTER SIXTEEN

T he concierge intercepted Ranklin as he was going into the lodging house to tell him that O'Gilroy and the gentleman were in the café at the end of the street. So, he plodded off there instead.

It was small and gently busy with that sense of cohesion, of customers and waiters in agreement that the place is just right, which marks a good pub or French café. You either try to fit in, or you go away, and O'Gilroy had clearly decided, some time ago, to fit. There was a waiter at Ranklin's side the moment he had squeezed into the little seat-back-high booth. Almost every table had such a partition, so you could either feel private or lean over the back to chat. Like garden fences, perhaps.

"What's going to keep me awake?" Ranklin asked.

O'Gilroy decided for him: "*Un grand café noir et une fine.*" His pronunciation was terrible, but the waiter didn't mind, which suggested how much O'Gilroy had come to belong. Jay offered him a cigarette and then waited patiently.

Finally, Ranklin said: "I didn't learn anything new, but I hope I put the fear of God into the Palace and stopped them having any more bright ideas. Did you find Gorkin?"

O'Gilroy nodded. "He's in that café I told ye of—"

"A very *intellectuel* place," Jay supplemented.

"—sitting in a corner scribbling away." There was a moment's gloomy silence while they thought of what he could be scribbling. Ranklin's coffee and cognac arrived. He sipped at each and whether either woke him up he couldn't say. But perhaps they made him feel he should try.

"Do we have any idea where Mrs Langhorn is? – the *real* Mrs Langhorn?"

Jay and O'Gilroy swapped glances. O'Gilroy shrugged. "Not with Gorkin, not with him running off to London and all. Be the people she knows around the *Deux Chevaliers* looking after her. And 'twas them sent the fake one, so like ye said, it's them must know where the real one's safe. Mebbe at the café itself, more like the barge now, if they're shifting their base to that."

"She could be anywhere," Jay said, "but of the places we know, the barge seems most likely."

"All right," Ranklin decided. "We can't do nothing: we'll raid that barge."

"Pistols 'n all?" O'Gilroy asked. It was an odd question for him, a man who probably slept with a gun under his pillow.

"Yes. Jay's experience suggests they're well-armed."

O'Gilroy nodded. "But one thing: if'n we find Mrs Langhorn, we don't kill her."

Jay, startled at the very idea, looked quickly from O'Gilroy to Ranklin and back.

Ranklin said: "I don't want to tie us down. She's no good friend of ours, and once we get aboard that barge we have to treat everyone as a likely enemy. Otherwise one of us could get hurt."

Jay certainly saw the sense of that.

"Only we don't kill Mrs Langhorn," O'Gilroy repeated.

"Look: we know they'll be armed and after this morning, they could be jumpy, there's no saying what could happen."

"I'm saying it. She don't get killed. That's all, and all there is to it."

Now Jay had become watchful.

"I'm only trying to give us all freedom of action," Ranklin said patiently. "If we tackle this with divided aims, then—"

"Ye can explain all ye want and talk fairy rings round me, but 'less ye give me yer word the woman don't get killed, ye do it without me."

There was a pause, then Ranklin asked: "Why?"

O'Gilroy said doggedly: "I know what we're in don't have rules nor laws. But mebbe that means we have to make our own. Sometimes, anyways."

"So, you're making a rule that—"

"And sometimes it means we should do more thinking than anyone asked us to do when we was soldiers."

There was silence between them. Not in the café: that was filling up as people, all men, drifted in for the French equivalent of afternoon tea. A man who looked like a lawyer was standing at the bar next to one who looked like a house-painter, the current job involving blue paint. The lawyer wasn't standing *too* close, but it was still an example of the café's *fraternité*.

And in their private corner, Jay was finding himself bridging a split in a team that moments ago he had thought legendary. He suggested tentatively: "Could we perhaps redefine the mission as going to rescue her? I mean, we should have an objective – shouldn't we?"

"And then what have we got?" Ranklin demanded. "A woman whose claim started all this, free to speak out whenever and whatever she likes."

There was another pause, then Jay said: "You *do* want her dead, don't you?"

"What do *you* want?" Ranklin flared. "*You* tell me how else we're going to kill off this conspiracy?"

Jay searched his mind for an argument that would get through to Ranklin, and hoping he'd found one, began cautiously: "Should we look at it this way? - suppose we killed off Gorkin's chief witness, couldn't he make something of that? I mean that whatever he then said she would have said, wouldn't it have the ring of a deathbed statement?" And when this had come out sounding like good sense, he was emboldened to go on: "And then there's the Paris police to think about. A shooting match on the barge is going to stir things up a bit. They may not mind a few dead anarchists, but when they establish who she is, I think we'd have some real explaining to do - and that's just what we don't want. Isn't it?"

And that, he thought, is a pretty well-reasoned argument - and to his chagrin, O'Gilroy brushed it a side. "Sure, sure, that's good thinking, but it's not what I'm saying. I'm jest asking what's she done to get killed for? Nobody says she ever killed anyone herself, nor ever like to. Ye said yeself she's no part of this plot, she's jest trying to get her boy out of jail, and probly a prisoner herself now. All she's done is spread talk about yer King, and ye don't know every word of that isn't God's own truth. And is *that* the reason she deserves killing?"

After a while, Ranklin said quietly: "All right. We rescue her. Where's the *toilette* in this place?"

When he had gone, Jay looked queryingly at O'Gilroy. "What's happened to him?"

"Never ye mind. 'Tis all right now. Ye heard him, din't ye? - we rescue the lady. Have ye still got that damn great pistol with ye?"

* * *

THEY HAD the taxi unload them at the corner of the Avenue d'Allemagne and the Rue de la Moselle, which led down to the *bassin* quayside. The narrow street ran between big warehouses and was in deep shadow.

"Have we all got pistols close to hand?" Ranklin asked calmly. "And fully loaded?"

Jay nodded. O'Gilroy said: "Got a spare magazine and can have it changed in three seconds. Tell us how long it takes with yer own little popgun."

Ranklin took his "popgun", actually a short Bulldog revolver, from his pocket and folded a newspaper over his hand. The simple professionalism of the move did a lot to restore Jay's faith in the near future. Then they came out into bright sunlight of the quayside itself.

O'Gilroy nodded along it. "'Bout a coupla hundred yards down on yer left. Tied up on the far side of one called the *Juliette.*"

Ranklin set the pace, neither skulking nor hurrying, just businessmen going about their business. They stepped over mooring lines and around piled sacks of cargo until...

"She's gone," O'Gilroy said. "Moved, anyways."

"You're sure?"

"There's the Juliette."

"Keep walking. And keep an eye out for her."

Jay suggested: "We could ask at that café."

But Ranklin had already summed up the café and its clientele; this one did not look fraternal. "No. Someone there might tip them off."

They kept on walking for another quarter of a mile, to the end of the *bassin* where the quayside merged with the Avenue d'Allemagne and paused among the more cosmopolitan crowd there. Without Jay noticing, Ranklin had pocketed his pistol again.

"We could search the whole *bassin,* but I don't see why they'd move at all unless they're going somewhere else. I think they got scared off by this morning's events."

O'Gilroy lit a cigarette. "So now d'ye want to charge into their café instead?"

"No, I damned well don't." He'd need three times as many men to rush the *Deux Chevaliers,* and probably wouldn't do it even then; if anyone was left there, they could be expecting that. "But we may as well look at the place while we're down here. If you remember where it is, see if you can find a taxi who'll drive us past it."

It took O'Gilroy a few minutes, but he came back with a taxi and said: "He'll do it but says the excitement's probly all over now. I asked him what excitement and he don't really know, but thinks it was police business."

"Does he mean the shooting this morning?"

"Doubt it. Not in the same street and more'n a quarter-mile away."

The taxi turned off the Avenue and chugged uphill into the tawdry streets Jay had walked that morning. From inside a taxi was a far better way to see them; he'd remember that walk for an awfully long time.

Then they were in a street with railway arches on one side, most filled in with rickety doors and occasional small businesses like a stone-mason's or jobbing builder's. On the other side a couple of identical touring cars were parked, and an inner group of arguing men, some in police uniform, surrounded by a ring of gawping locals.

"Apparently not all over," Ranklin observed.

"There's my chap from the *Sûreté!*" Jay exclaimed. "Should we stop?"

"Fine."

"Police raid," O'Gilroy said dourly, having an ingrained dislike of police raids.

While Jay chatted to the *Sûreté* officer, Ranklin stood in the street, lit his pipe, and looked genially around. O'Gilroy, unwilling to show his face unnecessarily, stayed in the taxi where the depth of the hood put the back seat in permanent shadow. The café was in the middle of a jumbled row of houses, was no wider than them, and had its windows – one cracked – mostly blanked out by dirty lace curtains and sports posters. Policemen went in and out, but not with any sense of purpose. To Ranklin, it looked like make-work, as if the raid had found nothing.

Then he became aware of sullen dark eyes watching him from among the spectators, looked again, and recognised Berenice Collomb. The hat was gone, and the coat replaced with a shawl, but it was the same faded green dress and dead-fish pout. He smiled, walked over and raised his hat.

"Bonjour, Mam'selle."

She muttered: *"B'jour."*

"I did not know you were back in Paris."

"We came this morning."

"We?"

"Your rich lady friend also." She almost smiled at his polite surprise.

"Is she around here?"

"Her?" She came close to laughing. "Not her, not down here. I came home by myself and I find…this. Did you start it?"

"Not me. I don't tell the *Préfecture* what to do."

"This isn't the *Préfecture*, it's the *Sûreté.*" But his mistake had been intentional, a false proof of genuine innocence. "Now the *Préfecture's* turned up as well and they're arguing about who owns us."

"Ah. Did they arrest anyone?"

"All the little birds had flown."

"Not swum?"

Her face died. He had suddenly re-joined the mistrusted ranks of Them.

Ranklin took his pipe from his mouth and examined it critically. "The *flics* don't seem to know about the barge. But if I can't find it, I suppose I'll have to tell them. They've got the men and resources."

"Why do you want to find it?"

"I want to talk to Grover's mother."

"Kaminsky and his mates will shoot your stupid head off."

"Kaminsky? Oh, the proprietor. Chap with smallpox scars? No, I wouldn't want to get shot. So perhaps I'd better leave it to the *flics*."

They had drawn back a little from the spectating locals, but still attracted glances whenever the fuss between the two police forces got dull. Berenice looked around uneasily. "*Alors,* I can't be seen talking so much to you. Give me some money and I'll come in the taxi with you."

Ranklin blinked, at least mentally. First, he was a gentleman gawper, now he was buying a lady of the streets. Oh well, it was all disguise, of a sort. "How much are you worth?"

"If you were young and handsome, five francs. To you, ten."

He handed over the coin. She frowned and bit it, but probably just to make sure the neighbours noticed. Then she pulled the shawl tighter around herself and got into the taxi. O'Gilroy moved to the jump seat and smiled uneasily at her.

Ranklin motioned to him to shut the partition to the driver, then said: "*Eh bien,* where has the barge gone?"

"Why do you want to talk to that old cow?"

"I have my reasons, but it should help prove Grover is innocent. Now—"

"Oh, I know he's innocent, all right. The pansy."

A bit puzzled, Ranklin said: "I know *you* know, you were... with him that night. But I'm talking about proving it."

"I wasn't fucking him that night! I'm never going to again! He has a tiny cock and fucks like a Ford auto: bang-bang-bang, pouf."

If Ranklin's face showed nothing, he must really be getting good at his job. Because even disregarding her language – which wasn't easy – his tactical base had dissolved. If that was really how Berenice now thought about Grover, he felt he'd been pulling on a rope and suddenly found it wasn't tied to anything. And he daren't look to O'Gilroy for support: when the translation seeped into the prim Irishman, he'd go into shock.

But the immediate point was that love's young dream had

somehow gone smash, and Ranklin had to start again from there. "Return to the barge. D'you think Mrs Langhorn is aboard it?"

"It's possible."

"Where else might she be?"

Shrug.

"And which way would it have gone?"

Shrug.

"Perhaps I'd better tell the *flics* about it after all. And if anybody wonders who told me, well, I was seen talking to you."

"You are a septic fat capitalist pig." She said it without rancour, as if it were a precise description. But it showed that Ranklin had got the rope tied back on to her.

"Continue."

"It will be going out of Paris, of course. Out of the *Préfecture's* area. Up the Canal de l'Orque towards Meaux."

"Do you know this or are you just guessing?"

She shrugged. "Did you really think they'd go down to the Seine through all those locks? And then upstream against the current? That way, they wouldn't be out of Paris until midnight." What Ranklin knew about the Paris canals he could write on his thumb-nail. "And I've heard them talking about some comrades in Meaux."

"How fast does a horse-drawn barge go?"

"It doesn't have a horse," she sneered. "Don't you know that Grover (stupid little boy) was helping put a motor in it?" Now he thought of it, Noah Quinton had said the lad had been putting an engine into a canal boat, that was his excuse for buying petrol. But Ranklin had forgotten it as just part of the defence. A good spy does not forget such details.

"Then how fast does it go now?"

She shrugged again. "He said it wouldn't go faster than you can walk." Which would be about three miles an hour, and they might have been gone four hours, which made twelve miles...

"And how far is Meaux?"

But this she really didn't know; it was just a name to her. And to Ranklin. So, the barge could be there already.

He yanked open the driver's partition. "How far is it to Meaux?"

"D'you want to go there? I'm not—"

"No, no. Just how far?"

Shrug. "Forty kilometres, perhaps."

Thirty miles. Ten hours. Thank God for that. He sat back, thinking.

Jay came back soon after that. "I had a word with—" Then he saw Berenice, swept off his hat and bowed. *"Bonjour, Mam'selle. Quelle surprise charmante – mais ça c'est votre ville natale, n'est-ce pas?"* Berenice didn't like Jay. Of course, she didn't like anybody much, but Jay was special since he looked like an anarchist's cartoon of an aristocrat. He smiled at her dull glare. "Does this mean the delicious Mrs Finn is also in town?"

"Apparently. We're going round there." He leant forward to give the driver Corinna's Boulevard des Capucines address.

"I'm sure Mrs Finn will be overcome to see Miss Collomb again. So soon."

"Quite." Ranklin turned to Berenice. *"Mille remerciements, Mam'selle—"*

"Pas possible. They saw you give me the money. They'll think it was for information unless it looks as if you've taken me away to fuck me."

Jay was listening, delighted.

"Oh, for God's sake... We'll put you down at a café and you have a drink and walk back. All right? Boulevard des Capucines!"

Jay squeezed on to the back seat. "And do not forget to tell the neighbours you did not know it could be so wonderful."

* * *

When they were under way, Jay asked: "You've learnt something, then?"

"We've learnt all sorts of things," O'Gilroy muttered.

"The barge is most likely going up the canal towards Meaux. That's apparently forty kilometres off, so it shouldn't be there until at least ten tonight. What did you pick up?"

"The—" Jay glanced across at Berenice and decided not to say 'Sûreté' "—rozzers were looking for the man who shot their chap this morning. At least that's their excuse; I think they hoped to scoop in a whole café-load of—" he decided not to say "anarchists" either "—freethinkers, charge them with something, and that's one in the eye for the...the competition. They didn't find Mrs You-know-who. Then the competition turned up and started arguing about jurisdiction. None of them knows where *they* have gone, but they've run away, so that's good enough reason to chase them."

Ranklin nodded; once the barge was outside Paris, the *Préfecture* was out of it, so now they were competing with only the *Sûreté* to find the barge. Or would be, once the *Sûreté* knew about it. And a slow-moving barge on a canal couldn't be difficult to track.

They were passing one of many cafés on the Avenue d'Allemagne, and Ranklin called on the driver to pause. "Here," he asked Berenice; "will this suit you?"

She got out slowly and didn't shut the taxi door. "Are you looking for Dr Gorkin?"

Remembering how she worshipped the man, Ranklin shook his head firmly. "We think he's back in Paris, but we're not looking for him."

More boldly, Jay said: "He's privileged, being an *intellectuel*. The Paris police daren't touch him."

She ignored him and asked Ranklin: "Do you think he was arranging...things? Like kidnapping me?"

The honest answer was Yes, but it suddenly occurred to

Ranklin that she could have decided to do some spying for Gorkin. He temporised. "We can't prove anything."

Her rather blotchy face folded into a frown. "The men who were going to kill me, they said...and it was the auto Dr Gorkin got from the drunken Englishman..."

Ranklin sighed. "*Alors,* get back in. We can talk about this later." Whatever she thought, it would be a good idea to stop her passing it on.

"Mrs Finn is going to love this," Jay said in English. "Why are we going to see her, by the way?"

"It may be the quickest way to get hold of a motoring map, perhaps a motorcar, and she may know where we can hire or buy a couple of bicycles."

"Bicycles? Why bicycles?"

"I don't imagine you and O'Gilroy want to *run* along the towpath searching for that barge."

At that time of day, the Paris streets were full of growling, hooting, rattling traffic. But inside the taxi there seemed to be a deathly hush.

CHAPTER SEVENTEEN

Corinna had brought forward her visit to Paris after finding that Ranklin had gone there already, but that didn't mean she wanted to see him right then. What she wanted to do was spread out the evening dresses she had packed hastily in London, compare them with those she had left in the Paris apartment, decide she had nothing suitable for a royal night at *l'Opéra,* and make an appointment with Paul Poiret on Monday.

But here he was, smiling apologetically, and behind him Conall O'Gilroy, of course, and that Lieutenant Jay who looked too handsome to be trusted and – dear God, not again! – Berenice Collomb. She instinctively looked at Berenice's hands: no absinthe bottle.

She summoned up a welcoming grimace. "Come in, come in, make yourselves at home. Jules will bring you some coffee. Or drinks?"

"No time for that, I'm afraid," Ranklin said. "D'you know where we can hire a motorcar?"

"I could lend... How long for?"

"Until tomorrow, say."

"Then you'd best rent one. Jules, telephone the garage and tell them to bring round a tourer of some sort."

"Your garage doesn't do bicycles, does it?"

"Bicycles? I don't know anything about *bicycles.*"

"Never mind, O'Gilroy thinks he remembers a place. And d'you have a motoring map showing the roads outside Paris?"

"There's probably one in Pop's study."

Ranklin followed her in there and, at her gesture, closed the door. She tossed a handful of folded and worn maps on the table, then let rip. "She isn't a little lost dog you have to bring back whenever you find her! I thought I was done with her for life when she went off back to La Villette."

"I know, I know. But she was some help and then I didn't want her telling anyone what we're up to."

"What are you up to?"

"Looking for Mrs Langhorn. We think they've taken her outside Paris... Tell me, did Berenice say anything about young Grover? She seems to have gone off him."

This time, Corinna's grin was real. "Oh yes, she's through with him."

"But he'll probably have all the charges dropped and be free in a couple of days."

Her grin widened. "That's the point. She's realised he's innocent. It seems that night she wasn't – well, she put it rather crudely—"

"Yes, she used some New Woman expressions with me, too."

"—but she assumed he really had been a big bold anarchist, setting fire to that police station-house. To prove his love for her, probably. So, when she realised he'd been tucked up with a good book instead, naturally she dropped him."

"Naturally," Ranklin agreed dazedly. "Then it was nothing to do with his performance as a lover?"

"She got graphic with you, too, did she? Oh no. That's just kicking him in the balls – metaphorically – after the event."

"I see… And did she say anything about Gorkin?"

"She may be cooling on him, too. I guess she's been figuring who wanted her bumped off, and it obviously wasn't those hoodlums who were going to do it. She was pretty quiet on the train and boat over – thank God. I think she was thinking."

Ranklin chose one of the maps. "If I can borrow this?"

"Sure. What are you going to do? – and what d'you want bicycles for?"

He hesitated, then decided it didn't matter, so told her.

"And what are you going to do with Berenice?"

"Well, unless you feel like—"

"No. Absolutely *no*. Pop'd have a fit and disinherit me if he came back and found her here. I truly am not going to do it."

"Quite, quite. You've done more than your share already. Actually, it may not be a bad idea to take her with us. Keep her from talking to anyone, and if she's really gone sour on Gorkin she may help persuade Mrs Langhorn to feel the same way."

"I wouldn't bet on her and Mrs Langhorn being best chums. Any mother's going to think her son can do better than Berenice Collomb." She led the way out.

Ranklin followed, recalling that Berenice usually referred to Mrs Langhorn as "that old cow".

* * *

IN THE DRAWING room Jules had, after all, found time to provide coffee and drinks. Ranklin gave the map to O'Gilroy and asked him to work out where they should start, then helped himself to coffee and went back to Corinna.

"There's another thing you might help on. You know journalists and their ways: is there anything we can do to stop the story being published?"

"By Dr Gorkin, you mean? How much does he know?"

"Most. The Grover-being-the-King's-son bit and a lot about us and the Palace trying to snooker it."

"A good up-to-date peg to hang it on."

"That's rather what I—" But then a voice-pipe whistled in the hallway and after a moment Jules came in to announce that the *garagiste* was downstairs with a new DSP tourer.

"Never mind," Ranklin told Corinna. "Later, if there's time."

He saw the indecision in her expression and said nothing. O'Gilroy had folded up the map, Jay had put down his cup and was putting on his charming farewell smile. Berenice was sitting slumped with half a glass of something.

"Oh, bugger it," Corinna said. "I didn't come last time, I'm coming this one."

"Look, I'm not—"

"Shut up. I was in on the first scene, I may as well be in on the last."

* * *

HALF AN HOUR later they had passed through the Porte de Pantin and were speeding up along the Chalons-sur-Marne road, O'Gilroy driving. Ranklin had automatically let him do that, knowing the man believed in mechanical things, but Jay wasn't so happy. He was prepared to defer to the back-street Irishman on back-street matters, but his family had owned motorcars since they were invented. He sometimes doubted O'Gilroy's family had owned so much as a bath.

But he had the sense to say nothing.

The taxi driver had been right: the map showed Meaux to be about forty kilometres by road, but the canal twisted around in the valley of the Marne itself and looked longer. There were locks, too, which should slow things up. They had no fear of the barge already being at Meaux: the question was where they should start looking. As a preliminary strategy they decided to divert and cross the canal wherever there was a bridge that might give a viewpoint.

But this wasn't as good an idea as the map suggested: the canal was lined with trees, and although these were still mainly leafless, they blocked the view past the first bend, which could be no more than a hundred yards away. Anyway, O'Gilroy was the only one, apart from Berenice perhaps, who had seen the barge before, and it certainly wasn't the only one on the canal. The one thing to set against this was that most of the rest were still horse-towed.

So, they soon reverted to Plan A: find a bridge that the barge should have passed already, then unload O'Gilroy and Jay to cycle along the towpath while the motorcar jumped ahead and waited for them at another bridge. They did the unloading just outside Claye-Souilly and went on about five road miles to a village called Trilbardou. There, the bridge was on a hill just before the village, and Ranklin and Corinna leant on the parapet in the still warmish evening air. Berenice stayed in the tourer, inert as a bundle of old clothes, perhaps thinking deep thoughts or possibly having an emotional overhaul, but in any case, silent.

Corinna said: "What are you going to do when you find this barge?"

Ranklin took out a pipe and began to fill it carefully. Finally, he said: "Pick some place to ambush it."

"You could fell a tree so that it fell exactly across the canal."

"With my penknife?" He sucked on the pipe to test its carburation. "If it were horse-drawn, we could shoo – we could hold up the horse."

"There's probably a towrope in the automobile; we could stretch that across."

"That wouldn't stop any of the barges we've seen."

She said impatiently: "No, I mean so that it caught and fouled the propeller."

"Would it?"

"Ha! If you knew anything about motorboats, you'd know they're always fouling their own mooring lines."

So, they routed and found a towrope – about twenty feet long. The canal was nearly twice that wide.

"I'll take the automobile down to the village and see what I can buy," Corinna announced.

"Will you find anything that thick?"

"It's better if it isn't. Clothesline would do."

A bit surprised that Corinna knew what a clothesline was, Ranklin let her go.

* * *

NEITHER O'GILROY nor Jay had ridden bicycles for some years; probably Jay hadn't touched one since he was a boy. But at least a canal towpath has no hills and no motor traffic. Against this, it can have ruts and muddy patches and a sudden swerve could be literally dampening. When they met a horse towing a barge in the opposite direction, they dismounted and stood well clear in the grass beneath the trees. O'Gilroy lit a cigarette.

Impetuously, Jay said: "Did the Captain really want to kill this woman?"

O'Gilroy looked at him. But perhaps guessing that Jay had kept this bottled up for the past two hours, didn't brush him off. He picked a shred of tobacco off his lip and said: "Goes back a long way. He was a good Gunner officer. He took me on in Ladysmith – that's near fifteen years ago now – 'n taught me to be a gun number. Was good at that. Would teach ye something but giving ye a reason for it, then leave ye get on with it. Weren't so many officers like him."

He looked again at Jay, who had been – was still – an officer, though not in the Guns. "Then they took all that away from him."

"Wasn't there something about his brother in the City and bankruptcy?"

"Never ye mind 'bout that. Point is, he wants to be a good spy, that's the job he's been given and he's damn well going to do it the best he can, but mebbe he's got more to forget than some of us. Mebbe we aren't all honourable, straightforward fellers like hisself. Mebbe we're more used to doing things sneaky and underhand. Jest sometimes, I mean, jest sometimes. But he reckons that's the way he's got to do things now – and it don't come natural. So, natural enough, sometimes he mebbe goes a bit too far. And that's where we help out. Jest like we did."

He said it with a finality that suggested the subject had been explored, explained – and was now closed.

Nevertheless, Jay said: "What actually made him change his mind?"

"Never know, will we?" But O'Gilroy's tone suggested he really meant: *You'll* never know. He flicked the cigarette into the canal and got back on to his bicycle.

It was growing dark now, and when they passed a tiny village there were several barges tied up for the night, cabins glowing with light, stove-pipes whisping smoke and a couple of horses grazing on the edge of the path. After that, they saw nothing for over a mile and then heard the sudden but stuttering roar of an engine. They stopped.

Sound carries well over water; perhaps it bounces like a skimmed stone, but O'Gilroy had no grounding in physics, just an empirical understanding of technology.

"It's an engine," Jay said unnecessarily.

"Missing on one cylinder, sometimes two of 'em. Running it up out of gear; ye'd never get them revs if it was turning a propeller."

He started off again, slowly, and after a minute the gentle curve of the canal showed lights moving slowly over a dark shape against the bank ahead.

Jay asked: "Is it them?"

"Can't tell. But probly. I'd best see if I can help get 'em moving again."

"*What?* You can't!"

"Why not? We don't want 'em stuck here until the *flics* find 'em. And I don't see us jumping 'em or getting Mrs Langhorn when ye can't get the motor within half a mile. No, ye jest go on 'n find the Captain."

Looked at tactically, Jay agreed that his stretch wasn't ideal for an ambush. It was too open, giving those on the barge as much a view as the darkness allowed. O'Gilroy handed over his pistol and spare magazines – he was sure enough about the other things in his pockets, but he didn't want a gun clonking around when he abandoned his jacket to get at the engine – and then started off again. Aware that his face might seem familiar from this morning's carryings-on, Jay followed in O'Gilroy's shadow.

When they reached the barge, one man was adjusting the bow mooring rope, while a second was waving an electric torch at the water near the stern, obviously hoping for some un-technical solution like finding a playful mermaid hanging on to the rudder. The engine was idling erratically.

The man swung the torch across the two cyclists. Jay kept going, screwing up his face apparently against the light, really to avoid recognition. O'Gilroy stopped. "*Vous avez un problème?*"

"*Je crois que c'est le moteur...*"

"*On dirait qu'un cylindre ne fonction pas. Deux, peut-être.*"

"*Vous êtes Anglais?*"

"*Irlandais!*" O'Gilroy corrected sharply.

In the reflected glow of the torch, the man's face creased into a smile. He eased himself up off the deck with slow, strong movements and apologised, then again for speaking only French. "You know about engines, then?"

"Something. I've been a chauffeur. What type is it?"

But the man didn't even know that. "American, I think. It has just been put into the boat and this is the first time we have tried it on a long journey."

"Ford, probably. Could be your sparking-plugs. Does the engine go fast when you move?"

"It goes very slowly."

Even unladen as it was, the barge would be quite a weight for a motorcar engine to push along. Now it sat high in the water, putting the deck at about chest height and, just below that, were two lit but misted-over portholes. O'Gilroy could hear a mutter of conversation from inside but couldn't identify a woman's voice. There were at least two people inside, along with the two men outside.

From along the towpath, beyond reach of the torchlight, Jay called: "Are you coming?"

"Jest a minute. Ye go on." He switched back to French and asked the man how far to the next village with a café, then called: "Jest a coupla kilometres to Trilbardou. I'll see ye in the café there."

Jay waved and pedalled off.

"A friend of yours?" the man asked.

"We work at the same place in Paris." The man waited for more, but O'Gilroy knew not to offer any: the innocent don't explain themselves. "Do you want me to take a look at this engine?"

The man stretched an arm and gave O'Gilroy a powerful heave up. There was an oil lamp hung on the little three-sided structure which would have been a wheel-house if it had had a wheel but was just to keep the rain off the man waggling the long tiller arm behind him and the engine lever sticking up from the floor. On one wall of the shelter there was a switch, like an ordinary light switch, and small levers that presumably controlled the throttle and spark advance/retard. That was all.

O'Gilroy grunted and looked at the man, who was studying him closely. He had a wrestler's build, squat and strong, with a heavy moustache above full lips and deep pouches under his eyes; the rest of his face was pitted with little smallpox craters. He didn't look very French, but La Villette couldn't afford patriotic snobbery. If you asked if this was a man who could handle café customers from that area, the answer was Yes, so this was presumably Kaminsky.

"All right, let's have a look then." O'Gilroy reached for the switch. "Does this turn it off?"

"You have to crank it to start it again." *You* have to; this was a man who told others what to do.

CHAPTER EIGHTEEN

From the bridge uphill from Trilbardou village, Ranklin could see perhaps three hundred yards of the canal, though he only knew it was that distance because of the view when it was lighter. Now the trees on either side were near-black shapes and the water fuzzed with evening mist or rising dew, if they were different things. He puffed on his pipe and only when he heard someone move beside him and he whipped around did he realise he was far less calm than he was trying to look.

But it was Berenice Collomb. He thought she'd gone to the village with Corinna she'd become so much a silent fixture in that motorcar.

"Hello," he said awkwardly. She didn't belong in these proceedings; he wished they'd managed to dump her somewhere. It was a pity human beings couldn't be switched off, like machines. "This is a bit prettier than la Villette. You come from…from Cherbourg, don't you? Is it anything like the countryside around—?"

"Was Dr Gorkin really trying to have me killed?" She wasn't interested in scenery.

Suddenly cautious, Ranklin said: "How can I know? The men

who kept you prisoner, do you think they were doing it for themselves?"

"I thought you knew everything." Truculently.

"Well, I don't. I only know what people tell me, and half the time that's lies. I just have to think what's most likely to be true."

There was a pause while she did this – or, more likely, realised that was just what she had been doing. "I think Dr Gorkin was making a plot... A true anarchist should not make a plot. Killing a king, or a president, that is honest. That is just helping history. History is on our side," she assured him. "So, one should not try to alter it, to manipulate people...one should not make plots. That is as bad as democracy."

"Oh." Ranklin reckoned this opened a topic a bit too big for casual conversation. But he certainly had no qualms about trying to alter history, at least the details that he could get hold of. Still, he just nodded and said: "And do you think he was trying to manipulate you?"

Annoyingly, she used his own trick of answering with a question: "What do you think?"

"Oh, you know me: I'm a monarchist and a soldier, and all sorts of things you don't believe in."

"Are you really a soldier?"

"By profession, yes."

"Just a slave, then," she said sympathetically (the damned little trollop). "But you aren't a big strong man, not like a proper tyrant. You're really just a tool of the tyrants."

"Perhaps," Ranklin said meekly, but on the clear understanding that this entitled him to inherit the earth in due course. "But we were talking about Dr Gorkin and what he's been doing."

There was a silence. The slight breeze had faded along with the light and the canal below was unruffled and glassy, reflecting the last light in the sky. Colour was draining away, too, leaving just tones of grey shading to black. Down in the village a cart rumbled along an unpaved road.

Then she said firmly: "Dr Gorkin is a traitor to the Cause."

"What about the café proprietor, Kaminsky?"

This was obviously more complicated, but she reached a decision in the end. She wasn't yet of an age not to reach decisions. "He is a tool of Dr Gorkin, he still believes Dr Gorkin is a great thinker. But you would say Kaminsky is just a criminal."

"Would I? Why?"

"He arranges things. Robberies, but only of banks, for the Cause. Perhaps assassinations."

"Setting fire to police stations?" Ranklin ventured.

Another long silence. "Perhaps. But he would do it because Dr Gorkin told him to... What are you going to do about Dr Gorkin?"

That was a question Ranklin really didn't want to answer. He wasn't in the business of justice, only manipulation. If he could prevent Gorkin publishing the King's-bastard article, or at least prevent him backing it with Mrs Langhorn's evidence, the rest was up to others.

"The police here regard him as an *intellectuel*," he said. "If they can't touch him...well, if we did anything to him, it would just make him a martyr."

"Then you will not try to kill him?"

"We will not," Ranklin promised virtuously. And when she said nothing, he went on: "When the barge arrives, will you promise to be quiet?"

"What are you going to do?"

"Rescue Mrs Langhorn, if she's on board. And if she's not... they can go about their business."

"I told you: Kaminsky will shoot your silly heads off. He always has plenty of guns."

"Let us worry about that. Will you promise to stay quiet?"

"She's a stupid old cow, but if you want to try and rescue her, that's your problem. Do you want me to swear by God? – I don't believe in God."

There was the growl of a big car in low gear from the direction of the village.

"No. Just promise as Berenice Collomb. That'll do me."

She may have been surprised at the idea, she may have shrugged, but she said: "I promise, then."

Its electric headlights blazing, the tourer slid past them and Corinna started to turn it around just past the bridge. This took a lot of to-and-froing and clashing of gears, but she managed it and cut off the headlights before they could shine back down the hill into the village. She parked just past the bridge and got out waving something.

"Got it." "It" turned out to be twenty-five metres of quarter-inch rope. Berenice climbed back into the motor and wrapped herself in the backseat rug.

Ranklin gave the rope a quite useless but masculine tug. "Fine. How d'you – I mean, how should I fix it up?"

"Tie one end to a tree on the far side, then sit in a bush holding the other end. Let it droop in the water, and when the barge is on top of it, pull it taut. And remember to let go when you feel it pull back."

"Splendid. Er – suppose it catches on the rudder instead?"

"The rudder is *behind* the propeller. Always," she said patiently. "And if you don't want to do it here, there's a side road in the village where you can get the automobile right up to the towpath."

"That sounds better, but we'll have to wait for O'Gilroy and young Jay here. And thanks, I don't know what I'd do without you."

Corinna could think of several replies to that, but no ladylike ones, so instead she said: "Were you having a nice cosy gossip with Berenice?"

"I think she's getting the idea that Gorkin isn't on the side of the ang—What do anarchists say instead of 'angels'?"

"No idea. What's she going to do about it?"

"That may be the problem; I was trying to persuade her not to do anything. She may think she's an anarchist, but she's young and still believes in justice."

"And you're too old and worldly-wise for such nonsense, are you? Everybody believes in justice. Or revenge. It comes to the same thing."

"Now who's being worldly-wise?"

"At least you didn't say 'old'. When are we going to bed together again?" Corinna tended to say such things – originally because it shocked Ranklin, now more or less out of habit. Of course, she also tended to mean them.

"Don't distract my thinking. I'm still wondering what we'll do with Mrs Langhorn – if we get her. Offer to take her back to London with us and meet Grover out of jail, perhaps. I can't see him wanting to come to France, and at least in London she'll be out of reach of the Paris Press."

"Ah yes: you were asking me what you can do to stop the story getting into the papers, weren't you?"

"Yes." Despite the petty successes of getting organised and out here, Ranklin had to remember they were still tilting into overall failure. Gloomily, he leant against the parapet again and stared at the still water. "Can you think of anything?"

"Can this Dr Gorkin get anything he likes published?"

"He's connected with some anarchist rag, the *Temps Nouveaux de Paris,* so I assume they'll print anything he wants. That must only have a tiny circulation, but I imagine the other Paris papers will—"

"They will, that's normal. And what you fear is he'll publish the whole thing about Grover being the King's bastard son and all your attempts to hush it up."

"Yes. All slanted and twisted and—"

"Yes, yes, I'm sure. Still, with a story like this any reputable paper would want to do some checking of its own... But if Gorkin can produce the boy's mother – Oh, I see: you want to grab her before she can back him up, is that it?"

"Something like that. And if she'll listen, tell her the whole tale about how Grover was set up and she was manipulated and impersonated. That's where I rather hope Berenice might come in. But I just don't know if Mrs Langhorn's on their side still or if she's being held prisoner on that barge."

"You aren't even sure she's *aboard* the barge, are you?"

"Well, no, but if they're running out, surely they'd take her along."

"Hmm. But you've got an awful lot of unknowns even before you start hoping she'll contradict the whole thing. And why should she? Even if she turns against Gorkin and all his works, she still stands to gain from telling about the King."

Ranklin nodded glumly. "The Palace is preparing a denial, but…"

"Nobody remembers denials. Your one hope would be to get your own story out first."

Ranklin stood up straight and peered at her, horrified. "You want us to announce this scandal about the King?"

"Oh no. No, no, no. It isn't a story about the King, it's about a conspiracy against the King. Then you go into the details of what they did: falsifying evidence, murder, kidnapping – the works. Get the Press seeing it from that angle and your intentions automatically become honourable, never mind your misdeeds. But only if you get in first."

"The only stable explosive is one that's exploded already," Ranklin suddenly remembered.

"Hey?"

"It was something I said to Gorkin. Actually, we were talking about a post-revolutionary society, but I suppose it applies to a good scandal as well."

"Like don't trust a volcano until after it's erupted? Yes, I guess that's about it."

But Ranklin was thinking of the obvious snag: that journalists, like intelligence officers, must surely ask first: Who says so? "But if I tell the Press all this, it's just gossip. And if I tell them I'm working for our government, then I'm obviously partisan."

She looked at him critically but sympathetically. "Yes, it's a great play, but you're not the right leading man... Couldn't you blackmail Gorkin to confess?"

"To perverting the course of justice, accessory to murder and kidnapping? What's left to blackmail him with?"

"Ah," she said thoughtfully, "we do have a bit of a problem there."

"And even then, we'd still need Mrs Langhorn to take a vow of silence." He sighed. "Well, it's no worse than I'd expected, but thanks for spelling it out."

"Are you going to be blamed for it all?"

"I'm not big enough to carry that much blame: they'll crucify the whole Bureau. Get invited to the Foreign Office that night: it'll be quite a party."

* * *

THE ENGINE WAS under a hatch behind and to the left of the steering shelter. A short wooden ladder led down into the glitter of thick, oil-black bilge water and an overpowering smell of petrol, oil and hot metal. O'Gilroy went down very carefully, found a place to stand clear of the water, and Kaminsky handed down the torch. O'Gilroy shone it around.

Perhaps the little windowless space had originally been a locker for ropes, paint and so forth. Recently someone with too little time, money or engineering skill had made it the engine room. The engine itself – it looked like a Ford Model T – was bolted to a slightly sloping wooden platform with an extended drive shaft running out through a dripping gland to the canal beyond. A flat metal bar stretched the gear lever through a slot in the roof above, and the cooling water pipe looked like a length of old garden hose. The rest was a child's scribble of pipes and wires, with items mounted anywhere: the coil box next to the gravity-feed petrol tank on the bulkhead, for instance, which made it a near-evens bet that everything would blow up before it shook itself apart.

There were a dozen things O'Gilroy wanted to check or improve, and he forced himself to remember he only wanted this boat to go less than two more miles. He sighed, tested the heat of the number one cylinder – that was the first to give trouble on Model Ts – and began unscrewing the sparking-plugs.

Two minutes later he climbed the ladder with two plugs in his pocket and began rummaging in an oil-soaked hessian bag of tools, bits of wire, nuts and bolts and anything else vaguely mechanical that was the engineering stores.

Kaminsky watched gravely. "Do you know what is wrong?"

O'Gilroy held up a sparking-plug in the lamplight to show the business end oily and crusted black. "That hasn't sparked for miles. The problem is, the engine's running too slow. You need a smaller gear-wheel in there."

"Will it make the boat go faster?"

"A little, perhaps. But more important, it'll let the engine run at a proper speed."

As he expected, there were no new sparking-plugs among the tools. He opened his penknife and began delicately scraping the crusted plug clean.

Jay pushed his bicycle up the bank to the bridge parapet, propped it up and reached down to pull off his cycle clips with delicate distaste.

"Well?" Ranklin demanded. "Did you find the barge? And where's O'Gilroy?"

"We found it, and he's stayed there to help them repair the engine."

"Bloody hell!"

"It does make a sort of sense. It's stopped on an open reach where we couldn't surprise it."

When Ranklin thought about it, that did add up.

Jay added: "If he can repair the engine, that is."

"Oh, he'll fix it." Ranklin's technical training had come just too early to involve petrol engines, so he believed that, for him, they ran or stopped according to how they felt. But O'Gilroy understood such things, so this one would work for him. "But will we know when it's coming?"

"You can hear it miles off on a night like this and across water. How do you plan to stop it?"

Ranklin told him, and Jay smiled admiringly at Corinna. "Brilliant, if I may say so."

She curtsied. Ranklin went on: "Did you see Mrs Langhorn – any woman – there?"

"I only saw two men. But I got the impression there's others on board. I was keeping my distance: they might have recognised me from this morning."

Corinna asked: "What happened this morning?"

But before Jay could admit to yet another shooting incident, Ranklin started giving orders.

CHAPTER NINETEEN

The first instinct of any self-respecting Ford T engine is to break the elbow of the man cranking it, but O'Gilroy knew all about that and caught it in the aftermath when it was so surprised that it fired up. It didn't run exactly smoothly: its condition and the sort of petrol sold in La Villette saw to that, but it ran. After a few moments, O'Gilroy climbed the ladder and, leaving the hatch open, adjusted the timing and throttle levers to the best sound he could find.

"*Il marche*," he announced to Kaminsky.

"You are very kind, *M'sieur*. Would you like us to carry you – and your bicycle – to Trilbardou?"

Probably Kaminsky wanted him to stay until the engine had proved itself more than he wanted to be rid of a stranger, but anyway, O'Gilroy accepted. He lifted his bicycle on to the foredeck, the second man untied the mooring-ropes and Kaminsky rammed home the gear lever without the engine stalling. It did indeed run far too slow under load, and O'Gilroy juggled the levers again to make it sound as happy as it could. Then he asked: "Do you have soap and water for my hands?"

Kaminsky hesitated about that but had to see the obvious

need. "Leon will show you where in the cabin. One of the ladies there is a bit sick in the head. Don't mind her."

There was a sliding hatch just ahead of the steering shelter and a companion-way – really a ladder, but wider and less steep than the one to the engine – down into a warm yellow fog. Gradually O'Gilroy's senses subdivided this into lamplight, tobacco smoke, cooking smells and a coke stove. And four people, two men and two women.

One man was the cheap swell who had been tailing the fake Mrs Langhorn that morning; seen front on, he had a thin, mournful face with big eyes. The other might have been one of the toughs he'd brought from the café, but O'Gilroy hadn't been watching them closely. The fake Mrs Langhorn herself was sitting by the stove watching a small saucepan of something. That meant the other woman, lying on a bunk against the hull, had to be the real article.

She was staring at the underside of the bunk above her and took no notice of O'Gilroy, so all he got was a glance of a perky young face, younger than he'd expected, above a full figure wrapped in a blanket. He made it a slightly frightened but intrigued glance, such as people give to the head-sick.

Was she really the cause of all this? A part of him said, Of course she must be: the discarded mistress of a prince, now wrapped in a tattered, dirty blanket and staring meaninglessly at rough boards a few inches above. While all Paris decorates itself to welcome her one-time lover, now King, in the spring sunshine...

Then his sense of romantic injustice was quelled by the voice of experience reminding him that life was a damn sight more complicated than that, and he looked around for soap and water.

* * *

JAY HAD BEEN SENT along the far bank with the rope to find a suitable tree nearly opposite the little lane up from the village. At this point, the motorcar could be brought up – really up: the canal was higher than the village – to the towpath itself. They didn't do that, partly because the sight of a big motor sitting on the canal bank would be very suspicious, and partly because of a cottage beside the towpath.

This was probably where goods were landed for the village, though it didn't look much used now, and the cottage had probably been built for the village harbour-master or whatever. It was silent and unlit, but that didn't have to mean much: countryfolk were more likely to save lamp-oil than read. Anyway, they weren't going to bang on the door and ask. They just left the motorcar fifty yards down the lane, facing the village, then whispered and tiptoed their way back along the towpath. As Corinna had pointed out, the barge wouldn't stop immediately even if the engine did: momentum would drift it on for several yards. During which time (they hoped) the steersman would bring it alongside the landing-place to find out what was wrong.

It was all a bit chancy, but at least it meant they wouldn't be climbing the bank at the bridge, perhaps dragging a reluctant Mrs Langhorn under fire.

Surprisingly, Jay hadn't got any cowboy skills when it came to hurling the free end of the rope across the canal, but he finally got it over tied to a piece of branch. By the time Ranklin pulled it in, the rope was soaked, cold and heavy. He tied it loosely to a bush and called in a hoarse whisper: "You get back to the bridge and wait for O'Gilroy, then join us here."

The dark figure waved and vanished.

"And when O'Gilroy gets here," Ranklin told Corinna, "you get back to the motorcar and be ready for a quick getaway."

* * *

THE ENGINE, or rather the sparking-plugs, held up for most of the two kilometres to Trilbardou bridge, but by then there was an occasional missed beat that O'Gilroy hoped only he himself noticed. The penknife scraping hadn't made the plugs like new, and Kaminsky would be stranded in the agricultural wilds well before Meaux. But his ears, luckily, were tuned to other troubles.

"What will you and your friend do in Trilbardou?" he asked.

"Have a drink, something to eat, and find a bed for the night. There's always somewhere."

"On holiday?"

"Just a few days."

"Where do you work?"

"In the export department of Renault. It's big business and could be bigger if we could get places like London to take up our taxis. Ask yourself this: how much does the average taxi driver know about his vehicle? How much does he want to know? Now think of how many problems you get with a chain drive and remember that we've been using Cardan shafts since before..."

The innocent may not need to explain themselves, but this has never stopped them boring their listeners to death.

On Trilbardou bridge, Jay heard the barge long before it came into sight as a dark shape moving, very slowly, on to a patch of sky-reflecting water. So why the devil hadn't O'Gilroy got here already? He could pedal three or four times faster than that tub. Oh God! – had they identified him? and killed him? or made him prisoner?

He moved into the shadow of a bush at the edge of the bridge, laying the damned bicycle on the verge beside him. He had half hoped that some enterprising villager would have stolen it when he got back from tramping across farmland to rig the rope, but no such luck. And he still needed it to circle back through the village and come up to where the barge would be ambushed; he and O'Gilroy daren't be seen overtaking it along the towpath.

Then he just waited impatiently as the barge puttered nearer at a pace that would have sent a snail to sleep. Unconsciously, his more mechanically sensitive ear picked up the occasional hiccups in the engine note, showing that O'Gilroy had fixed but not cured it. Then, consciously, he chided himself for being pleased about that; he might be thinking of a man already dead.

Or one who had simply accepted a ride on the barge, he thought. That sounded more like O'Gilroy's opportunism: get to know the barge and its inhabitants better. In which case his bicycle should be on the deck somewhere, so Jay peered for it. And saw it glitter among the dull, matt tones of the barge and its rusted gear. That was better; if they'd killed him, they'd surely have thrown the bicycle into the canal after him.

Then he realised the barge wasn't stopping. It crept up to and then under the bridge, staying several feet out in the channel, its slogging engine note unchanged. Stooping, Jay hurried to the other side of the bridge and thought he saw O'Gilroy's tweed suit and flat cap standing beside a wider figure in the faint lamplight of the steering shelter but couldn't be sure. He thought for a moment, then grabbed up the hated bicycle and charged downhill into Trilbardou village.

The simple fact was that O'Gilroy didn't know Trilbardou bridge from any other bridge they had passed under. It didn't obviously belong to a village, which was to one side and downhill, behind a high bank. Kaminsky had mentioned – once O'Gilroy had stopped extolling the position of Renault's radiators – putting him off at the village's landing-place. Which sounded reasonable: such a place must be obvious to Jay and Ranklin as well.

So, they passed beneath the bridge and Jay, with Kaminsky explaining that he did indeed come of a canal-barge family but had worked ashore for the past twenty years. Handling canal-borne goods to start with, expanding to other items...a "man of affairs", as he called himself. Lies, but Kaminsky seemed to enjoy lying. Most crooks did; some wrecked themselves by enjoying it too much and lying about unnecessary and easily checked things.

The canal curved gently to the right and then ran straight past the landing-place and the dim blur of the towpath cottage.

"That's the place," Kaminsky said. "Where that house is. Leon!" And after a moment Leon climbed the ladder from the cabin to take the bow mooring rope.

From the undergrowth beside the towpath Jay and Ranklin saw him walk forward along the barge in the faint starlight.

"They're stopping," Jay panted. "Two of them have to come ashore to moor the thing. Then...then what do we do?" He had arrived just two minutes before, throwing the bicycle into the undergrowth and gasping out his tale.

"We wait," Ranklin said firmly. "We wait until O'Gilroy's ashore and clear before we do anything." Certain that the barge was stopping, he let the now-pointless clothes line slip into the water and took out his revolver. "Then we tell those ashore to surrender and threaten to...to throw burning petrol down over those left inside if they don't give up, too. We don't mean it, but we threaten it. Unless O'Gilroy's got any better ideas," he added.

The engine beat faster as Kaminsky yanked the lever out of gear and angled the gliding barge towards the landing-place. Liar or not, he knew how to handle the thing, barely grazing the bank as it drifted to a stop. Leon scrambled down, carrying a thick rope and tied it to a mooring post.

And then O'Gilroy jumped down, himself carrying a rope: with Kaminsky around, others did the work. He wrapped it around another post, just behind the barge's stern, bringing himself within a few yards of Ranklin and Jay.

From the darkness Ranklin hissed: "When you've got the bicycle, bugger off!"

O'Gilroy nodded to show he'd heard and finished his knot.

"Not too tight," Kaminsky called. "Leon will pass down your bicycle." Already Leon was climbing back on board.

"Oh, *shit!*" Ranklin groaned. Now neither of the barge crew was ashore.

"Shoot the buggers," Jay muttered. He had a gun in each hand, O'Gilroy's in his left.

"Wait."

O'Gilroy moved forward to take the bicycle, promptly got on it, shouted: "*Bon soir, M'sieur,*" and shot off down the little lane.

Kaminsky stepped to the side of the barge, staring and then exploding into language that should have boiled the canal dry. The *Irlandais* was supposed to cast off for them, the ungrateful, lazy, dog-begotten, whore-born...and quite forgetting in his anger that Leon could do it just as well, Kaminsky jumped heavily down.

"Get him," Ranklin ordered.

Kaminsky found O'Gilroy's idea of a mooring knot and a new fund of language immediately after; you could say this for the man, he wasn't repetitive. Then he saw the movement beyond and looked up.

"*M'sieur Kaminsky, je crois?*" Ranklin guessed and then, because they were too far away to grab him, and he wasn't sure Kaminsky could see the guns pointing at him, fired past him into the canal.

Kaminsky straightened up carefully.

"The other one's gone to ground," jay warned. "Still on the boat."

"Only to be expected. *Venez ici, M'sieur.*"

Kaminsky lumbered towards them, breathing heavily. Ranklin put his revolver against his chest and ran his hand across the man's pockets, finding only a modestly small pistol. However, doubtless the barge was crammed with bigger, more powerful weapons; a certain breed of anarchist never seemed to leave home without an arsenal. He stepped back out of range of Kaminsky's breath.

"I think you have to speak some English, but so that I'm sure you understand me, I'll stick to French. Now, I won't introduce ourselves, just bear in mind our pistols. I have a simple proposition: we'll exchange you for Mrs Langhorn. The *real* Mrs Langhorn this time, if it pleases you."

Kaminsky absorbed this. "Why should I trust you?"

"Why *do* people say things like that?" Ranklin sighed. "I'm sorry, but whether you trust us or not is not important. Only, if we don't get Mrs Langhorn we'll all just wait until the *Sûreté* arrive."

"Why should they come?"

"Hmm. No, probably just one shot is not sufficient. Fire three more, Mr Jay."

Jay loosed off the automatic into the air.

In the ringing silence, there was a scrabbling in the bushes behind them and O'Gilroy saying: "Hey, that's my gun yer emptying."

And he stumbled out on to the towpath to take the pistol from Jay's hand. Kaminsky peered through the gloom. "You? You perfidious maggoty turd—"

"Sure, sure," O'Gilroy said. "But we're all in plain sight from the barge – or would be saving the dark. Would anybody mind stepping into cover?"

So, they retreated a few yards to a stand of trees and got, more or less, behind them. O'Gilroy explained about the others left on the barge, and then Ranklin suddenly remembered Corinna, waiting in the motorcar with Berenice and wondering what the hell those gunshots meant. And also, with nothing and nobody but fifty yards of the lane between them and the barge.

"Jay, double back and tell Mrs Finn we're all right. And then stand guard there. We'll be along in a minute." And when Jay had moved off through the bushes back the way O'Gilroy had come, he changed to French for Kaminsky. "Now, call to your friends on the barge and tell them you'll be set free when we've got the real Mrs Langhorn."

"No, you will let me go at the same moment they let her go and—"

"Please just say what I said."

There was a pause filled with more heavy breathing. Perhaps Mrs Langhorn was Kaminsky's ace, his one hope of saving something from what, for him, was becoming a costly mess. Or perhaps she was just an insurance, a bargaining counter. Either way, he wouldn't have guessed what she might be used to bargain for: himself, his own freedom, possibly his life. So, in the end, Ranklin was pretty sure he would do what he'd been told; it was the sensible thing. But his pride required this pause, and Ranklin was willing to allow him that. Wipe your feet on a man's pride and he might do something not sensible at all.

Then Kaminsky pulled himself up straight and shouted in French, just what Ranklin had told him. After a moment, a voice shouted back in another language – it sounded Slavic, but Ranklin didn't know it – and Kaminsky began to reply in the same before Ranklin rammed his pistol against the man's back. "Speak French!"

"Go on," Kaminsky called. "Send her out."

There was a muffled shout from the barge about Mrs Langhorn needing to get some clothes on. So, they'd have to wait.

Kaminsky asked: "Can I smoke?"

"Sorry but no lights, please." And then, mainly to get Kaminsky thinking about something other than trickery, he asked: "How did a man like you get mixed up with Gorkin's schemes? You aren't an anarchist, are you?" He had had to stop himself saying something like "You're an honest, straightforward criminal, aren't you?"

Kaminsky snorted. "Anarchism, anarchism – it's an affair for dreamers who've got nothing. Or everything. For those who've got time to dream. What I am, the good God knows – if He exists. On Sundays I'm a late sleeper, that's all."

"Are you saying this was all Dr Gorkin's plot?"

Kaminsky paused, probably wondering how much Ranklin knew. Then: "Him. If Gorkin doesn't believe in God, it's because he doesn't need to: he thinks he is God. A Messiah for himself. Do what I tell you of your own free will – that sort of anarchist. I just wanted to put some sense into their schemes, stop them plotting themselves up their own arse-holes." His bitterness sounded sincere, perhaps because it also sounded fresh. He could hardly have felt that way about Gorkin when the scheme was hatched.

Or had he joined in because he liked to think of the thugs who sat around his café as *his* followers, and Gorkin the Messiah looked like walking off with them?

"But a man like you must have seen a profit in it."

He had the feeling that, in the darkness, Kaminsky was staring at him as if he were the dunce of the class. "Well *of course* I saw a profit it in. A woman who knows the King's darkest secret – there must be a few jewelled goblets in that, mustn't there? Or hefty payments from the Paris newspapers, the world's newspapers. What do *you* want her for?"

"Not for profit," Ranklin said instinctively. But then he thought of his own standing within the Bureau, and of the Bureau's standing with the Palace in its perennial battle with the Foreign Office... But not profit. You couldn't call it profit.

Kaminsky gave a disbelieving snort. Then there was a shout from the barge: "She's coming."

Ranklin leant out from behind his tree and peered. The barge was just a black shape against the blackness of the trees beyond, centred on the dim oil lamp in the steering shelter. Movement interrupted the lamp, there was a thump and a shape on the slightly lighter background of the towpath. And another. Then one shape seemed to be moving towards them.

"Are you going to do the honourable thing?" Kaminsky asked. So, he had learnt, or guessed, a certain something about Ranklin.

"When I'm sure it's Mrs Langhorn." He added: "And then we won't stop you unhitching the barge and moving on." In fact, we'd be very happy if you'd lead the *Sûreté* away from here and us.

"Run the engine up to full power a few moments to clear the plugs first," O'Gilroy advised.

Reminded, Kaminsky began: "And you, you puppy of diseased bollocks—"

"Shut up." Ranklin stepped forward to meet the approaching figure which moved cautiously along the uneven dark towpath. They stopped and looked into each other's faces, just a few inches apart. She was, he realised, barely shorter than he, but was certainly the woman he'd met at the Portsmouth hotel.

"I remember you," she said. Her voice sounded slow and thick, as if she'd just been woken. "You work for Mr Quinton."

For a moment Ranklin was baffled, the London lawyer seemed so far away, then he remembered. "In a way, yes. Have we rescued you or did you come just because you were told to?"

"I...I don't know. Have you?"

"Let's assume that we have." He took her arm and steered her back behind Kaminsky. "All right, you can go."

Without another word, Kaminsky strode off towards the barge.

"By my reckoning, they're jest about all—" O'Gilroy began.

"Get her under cover and lead her back to the motorcar. And warn Jay you're coming," Ranklin ordered. He himself stayed half in cover of the trees, watching Kaminsky's retreating back. He heard O'Gilroy and Mrs Langhorn blundering through the undergrowth, then O'Gilroy calling to Jay.

The copse or wood or whatever – anyway, a tangle of trees, bushes and long grass – lay on the corner of the little lane from the village and the towpath, opposite the dark cottage (which hadn't come to life at the sound of shooting, so must be empty. Or inhabited by somebody with extraordinary good sense.). Anybody going through the copse cut across the corner and was in complete cover from view, and pretty good cover from fire: you could shoot a machine-gun into that tangle of trees and bushes without being sure you'd hit anybody. Equally, of course, it meant that O'Gilroy couldn't see or shoot out of it. For the moment, they were down to two guns; two *divided* guns, and Ranklin felt a twang of unease...

Kaminsky's shape blended into the bigger shape beside the barge. Considerably bigger: had O'Gilroy been about to tell him that everybody seemed to be coming ashore? Ranklin was taking an instinctive step forward when the whole shape charged into the lane. In the moment before he was unsighted by the trees, Ranklin fired twice. And he'd been right about the arsenal on the barge: his shots touched off a blizzard of gunfire.

JAY HAD PLACED himself on the lane-side between the motorcar, fifty yards down, and the cottage and barge at the canal. He could hear O'Gilroy and Mrs Langhorn crackling through the bushes on his left, the throb and occasional hiccup of the barge's engine, could see the dark knot of people on the towpath. A funny thing, darkness: you could see something but couldn't be sure you could see it until it moved suddenly.

And then it was moving suddenly. Along with the gallop of feet, a shout and then a burst of shots and flashes. Jay knelt and steadied the heavy revolver with both hands, feeling how familiar it all was. Just like all those pictures from his childhood: the young officer facing the charging tribesmen. And now it was him in the picture.

Remember to aim low. He fired once, re-cocked, fired again. Bullets snapped past. He heard the clatter of the motor's self-starter and the roar of the engine. How very sensible. He fired, and a dark figure tumbled, then he felt a punch in the chest. No pain, but it had knocked his aim off. He tried to steady the gun but found instead that he was toppling forward. No matter; on the ground I'll be steadier, I'll re-aim from there... But when he hit the ground he found he couldn't; it no longer seemed to matter.

CHAPTER TWENTY

Rushing – as much as he could rush through those bushes – O'Gilroy began firing before he could see what he was shooting at. Beyond, he saw a muzzle flash, so he'd distracted one gun from Jay. Then renewed shouting and scampering, and a last shot overhead.

Cautious as he reached the edge of the lane, O'Gilroy crouched, gun roving for a target. Nothing moved. Gradually his hearing expanded with his vision. From down the lane he heard the motor: good, Mrs Finn was out of it. Forget her. Mrs Langhorn blundering in the bushes behind him. No problem yet. But then he realised there were still occasional shots from up by the canal. So, somebody had stayed on the barge to pin Ranklin down.

"Captain! I'm at the road! Can't see nobody! Jay's…" A figure lay in the middle of the lane up to his left, in that poured stillness that usually meant death. Another, that must be Jay, lay just as unmoving a few yards down to his right. "Mebbe dead," O'Gilroy finished, more quietly.

"I'm coming!" Ranklin called back.

"Wait! They're mebbe in these trees!" But then the sound of his voice attracted a couple of shots from the cottage across the lane. At that range you don't hear a bullet go past: it's lost in the sound of the shooting. But among trees you hear the patter of twigs – there were few leaves in April – it cuts down and know that somebody is being personal about you. And in this case, doing it from the safety of the cottage.

Thinking it through, he reckoned that once their charge had been disrupted by his flank fire – and when they saw they weren't going to capture the motorcar, since they must have been trying for that – the instinct for brick walls had taken over. They wouldn't necessarily stay there, but when bullets are flying, walls are hard to give up.

He crept back into the bushes, calling to Mrs Langhorn to lie down and stay still, and then to Ranklin: "It's all right, Captain. Take yer time and come careful." Then he crawled off in a half-circle to reach the lane again beside Jay.

A couple of minutes later Ranklin snaked up to Mrs Langhorn and found her lying as flat as her cottage-loaf figure allowed. "Are you all right?"

"I don't know. I'm all scratched and torn... What's going on? Where *am* I?"

"A place called Trilbardou, up the Canal de l'Ourcq from Paris. How long have you been aboard that barge?"

"I...I don't know. I don't remember when..."

Unless she was lying, and she was certainly capable of that, it occurred to Ranklin that she could have been drugged. As complications piled up on Kaminsky, it would have been tempting to pigeon-hole one problem female with a hefty dose of laudanum.

He switched to reassurance. "Well, never mind about it."

"Who are you, then? Who are you really?"

"Oh, private investigators. Rather superior ones."

"Then you're still working for Mr Quinton? – what's happening to Grover?"

This sounded like the real Mrs Langhorn. "Unless I miss my guess, then – what's today? It's still Saturday, yes – then on Monday the French will drop the case against him and he'll be free. However, right now he's safe in a cell in Brixton while we're lying in these bushes hiding from some armed men who want to get you back. Now, I can't stop you going back, though I can tell you the *Sûreté Nationale's* looking for them. And unless everyone around here's stone deaf, they'll be here soon. I've got a motorcar down in the village, so if we can get to that..." He left the idea open.

A few hours ago, I wanted to kill this woman, he remembered. *A lot's happened since then, but...it would still be a solution. For us.*

There was a crackling from the bushes and O'Gilroy calling a soft warning. A few moments later he bellied his way out of the long grass. "He's dead, all right. Jay."

Ranklin said: "Yes," just to show he'd heard.

"I got his gun."

"Yes. Good."

Mrs Langhorn asked: "Do you mean one of your men?"

"Yes."

"I'm sorry."

"It happens." He could have feelings about it later, when there was time. "Can we get out of this cover and down the lane without being seen?"

"Surely. Trees'n stuff go way down on this side. What then?"

"I want to get Mrs Langhorn to the motor. Then keep those bastards bottled up here until the *Sûreté* arrives."

"Ye think they'll wait that long?"

O'Gilroy had a point there. Whatever questions the *Sûreté* had had for Kaminsky before, there were now two dead men to ask about. The safety of the cottage could be palling.

There was suddenly a blast of shooting, but nothing came their way. The firing seemed to have been wasted on the corner of the undergrowth back by the canal. Now there was nothing – but then a clatter as something was knocked over in the dark cottage.

"Covering fire. Bringing in the feller that's stayed back on the barge," O'Gilroy whispered. "Now all of 'em's in that cottage."

So, not surprisingly, they had abandoned the walking-pace barge and concentrated in the cottage. They could either stay there, or— "They're going to break out and look for a motorcar to capture."

"That figgers."

The motor Corinna was in was probably the nearest; if Ranklin knew her, she wouldn't have gone far. But any hapless motorist would suit Kaminsky now.

"Hell. Can you hang on here until I get back? Stop them breaking out?"

"Ye'll hear if it happens," O'Gilroy said calmly.

"And they might get across into these trees to…"

"They're welcome." And given O'Gilroy's mood and his infantry training, that was probably the simple truth. A bunch of men moving in a dark crackly wood was at a fatal disadvantage to one who lay quiet and knew every sound was an enemy. Come to think of it, even Kaminsky and his townies would probably work out that much.

"All right. I'll be back." And Ranklin began crawling, Mrs Langhorn gasping along behind him. After he had gone a few yards without attracting fire, he rose to all fours, and by the time he reached a solid stretch of fence was moving in a crouch.

The fence led them to the lane, and from there the cottage was just a pale blur. "Don't run," Ranklin warned. "Just walk quietly."

At the corner where the lane met a proper street and became suddenly the heart of the village, lined with cracked stucco walls and shuttered windows, there was a small crowd gathered under one pale gas light. In front was the local gendarme. He had his pistol holster undone and laid a hand on it as Ranklin and Mrs Langhorn came out of the darkness.

Ranklin braced himself, made no attempt to hide the revolver in his hand, just brushed bits of copse out of his hair. It was the time to remember he was an officer. "Ah, *M'sieur le gendarme*. Have you called the *Sûreté*? Good. I'm Spencer of Scotland Yard—" well, within a few hundred yards, anyway "—and it's an international anarchist gang up there. They kidnapped this lady and we've rescued her. Now listen, everybody—" he raised his voice "—their one hope is to escape this way and steal a motorcar. So, if there's any motors about, please make sure they're hidden, or their starting-handles are." The village might well have no motorcars, but the mention of "escape this way" had already reminded several citizens that they'd get just as good a view from their bedroom windows. But one of those remaining, towering over the rest, was Corinna. Thank God. "The lady's employer will take care of her." And to keep the gendarme from interfering, he added: "The *commissaire* will wish to question her personally." Now Ranklin addressed him directly. "I won't presume to give you orders, but may I suggest that you tell these people to find somewhere safer? It's the bandit Kaminsky from the *Café des Deux Chevaliers* up there. Perhaps you'd tell the *Sûreté* that. Kaminsky, they're already looking for him. And then possibly you'd guard this corner and show them the way when they arrive?"

"Very good, sir." The gendarme even saluted him. He was a sizeable man, and probably a brave one. But in this situation, he was just out of his depth.

Ranklin nodded politely – he'd long since lost his hat somewhere – and led Mrs Langhorn over to Corinna. From there he could see the motorcar parked just along the street. "This is Grover Langhorn's mother. Get her to…to the village café, wherever it is, then put the motor out of sight."

"Are you all right?"

"Jay got himself killed." Why did people have to keep *reminding* him of it? He'd remember it when he had *time,* damn it.

"Oh God."

"Yes. Well, it happens." He turned away. "I was serious about all that stuff. O'Gilroy and I'll keep them pinned down until the *Sûreté* gets here. Don't worry."

"What d'you mean, don't fucking *worry?*"

* * *

THERE WAS another spatter of shots as he went cautiously back up the lane, and he crouched in the cover of a fence, but nothing came his way. And then, after he had turned off into the copse and begun crawling again, he and O'Gilroy had to reveal themselves with husky calls before they met. But that attracted no more shooting.

"They tried coming out've the back door," O'Gilroy explained. "I sent 'em back. Next time, they might have the sense to come out crawling and I'd never see 'em behind that fence." The cottage had a tiny fenced garden at the back. Once Kaminsky and Co were loose in that, they would slip among the trees beyond and filter down into the village.

"No..." Ranklin stared at the cottage roof, dark against the starry sky. At the far end there was a chimney stack, and a wall with a chimney wouldn't have a door, and probably no windows either. So, there was just a front door on to the towpath, a back door on to the garden, with windows on those sides and the narrow end facing them.

One man up in the corner of the copse and the towpath could cover the front and this side, but the second would have to be across the lane, able to contain any who crawled out into the little garden.

"That's my job," O'Gilroy said firmly. "Yer a Gunner." With the gentle implication that Ranklin was most effective when several thousand yards from the enemy. And Ranklin couldn't really argue.

But: "We're *not* after revenge. We're still doing the job we came to France for. Right now, that means keeping them penned up until the *Sûreté* gets here."

O'Gilroy said: "Uh-huh," and then started asking how many cartridges they had left. Ranklin knew that revenge for Jay's death made a lot more sense to the Irishman than saving the King from embarrassment. It made it straightforward and personal. But he would obey orders...or rather, he wouldn't *disobey* them.

So Ranklin crawled off through the undergrowth to the corner by the tow-path with Jay's big revolver. It was the familiar Army issue, with the disadvantage that he'd never known it to be accurate for anything but killing off wounded horses.

It took O'Gilroy five minutes to cross the lane and creep through a patch of waste ground studded with small bushes and goat droppings, to the trees by the far corner of the garden fence. Shielded by a trunk, shadowed by the almost bare branches overhead, he rose carefully upright and peered around and over the low garden fence.

The cottage was only a few yards away, the little garden between just a shapeless mess of scrawny bushes and long grass. He was pretty well diagonally opposite where Ranklin should now be, the cottage in between, so there was no risk of their shooting each other. War Office letters to sorrowing parents never mentioned getting in the way of a mate's shooting, but it happened often enough.

All right. Suppose he now fired a couple of shots through the door or its flanking windows: that would tell Kaminsky this side was covered and not to attempt anything. That would certainly be obeying orders. On the other hand, waiting for such an attempt wouldn't be *disobeying* orders, would it? It would just be a sensible saving of ammunition, and he only had six rounds left. Far better, really, to keep them until he could see a target. That was what the Army had taught. It had also taught patience.

It was very quiet, a silence such as cities like London and Paris never know. The excitement might be causing untypical noise down in the village, but the houses and trees blocked it off. Even the barge's engine had stopped – seized up, perhaps – and half a dozen people with cocked guns waited within yards of each other in dead silence. And two more, in real dead silence, in the lane.

Suddenly there was shouting from the far side of the cottage. Something in French about a woman, and then an English female voice. *God* damn! They were sending out the fake Mrs Langhorn on Ranklin's side. And him an English officer and gentleman who'd be quite unable to handle that, who wouldn't see it for a trick...

Then he realised the back door had opened, slowly and quietly, so slowly and quietly that he wondered if it had moved at all. But then a shape slithered over the doorsill. Moving as slowly as the door had, he leant his gun hand against the tree and aimed.

For a moment he had cunning thoughts about waiting for a second creeping shape and shooting that to block the retreat of the first... But it was too dark, the shooting too uncertain. He just fired, twice.

The figure gave a grunt, and then came a wild blast of firing – from the door, from the windows. Whatever anarchists really believed in, having enough ammunition came near the top of the list, and it was too much for O'Gilroy to risk. With his back to the tree trunk, he slid down to the ground while twigs, bark and even branches pattered down around him, and when the firing died down, he bellied away to a new position.

By the time he had raised himself to see over the fence again, it was quiet, and the back door was shut. Then there was a clattering from inside the cottage, a muffled screech of pain, and O'Gilroy smiled in the darkness. He didn't know if it was Kaminsky he'd hit, and anyway, there was no reason to suppose it had been

Kaminsky who'd killed Jay. So, it was just his hope and imagination, and all very primitive. He felt much better for it.

Moreover, those in the cottage now knew he was waiting out there, so in the end he'd done just what he'd been told.

* * *

IT TOOK TEN MORE MINUTES, silent except for groans from within the cottage, for the first of the *Garde Mobile* of the *Sûreté* to arrive. Eight men in two motorcars (Ranklin worked out later) who first questioned the village gendarme, then advanced cautiously – except for shouting loudly – up the lane. Ranklin called back and, after a time, handed over control of the copse to them. It took longer still to get a couple of men across the waste ground to take over from O'Gilroy, but that was managed, too.

He met up with Ranklin halfway back down the lane, and after they had both said they were unhurt, O'Gilroy asked: "What happened with the woman coming out the front door?"

"Oh, she just wandered along the towpath calling to me."

"What'd ye do?"

"Nothing, of course." Ranklin sounded surprised. "She was obviously a ruse, but I knew she couldn't see me. And when the shooting started on your side, she turned and ran back inside. What should I have done?"

"Nothing. Jest what ye did." After all, O'Gilroy was recalling, *I had to talk this man out of killing the real Mrs Langhorn just a few hours ago. Maybe he's learning.*

There were a few official-sounding shouts behind them, then a *Sûreté* voice calling on the cottage to surrender. That brought a burst of shots, and Ranklin was a bit surprised to feel himself relaxing. Firing on the *Sûreté* clearly established the besieged as villains, but more than that, it suggested that the siege would go to a fatal end. Odd how anarchists fought to the – quite pointless – death: at Sidney Street and here in France, too, at Choisy-le-Roi

last year. Of course, Kaminsky had said he wasn't an anarchist –
but was he really? Or would he just prefer to die than be thought a
coward? Either way, it was a deplorable waste of life, but if
Kaminsky opted to be dead and silent – unless, of course, he
already was – Ranklin wouldn't complain.

Which left the problem of Gorkin – and Mrs Langhorn.

CHAPTER TWENTY-ONE

The village café was along the high street and left, beside a village green that seemed more English than French. The evening was turning chilly – it was still only April, after all – and the pavement tables were unoccupied while the interior was warm and steamy. But the tables inside weren't much occupied either; most of the regulars would be hanging around the fringes of the siege. There were just a couple of old men whose minds weren't in the present day, and in a corner banquette, Corinna, Berenice and Mrs Langhorn.

They made a strange trio: Corinna, who didn't own any clothes that were less than elegant, alongside Berenice doing her usual impersonation of a bag of washing. And Mrs Langhorn, who at least knew how to wear clothes, had Corinna's motoring dustcoat over a skirt and blouse that hadn't been improved by crawling through the copse. But she had done something to tidy her hair.

Corinna watched them approach with anxiety turning to relief. "You look all in one piece. Have the cops finally ridden to the rescue? I heard automobiles."

"The *Garde Mobile*." Ranklin and O'Gilroy sat down. "It could turn into a proper siege, army and all, if it lasts much longer."

Corinna glanced cautiously at Mrs Langhorn, then asked: "And you had no trouble getting away?"

"No, the *Sûreté*—" but then the proprietor, fat and gloomy, arrived. He delicately picked a bit of twig off Ranklin's shoulder with his pudgy fingers and dropped it into an ashtray. Ranklin ordered cognac and beer for himself and O'Gilroy, and whatever the ladies were having again.

"That boy's going to make his fortune tonight," Corinna said. "When the journalists get here. He's got a telephone." Ranklin nodded: he hadn't thought of journalists. Then he took the hint from the "boy" – probably twice Corinna's age – and went off to the *toilette* to try and clean up.

When he got back, Corinna said: "You were telling us about the *Sûreté*."

"They're still getting organised up there and hadn't really got time for us. And my French wasn't too good." He glanced at O'Gilroy. "You seemed to have forgotten yours entirely."

"No spikka da lingo."

"Then," Corinna asked, "d'you want to get away before they've got time for you?"

Ranklin shook his head slowly. "No, I'll have to stay and give them some sort of explanation. But I'm hoping by then there'll be a *commissaire* or even a *prefect* along: they're more likely to settle for a nod and a wink. It's the lower ranks who ask awkward questions."

"And there's still…" She had suddenly remembered Jay, lying in the cold lane.

Ranklin nodded.

"D'you want to tell me how—?"

"No. Later." Then a tray of drinks arrived and he and O'Gilroy finished their beer in a few gulps. It was funny how action made your mouth dry. Then they sipped the cognac for their nerves. Corinna watched their duplicated actions solemnly.

Mrs Langhorn had been silent, looking from them to Corinna and quite ignoring Berenice. Now she asked: "Well, you've rescued me. What happens to me now?"

Ranklin felt he had already hauled himself up a vast mountain, only to find another false summit and an indefinite way yet to go. Had it been worth it? Why not stop now, before it cost him anything – anybody – more? Let the damned woman say what she liked to whoever she liked. But...but maybe he had to go on a few more steps.

He said: "You were on that barge, so the *Sûreté* will want to talk to you, too. What will you tell them?"

She was a bit taken aback; perhaps she thought she'd reached a safe peak, too, and now he was pushing her off.

"What do you want me to tell them?"

Ranklin shook his head. "Firstly, just tell me what you've been doing. From the start."

"Just trying to do my best for Grover. Anything they told me to."

"Such as?"

"Writing a letter to the American Consul and moving into horrible lodgings where Kaminsky said I'd be safe from the police... And then going to Portsmouth with him. And meeting you. All that was his idea, he said it would be best for Grover."

There was a distant crackle of firing, but it didn't sound final, dying away in a series of individual pops.

"Go on."

"Then...then he made me move on to the barge, and I was kept prisoner. I was really a prisoner there. He didn't tell me what was going on in London, just said it would be all right. He'd taken my papers, too, and my passport. In France, if you haven't got papers you're *nobody,* you don't exist. I felt he was...was just turning me into *nothing.* I was frantic, I was going *mad.*"

Ranklin glanced at Corinna's cool expression to help remind himself that this woman had once been an actress.

"And he said he'd give me some medicine to calm my nerves. I got some sleep then, and when I woke up he made me drink some more... I knew the barge was moving... And then you rescued me." And she smiled, bright and thankful. And quite ready, he felt, to tell her story again with a different slant and new stage effects if that suited better.

"I went through it all for Grover," she reminded him. Which was probably true, but to her mind, it also excused everything. Whatever happened, she and Grover were going to come out unscathed.

"Did you see Dr Gorkin at all?"

"He used to come down to the *Café des Deux Chevaliers* sometimes. And when Grover was arrested in London, he asked me if I'd swear to the King being Graver's father."

"And you said you would."

"It was to save Grover! They told me it was the only way... Anyway, why shouldn't we have a bit of proper living?"

"In Buckingham Palace?"

"And why not?"

"Mrs Langhorn, I told you – when I thought you were Mrs Simmons – that no power on earth could make Grover the next king. That's still true."

"But it's still true he ought to be."

"It's also true that because you started saying that, four people are now dead, they tried to kill off Berenice—" at that, Mrs Langhorn really did look at the girl, in genuine, wide-eyed surprise "— and probably more by the time this siege is done."

After a moment, she muttered: "That doesn't change the truth."

Ranklin sighed. "No, none of it does. But there's been one other development: somebody...somebody close to the Palace is offering a pension if you abandon this story."

"They admit it!"

Ranklin repeated patiently: "They're offering a pension. But if the story comes out, the pension stops. I should think about it." He turned to Corinna. "I think it would be best if you just got them back to Paris. Just where..."

"I can find somewhere." In this situation, in front of this audience, Corinna wasn't one to raise objections. "I'll send our chauffeur back for you. Er...who will you be?"

"Tell him to look for Spencer. And thanks – as much for running away from that lane as anything."

Her expression turned serious. "If I'd stayed, I might have helped that Jay to—"

"No, you wouldn't!" Ranklin shook his head firmly. "There were three of them and you'd just have got yourself killed and let them get away in the motorcar. You did *exactly* the right thing." For once, he didn't add.

He saw them to the hired tourer parked around the corner. As he closed the door on Mrs Langhorn, she said: "You said you were working for Mr Quinton."

"And you said you were Mrs Simmons."

* * *

THEY STOOD for a moment on the doorstep of the café, listening to the siege. By now the shooting was constant but low-key, just individual shots. O'Gilroy said: "If'n we'd jest shot that barge to hell, we'd be rid of that old bitch and young Jay'd be alive yet."

"Nobody can be sure of things like that."

"He'd be alive," O'Gilroy insisted. "Only I stopped ye going for Mrs Langhorn and—"

"*I'm* in command," Ranklin said sharply. "I decide things like that." And will people just stop reminding me of "ifs"? The man is *dead*. Let him lie.

After a time, O'Gilroy muttered: "Stupid honourable bastard of an officer." Ranklin chose not to hear.

Soon after that, the first journalists arrived. First came obvious "lines-of-communication" people, a couple of youngsters and an elderly chauffeur, setting up trays of drinks, establishing there was a telephone, interrogating the proprietor. His instinct was to be taciturn and surly, but as he saw Corinna's predicted fortune coming true, he began to flower; Ranklin overheard several dramatic and imaginative details. Whether the young reporters believed him or not, they wrote it all down.

After maybe half an hour, a bunch of more seasoned reporters hurried in and, without seeming to try but rather as if it was their right, took the place over. They had clearly been up as near to the action as the *Sûreté* allowed, had got little but statements from police officers and some villagers' rumours, and immediately, to Ranklin's surprise, sat down to swap notes. Where was all this deadly rivalry and "scoops" he had heard so much about?

Mostly they ignored Ranklin and O'Gilroy, but eventually a middle-aged man strolled over and said: "D'you mind if I join you?"

He had an American voice, and Ranklin said: "If you want," but the man had already sat down.

"Wendell Lewis, Associated Press." He stuck out a hand, and they both shook. He hung on to O'Gilroy's hand a moment too long, then asked: "What's your connection with all this?"

"Just innocent bystanders."

Lewis smiled quickly. He was in his thirties, with a narrow, sharp face and heavy glasses that gave him the look of a scholarly fox. "His hand's all scratched up and you've got a fresh cut on your cheek." Ranklin instinctively touched his face; it had just been some thorn, and he had washed the smear of blood off in the *toilette,* but it still stung. And showed, it seemed.

"Why aren't you beavering away like your colleagues?" Ranklin asked.

"Time difference. Those boys are up against edition times, but I've got five hours' leeway. I needn't file for our East Coast papers until five in the morning French time. D'you think it'll last out until then?"

"I've really no idea…" It hadn't occurred to him that Kaminsky might time his Last Stand to suit newspaper schedules, and he doubted it had occurred to Kaminsky either. But this raised a thought… "But d'you mean that if it doesn't end soon, they won't have anything to write?"

"Hardly that. A shoot out with dozens of police is quite a story; it's just if you don't have the ending it's a bit like writing up a ball game without the box score. We'll all be filling in with background and colour, who they are, how did it start."

"Do you know most of the journalists here?"

"Most." Lewis looked back over his shoulder. The room was full and busy, particularly for the proprietor and his wife. For the moment the telephone had been taken over by a uniformed *Sûreté* officer but there was a pack of young reporters behind him, ready to pounce.

Lewis peered through the wreathing tobacco smoke. "There's Lebrun of *Figaro*, and Davidier from *he Matin*, and *he Gaulois, Echo de Paris*, and Jake Jacobs of our *Herald*, and a couple of stringers for your Sunday papers…pretty good turnout, for a Saturday night. It must be the rumour they're anarchists – are they?"

"You shut your mouth, Connelly," Ranklin suddenly told O'Gilroy. And since O'Gilroy hadn't been about to say anything, and he'd never used the name Connelly, he looked briefly surprised. But then decided he'd better be abashed and sullen until he found out what the hell Ranklin had in mind.

"They may call themselves anarchists," Ranklin told Lewis, "but for my money, they're just trouble-makers and crooks. Pure rabble, no matter what Connelly says."

Nothing had changed in Lewis's face, but at the same time everything had. He was now twice as alive.

"Connelly" muttered: "Bloody English bastard," a comment that was, in context, non-committal.

"Shut up, you damned Irish renegade."

"I could tell ye a tale—" "Connelly" ventured.

Ranklin snatched his pistol from his pocket and thrust it in O'Gilroy's face. "I said shut up!"

Lewis's chair clattered backwards on to the floor, stopping the room in mid-gabble. A couple of dozen faces turned to the banquette in the corner but saw no more than Ranklin's back and a glimpse of his gun as he whispered fiercely at O'Gilroy.

Then Lewis, who'd backed away several steps and felt somehow responsible for this outburst, said: "Hey, I didn't mean to start anything…"

Ranklin straightened up and turned to face the other journalists past him. "My name's Spencer from the British War Office and that's all you need know about me. This *gentleman* wants to say a few words to you gentlemen of the Press, and I've agreed he can do so on his promise that he'll then accompany me – voluntarily and quietly – back to London. Now say your piece."

The *Sûreté* officer, who'd felt he should have something to say about a flourished pistol, paused uncertainly.

O'Gilroy shambled to his feet. As the would-be-inconspicuous O'Gilroy, he would rather face the Inquisition than this group. But he was no longer O'Gilroy. As Ranklin watched and listened, he gradually became Connelly. It was like seeing a man become possessed, in this case by an Irish braggart who would far rather talk than do.

"Yer here because of some fellers I know holed up in a house by the canal 'n like to gettin' their selves killed. I don't say Good Luck to 'em, I'd jest say God go wid 'em – whether they believes in Him or not. Meself, I'm no sort of anarchist, 'n niver was. I'm a good Irish republican that wants no truck wid kings 'n queens 'n all of the aristocrats that's been bleedin' Ireland white for centuries past. The only raison I'm not home in Ireland now is the traithors av the Irish poliss that hounded me out av family 'n home 'n if ye think yer gettin' me rightful name, good luck wid it.

"So I'm livin' in stinkin' lodgin's in La Villette wid a bunch that calls thimselves anarchists. 'N mebbe they are: seems ye can call yerself an anarchist long as ye believe the world's an unfair place 'n better off wid no laws 'n nothin'. Meself I believe in Irish laws made by Irish folk for the runnin' av a proper free Ireland."

"Get on with it," somebody called.

O'Gilroy looked sullenly truculent, paused, then hit them between the eyes. "All right. So it began wid this feller claims he's the bastard son av King George 'n the next king av England by rights. Said his mother'd told him so."

That hushed them. It was a hush of disbelief, but most of the audience scribbled a note or two. Some of the French journalists who couldn't follow his "English" demanded what he'd said and were themselves hushed. Ranklin saw the *Sûreté* officer slip out into the street.

"So ye let loonies like this," O'Gilroy continued, "in ivry pub in the world. But the feller Kaminsky gits to hear av ut – he's one av the fellers shootin' at the poliss right now, runs the *Café des Deux Chevaliers* in La Villette. 'N he told Feodor Gorkin, the intellec'chul feller that came down slummin' at the place. So they got the idea they'd use this to show what a rotten place England was. Have ut all come out when the King was visitin' Paris.

"'N sure, I wint along wid that. But I didn't know what I was gittin' meself into. Anyways, this young feller was the waiter in Kaminsky's café 'n he'd bin workin' on Kaminsky's barge, puttin' an injin in ut—"

"What 'fellow'?" an English reporter demanded. "Who're you talking about?"

"Did I not say ut?" It was a nice touch, making them drag bits of the story out of him. It involved them. "'Twas a feller Grover Langhorn, 'n American, 'n his mother Mrs Langhorn who'd bin English. 'N he'd bin workin' on the barge, like I said, so they sent him to buy petrol, then one night when they know he's off duty at the café 'n safe alone in his room, a couple av the boyos set fire to the poliss station up the road."

By now he *was* Connelly, sitting in on the betrayal of Grover to the French police, his flight to London and second betrayal to Scotland Yard. And going with Gorkin to London for the extradition hearing, learning of Guillet's failings in court and the decision to kill him off. He even had himself – Connelly – asked to do the killing but getting cold feet, "unconsciously" showing himself fonder of words rather than deeds.

"Anyways, he borries a motorcar off'n the fancy people he was stayin' wid, while I gets a coupla fellers from the Anarchists' Club. 'N he sends 'em to pick Guillet up 'n bash him on the head 'n roll him into the river. Mind ye," he added quickly, "I din't see nor know of this, I jest heard tell of it later."

They didn't believe that. It was too like a snake wriggling out of its old skin and claiming he'd left his sins behind, too. But paradoxically, they had to have something to disbelieve so that they'd believe the important parts. And "Connelly" was giving answers to questions everyone else had shied off, answers that strung together into a logical story. They were all scribbling flat out by now.

Of course, there was no mention of the Bureau, and not much of Mrs Langhorn. Her trip across to Portsmouth was ignored (but why, come to that, should "Connelly" know anything of it anyway?).

And standing at the door were two new *Sûreté* men and another in plain clothes.

"Ony then things really did start goin' wrong. Seems Berenice Collomb'd gone round to find Guillet 'n ast why he's tellin' such lies 'bout her boy, 'n the London poliss grabbed her for the murther 'n whin they lets her go, it's in the keepin' av an American lady runnin' the fund that's defendin' Grover. 'N Gorkin, he's bad worried she's mebbe goin' to talk too much 'n he sez I should kidnap her 'n give her the treatment same as Guillet. 'N I sez I told ye I'm niver doing things like that, I come across to help banjax the English government 'n now yer killin' poor Frenchies, the same people yer say yer doin' all this for, and I'm off back to Paris. 'N I am.

"'N seems I did right, 'cos what I hear, Scotland Yard caught these fellers 'n rescued Berenice 'fore they could do her in. 'N seems Gorkin agrees wid me, 'cos he comes on the next boat 'n to hell wid those poor fellers from the Anarchists' Club.

"'N then, I heard of some English fellers in Paris tryin' to find out 'bout Kaminsky and the boyos from the café, 'n I kinda fell in wid 'em, becos killin' people's not what I signed up for, nobody told me 'bout that, 'n when the poliss from the *Sûreté* raided the café 'n Kaminsky gets away in the barge, I only went along 'cos they made me. Needed a feller to fix the injin. 'N first chancst I got, I'm away."

One of O'Gilroy's great talents was believing in his own lies, at least while he was telling them.

An English reporter who was quicker on the uptake than the rest asked: "You mean you'd changed sides and were working for the British War Office all the time you were on the barge?"

"Ye think what ye like," O'Gilroy mumbled.

"Did you stop the barge here and tip off the *Sûreté*?"

Ranklin stepped forward. "I think that's enough. Now—"

An American voice called: "This story about Grover Langhorn's parentage – d'you think there's any truth in that at all?"

This was the heart-stopping moment, when the reporters could decide that anarchist plots ran a poor second to royal bastards. And typically, Ranklin's mind flew off at an absurd tangent, reckoning that that fatherhood wasn't a matter of "*any* truth" but plain true or false. But O'Gilroy was hardly likely to take up such a quibble, yet everything hung on his answer. And he surprised them all.

"Sure 'n it's true. Isn't ivry English king pokin' ivry woman in the land 'n 'nough bastards to fill a rij'ment?"

There was a deathly hush. Then Ranklin recovered and called sternly: "Will you stop these filthy, irresponsible accusations against our monarch?" Everyone looked at him. "I'll ask you to disregard those last remarks of Connelly's."

"Where's this Mrs Langhorn"

O'Gilroy hesitated, and Ranklin held his breath again. Of course, they'd want to know that – but where, for the sake of this story, should she be? He should have thought of it. Oh God...

"Last I saw, she was on the barge wid Kaminsky." When all else fails, try (almost) the truth.

Anyway, it brought a pause while they thought about the implications of this, but then: "Is she one of the people being besieged, then?"

O'Gilroy shrugged, and Ranklin stood firmly forward to rescue him. "Connelly wanted to tell you his story. He's now done so, and I take no responsibility for it. I'm sure that Scotland Yard and their French counterparts are investigating, and you'll hear the truth of it in due course." Ranklin wasn't so obtuse as to think any journalist cared about "due course"; they were interested in *now*. But he too was playing a part. "Now I ask Mr Connelly to honour his promise and return quietly to London with me."

"What will happen to him?"

"We do not regard Mr Connelly as particularly important—"

"Me 'n ivry other Irishman!" O'Gilroy shouted.

"—we regard him as a useful – if not entirely trustworthy – informant."

Playing the part to the last, O'Gilroy yelled: "'N mebbe ye've royal blood in yeself!"

"English is quite good enough for me," Ranklin said with dignity. He took O'Gilroy by the elbow and pushed him, protesting sullenly, towards the little group of *Sûreté* men by the door. He couldn't say they looked pleased, but they were, in their way, welcoming.

CHAPTER TWENTY-TWO

A round two in the morning a company of infantry – about two hundred men – arrived. Despite the urgings of dead-line-conscious journalists, they took time to be briefed and then to replace the *Sûreté* men, which wasn't easy in the darkness. Two soldiers were wounded, which was blamed on the anarchists, and this took up more time. At last two machine-guns were set up: one in the lane and the other on the far side of the canal, firing in arcs which would miss the village if they first missed the cottage.

The machine-guns opened fire at 3.43 am and fifteen seconds later, both had jammed. The first versions of the French Hotchkiss had a reputation for unreliability, and their crews were unfamiliar with the weapon. But from about 4 am firing became more or less continuous, and if anybody was by then shooting back, it wasn't reported: most soldiers wisely had their heads well down to avoid howling ricochets. But even the humblest, most deserted dwelling-place has plenty of inflammable material in it, and with thousands of bullets arriving already red-hot and then striking sparks if they hit even a metal nail-head, the next step was inevitable: the cottage caught fire.

Shooting was stopped, and the flames – mostly in the roof –

left to burn out in the slow light of dawn. When a cautious patrol went in, four not-too-badly-charred bodies were found, all with several bullet wounds (the autopsies confirmed). Three men and one woman.

* * *

RANKLIN HAD the car stopped outside the Gare du Nord and so arrived at the Sherring apartment with three newspapers, just before 7 am. The housemaid was already up and about, and she went to rouse Corinna while the chauffeur started making coffee.

She appeared ten minutes later, wrapped in several layers of mauve taffeta negligee with a white fur collar. She looked pink and scrubbed but not truly awake. They sat down around one end of the big dining table while the maid poured coffee.

"It's over, then," Corinna said.

"The siege, anyway." Ranklin passed over the newspapers. "But it ended too late for these papers, so they had to make do with what they'd got by the time that…what's the phrase?"

"Newspapermen talk of 'putting the paper to bed'."

"What a lovely thought." Ranklin hadn't been near a bed in forty-eight hours. They drank coffee and Corinna skimmed the papers. O'Gilroy offered a cigarette to Ranklin. Corinna half-raised her head to complain, then decided the world was full of worse things, and went on reading about them.

Then she said: "Connelly. An Irish renegade called Connelly. I don't think I know anybody of that name, so tell me why it sounds so dreadfully familiar."

O'Gilroy smiled his twisted smile and Ranklin said: "I couldn't say. You know so many strange people."

"I do seem to, don't I? Well, you appear to have taken mama's advice and got your story in first."

"Yes…d'you think it'll do?"

Her face showed hopeful uncertainty. "Newspapers hate

saying 'Sorry, we got it all wrong, let's start again'. But what will your café proprietor and his pals be saying?"

Ranklin shook his head. "Nothing. They do tend to fight to the end – anarchists."

After a while, she asked: "Were you counting on that?"

"A gentleman always gives up his seat to someone who wants to be a martyr. But will this stop Gorkin publishing his version?"

She thought about this while she drank more coffee. "You can't really ask me what that man would do... But at least you've put him in a difficult position. He can't say that all of 'Connelly's' story is rubbish because the Press knows it isn't. And he'd be asking for trouble if he started quibbling about details, saying 'Yes, I did this, but the Secret Service did that'. If he admits he was involved at all, he can't tell how much he'll get sucked in... But then again, if Mrs Langhorn is still ready to back him up saying Grover's the King's son, I can't say how much it's worth to him as a trouble-maker to risk himself in stirring up more trouble."

"And Mrs Langhorn's got her own row to hoe," Ranklin reflected sombrely. "Even if she now thinks Gorkin's a bad hat, she may still be dreaming of eating off gold plates in Buckingham Palace. Is she here?"

"Good God, no. Pop's here." To O'Gilroy's amusement, Ranklin flinched, though as far as Corinna's father went, his conscience had been clear for over a week. In a manner of speaking. "He came home good and late; he'll probably sleep till noon, it being Sunday. No, I got her and Berenice in at a hotel down the street. What are you planning for Mrs L?"

Ranklin shook his head. "That's up to the Sûreté. When they let us go, they were still trying to prise control back from their army, and what with wondering how an Irish renegade was also a British agent, and telephoning St Claire to confirm there *was* a plot against the King – so all in all, they hadn't got any sort of clear picture. But this morning they'll start putting things together and when they realise we spirited Mrs Langhorn away, they'll want to hear her story. That's her chance to start dropping matches in the powder magazine."

Corinna finished her coffee and refilled her cup, then added milk and sugar. Her actions were deliberate and thoughtful. At last she said: "Perhaps it's a pity a stray bullet didn't take her out of the reckoning."

Ranklin and O'Gilroy didn't look at each other.

"And the same goes for Gorkin," she went on. "But if anybody were to bump him off now, it would make him a victim."

"A martyr," Ranklin agreed. "I was warning Berenice of that. Probably unnecessarily, but God knows what she might do. She's decided that Gorkin is a traitor to the great cause. He's been trying to manipulate future history and apparently that's unsporting."

Corinna gave an unladylike snort. "What the hell else are we put in this world to do?"

Ranklin nodded. What else did anybody form a Secret Service Bureau for? Then he levered himself stiffly to his feet. The moment he let himself relax, every bone in his body started to ache. "Well, I suppose I'd better find this hotel and do what I can to manipulate history for myself."

"I'll show you."

* * *

ONE OF THE Paris papers had brought out a two-page late extra edition covering the end of the siege, and Ranklin bought a copy as they walked down the Boulevard des Capucines. It was another sunny morning, with the street empty except for a few scurrying churchgoers responding to the call of the bells.

The hotel was a small family place just off the Boulevard, with no restaurant but a small breakfast room in the vaulted basement. This was for residents only, of course, but as usual, Corinna assumed this didn't apply to her, and as usual the hotel agreed.

So, they sat down to more coffee while Ranklin tried to work out just how late the special edition had gone to press. About six o'clock, he reckoned, since it covered not just the army patrol finding the bodies but had the journalist himself tromping among the ashes and fire-tarnished cartridge cases, smelling burnt flesh and wood-smoke, and feeling the warmth still in the iron door-hinges. There was too much of that sort of guff, but it sounded genuine. The rest was a reprise of the earlier Connelly back-ground story.

Of the bodies found, Kaminsky had been identified, and a Raymond Cuchet, and – "Good God," Ranklin said softly, and put the paper down to think.

Corinna said: "What is it?" but O'Gilroy, who either knew Ranklin better or was less impetuous, shook his head at her. Ranklin went on staring, luckily unseeing, at a mural of beach and palm trees which the hotel had thought would improve the vaulted wall.

Mrs Langhorn came in, wearing a skirt and blouse of Corin-na's, the blouse too tight and the skirt hem trailing several inches on the floor like a ball gown. She smiled confidently at them and sat down. A waitress hurried over with a fresh cup and poured her coffee.

"Is Berenice up?" Corinna asked.

"Don't know. Shouldn't think so." Then she added: "Little trol-lop," but as automatically as she might have said "May she rest in peace". "What happened last night after we left?"

Ranklin held up the newspaper for her to read the headline, but from her frown and the moving of her lips, she wasn't too good at French journalese, so he read it for her. "'Four anarchists dead in flames of besieged cottage – plot against the King of England – Irish revolutionary confesses all.' Don't trouble your-self with that last one, it needs some explanation."

O'Gilroy reached for the paper and Ranklin handed it over, tapping a paragraph halfway down the first column.

Mrs Langhorn asked: "Is it all over, then?"

"Perhaps, but that's up to you."

She understood exactly what he meant. "When you said Grover would be let free, did you really mean it?"

"Oh yes. It was sure enough before, but last night made it even more certain. What are you planning to do then?"

O'Gilroy gave a sudden cackle of laughter, shook his head, and looked at Mrs Langhorn with new interest. She blinked, disconcerted both by him and because this time she wasn't sure what Ranklin had meant. So, she chose for him to be asking where she'd go. "When he's free, I don't fancy staying in Paris. I only come because of him, and now, well, there's going to be too many of his anarchist friends around probably blaming me..."

"That does seem likely," Ranklin agreed politely.

"We'll have to get back to the United States."

"Are you an American citizen?" Corinna asked. The question surprised Ranklin, who'd assumed it was automatic for a woman marrying an American. But Corinna should know.

"No, I never did. But Grover is. I shouldn't have any trouble."

"You didn't have in the past. But now you've been mixed up with anarchists and murderers. I should wait and see what the New York papers say about you before you book a passage."

Suddenly unsure, Mrs Langhorn looked from her to Ranklin. "I'm not going to be welcome in England, am I? I should think you'll see to *that*."

"That rather depends on who you are."

She frowned, puzzled.

He reached to tap the newspaper. "I don't think there's any easy way to break this to you, but you're dead."

A procession of emotions flickered across her face: fear, then bewilderment, finally mistrust. He smiled reassuringly. "The charred body of a woman with your identity papers and passport on her was found in the cottage at Trilbardou. The false Mrs

Langhorn sent to the Ritz yesterday, of course, but the *Sûreté* don't know that."

"But I can prove I'm alive! All sorts of people...and Grover – when he's free – will say I'm me."

"Oh yes, you shouldn't have any trouble about *that*. But not many people get the chance of a new start, and I suggest you think of the alternative before you turn it down. You were on that barge, you have been part of Kaminsky's gang, and as the only surviving member, the *Sûreté* will want to ask you all sorts of questions. The *Préfecture*, too. And if you tell the story about Grover being the King's son – which you can't actually prove, can you? – I'm sure his birth certificate gives your husband as the father. In fact, I don't think you can even prove you were the King's mistress: we couldn't. And the more you try, the more you'll tie yourself up in the plot against the King. And even if you talk your way out of that, you'll have all your enemies back in force. Er...that'll include me." He smiled apologetically. "Sorry and all that, but we really will make life hell on earth for you and Grover if you come back to Britain, and also see what we can do to keep you out of America. As for what France does to you... well, that's up to the *Sûreté*. But we'll give them any help they need."

She looked at him, letting all this sink in – then broke down. Her pert face crumpled, and her shoulders shook with sobs. "What can I do?" she wailed. "I'm just one poor woman against all you police and authority and all... You stamp on me like an insect, you do... The poor people in this world have got no rights, they've got no justice. None at all."

Corinna had got hold of the paper by now. Without looking up, she said unsympathetically: "You sound like an anarchist."

And again, Ranklin had to remind himself that the woman had once been an actress. He waited in silence, and she dabbed at her eyes quickly. Was it cynical to think that was so he wouldn't see how few tears there had been?

She gave one last sob and stopped.

"Or," he said, "you could start a new life with a pension. And if you pick that, we'll give you all the help we can."

There was a long, long silence. Then Mrs Langhorn asked: "How much?"

* * *

"THIS TIME," he told St Claire and Harland, "I'm vouching for her. Don't worry about passports and papers, just get her to sign up and hand over the first dollop of pension."

That flummoxed them. Harland frowned and said: "We haven't got any *cash* to disburse."

"Good God, man, you weren't expecting her to settle for a cheque or some vague promise? Get it from the bank—"

"On Sunday?"

"Then from the hotel. Haven't you ever seen soldiers at pay day? They'll stand for all sorts of stoppages and allotments if they can see real money on the table."

Luckily St Claire *had* supervised at pay days. "We'll get it, never fear. And perhaps it would be a good idea to throw in a passage to England?"

"Distinctly good idea."

"But who will she be when she gets there?"

"Luckily, she's got a part half-written for her already: her own sister, the widowed Mrs Simmons. It has to be some relative, so she can scoop in Grover. And she plays the part rather well, I can vouch for that, too."

"But she won't have any of the paperwork, birth and marriage certificates and... Oh." He caught Ranklin's patient look. "Your Bureau, of course. Perhaps we'd better not know about that." He and Harland exchanged glances. "Then just give us an hour to raise the wind and send the lady up."

"And what are you going to do yourself, now?" Harland asked.

"I'll probably escort Mrs Simmons back to London and help

find her lodgings there until she decides where to go. But first—" he sighed "—I've got an interview with the *Sûreté* to get through. Still, they have killed off an anarchist gang and wiped the eye of the *Préfecture*, so if I can convince them they've saved the King's visit here, they may settle for that. I used to laugh at the French police for being so political but thank God they are. And then arrange with the consulate to get Lieutenant Jay's body shipped home."

"If you need any help from the Embassy..." St Claire said quickly.

"Thank you."

There was a silence that became awkward with unsaid things. Ranklin gave a little shrug and turned towards the door. St Claire said: "I hope you think it was worth it. It was, you know."

Ranklin nodded, meaning nothing. St Claire went on: "All sorts of things that could have happened now probably won't. There are always casualties; that's what we're for. And to do the best job we can. Nobody can ask more than that."

Ranklin nodded again. It was the right speech for a major to make to a junior.

"What will you tell Jay's parents?" St Claire asked.

"That he died on His Majesty's service, I suppose."

CHAPTER TWENTY-THREE

Gorkin wasn't in what O'Gilroy said was his usual café, though the posters on the walls and the intensity of the conversations at the tables told Ranklin he'd got the right place; this was the *intellectuel* version of the *Deux Chevaliers.* He felt badly out of place there and stayed only long enough for a small coffee. He didn't ask about Gorkin, either. He wanted it to be a casual encounter. After that, he tried several more cafés along the Boulevard Saint Michel, then headed for a smaller place which Gorkin seemingly didn't use but was almost opposite his apartment house.

O'Gilroy was slumped at a table one row from the window, reading a newspaper.

"He could be in, could be not," he reported. "But he had another visitor half an hour ago: Berenice. Dressed up like...like a real tart. All paint and an orange fur stole and a purse." He was trying to keep the censoriousness out of his voice. "Only there twenty minutes, so mebbe he was out, and she waited jest that long."

"Damn. Was the little bitch reporting to him what we'd been up to?"

"Don't know. Like I said, mebbe she didn't see him."

"And the concierge let her in dressed like that?"

"One of these places that only has a concierge night and mornings. Afternoons, ye jest walk in and knock on the door."

"Damn," Ranklin muttered again, thinking. Maybe he should cut and run now, concentrate on getting Mrs Langhorn back to England. But he'd be leaving a loose end: if Berenice had been blabbing to Gorkin, he had to try and find out what she'd told him. Which meant either trying to dig her out, down in La Villette – which he didn't fancy – or seeing what Gorkin might say. And of the two, Gorkin was the talker; Messiahs are.

He sighed. "I'll go up and see. You hang on here."

The building was quiet, except for someone practising on a violin somewhere; perhaps that itself told how empty it was at that time. Gorkin's apartment was at the front on the first floor, and the door was slightly open. Ranklin pushed, then knocked and called softly, but got no reply. The open door surprised him and made him wary of a trap, but he still wasn't going to pass up the chance of a look around.

He was in a small living room, the walls lined with books and stacks of small periodicals and manuscripts. A large typewriting machine stood on a solid table by the window, a large comfortable office chair behind it. Ranklin tiptoed across to see if there was anything half-written in the machine, but there wasn't. And there was too much paper everywhere to make a hasty look worthwhile. He went over to the inside door, listened at it, then pushed that open. It was the bedroom –

– and Berenice hadn't been telling Gorkin anything. Or if she had, it didn't matter now.

When he had fetched O'Gilroy, they stared down at the sprawled, half-clad figure at the foot of the bed. Gorkin looked pallid, wide-eyed – and bloody. You have to be very adept with a knife to avoid bloodiness, and Berenice hadn't been. But she'd certainly been thorough.

"I *told* her if anything happened to Gorkin it would only make him a martyr!"

O'Gilroy shrugged. "Gave her a good reason, didn't ye? Feller's let down the Cause with his plotting and suchlike, but at least he can be a martyr." He smiled lopsidedly. "She's a dedicated kind of girl, that one."

Ranklin said grimly: "He's only a martyr if his death's tied to the King – and us. She might have thought of *that*."

"Mebbe she did."

"Hm. But if he was just killed by a casual whore…that could happen to anyone."

"Yer not going to give her to the *flics?*"

"Of course not: *she's* tied to us, damn it, if anybody starts looking. All right, we'll re-write his ending for him. Just stand there and look around. What can you deduce?"

"I'm no *flic.*" Offended.

"Just pretend you are, man."

Somewhat mollified, O'Gilroy gazed around. "She waited until he was taking off his trousers. Feller with his trousers round his ankles can't fight back. Then *wham* with a knife… Where is it?"

"The silly bitch must've taken it with her. I'll see…" He went into the kitchen, found a selection of worn cooking knives, and called: "How long a blade?"

"Short, she'd be carrying it in her purse… Not too short, though. Got to be as deep as the wounds and nobody'll know how much 'til they cut him open."

Ranklin momentarily shut his eyes in exasperation, then brought two knives out. "Which, then?"

O'Gilroy judiciously chose one. Then he wiped it in Gorkin's blood and tossed it to the floor. "Probly won't bother too much: ye got knife wounds, ye got a knife, why make tests?" He resumed his gazing. "They had a drink first."

There was a bottle of wine and one of absinthe on a little table, along with two used glasses. Ranklin asked: "Does the *Préfecture* use fingerprints yet?"

"Surely."

"And was she wearing gloves?"

O'Gilroy thought, then shook his head. "Damned if I can remember. Likely worn through at the fingers anyhow."

So Ranklin sniffed the two glasses, took the absinthe one to the kitchen and washed it out – a rather messy business if one is, quite properly, wearing warm-weather doeskin gloves. Then he tipped a little wine into it, tasted it to leave a blur on the rim, and put it back on the table. He wiped the absinthe bottle clean of fingerprints and put it back in a cupboard. Could she have touched the wine bottle as well? Best to be safe: he wiped that, then shut his mind to what he was doing and clenched Gorkin's dead hand around it to replace his own prints.

O'Gilroy watched, then re-enacted her entrance – wiping the front door-knob and around it; then the bedroom door; sitting down – wiping off the wooden parts of the chair; then – "Would she go to the *toilette*?"

"Could have done."

O'Gilroy found the bathroom, looked at it and said: "Jayzus!" because any cleaning was going to show up there. But he wiped delicately at just the most likely places, then came out holding a crumpled, stained length of toilet paper. "She wiped off the knife in there. Didn't want blood insider her purse." But the stains gave a good impression of the shape and length of the knife and prompted him to choose a more suitable one from the kitchen and bloody that instead. Then he flushed the blood-stained paper away.

Ranklin had been exploring. A wardrobe held several of Gorkin's suits including a set of evening dress tails, so the anarchist hadn't been averse to a little capitalism. Or once hadn't been: the suit was pretty old. Surprisingly, there was also a small clutch of women's skirts, blouses and shawls.

Relics of a semi-permanent mistress? Then he found a woman's hat, heavily veiled, and remembered from Constantinople the stories of women going to clandestine affairs under cover of the veil. Perhaps there were some Parisian women who wanted to step out with Gorkin but not be recognised.

He turned to the paperwork in the living room: he might just be lucky, but at the same time he was very cautious, because any sign of disturbance would lead to a far more thorough search by the police. He had had some idea of taking any notes about the King, but soon gave it up.

Nevertheless... "We still haven't given them a motive. If they look for one, they're bound to think of his involvement in the plot against the King."

"Robbery? Whores do."

Ranklin nodded but left that to O'Gilroy who went through the rooms quickly and quietly, leaving an extraordinary mess for a haul of just the money from Gorkin's pockets, his cufflinks, a few bits of cheap jewellery and a diamond pin that alone looked worth anything. It wasn't much, but any detective would long since have stopped being amazed at how cheap life could be. O'Gilroy did it all very professionally, and Ranklin asked no questions. He just pocketed a bunch of letters and Gorkin's passport and papers for the Bureau to study.

"We'd best be going," O'Gilroy proposed.

But Ranklin hesitated. "You really don't want any suspicion to fall on Berenice?"

O'Gilroy squinted at him curiously. "'Course not. The feller deserved the killing, and never mind her reasons. Why're ye asking?"

"She's short and dumpy. Suppose a tall, thin woman was seen going out of here?"

"Yer never going to get Mrs Finn down here to—"

"Good God, no. But there's some woman's clothes in the

wardrobe, including a hat with a thick veil...and I'm short and dumpy."

O'Gilroy was so appalled that his profanity deserted him. At last he croaked hoarsely: "Ye can't ask me to do that."

"I just thought it might help Berenice."

"Anyways, how can I leave me own clothes here?"

"I can carry them out in one of Gorkin's bags."

"But I... Ye jest can't..."

"If you can't do it, you can't. Never mind." Ranklin's face was all innocence; he might have been asking for the loan of a match.

"Ye connivin', stinkin' bastard..."

WHEN THE STROLLING gendarme was about forty yards from the apartment house entrance, Ranklin turned that way, put the bag down on the pavement, took out his pipe, and lit a match. That was the signal. The gendarme was only ten yards away when O'Gilroy came out, turned towards him, then abruptly turned about and hurried off the other way, skirt swirling and shawl clutched around his shoulders, face invisible behind the thick veil. He even had a surprisingly feminine tittuping scurry, given that he had to have kept his own shoes. First Connelly, now a Woman of the Streets; next King Lear? Or even Portia?

And he had certainly impressed his audience. For a moment, the gendarme looked like hurrying after the "woman", and Ranklin was ready to intervene with a query. Then the man checked and went back to strolling. But he should remember. (And would probably get a roasting for having failed to catch a murderess, too. Still, that would be a helpful lesson for him.)

Walking briskly after O'Gilroy but on the opposite side of the road, Ranklin wondered if he would ever put this in his report. Jay, in particular, would get a kick out of...

Damn. He kept forgetting.

Some people take a long time to die – in your mind, that is. Some people are struck off the memory immediately; you remember them only as dead. But others, you keep expecting them to come into the room, are constantly thinking "I must tell so-and-so that" before you remember. Unfair, really.

* * *

IT TOOK until Tuesday for St Claire to squeeze a passport out of the consulate for "Mrs Simmons"; strictly, she didn't have to have one, but as Ranklin kept patiently pointing out, it's the guilty who actually need paperwork to prove their innocence. He didn't want her meeting any officials, French or British, without some proof of who she now was. If she got flustered and relapsed into Mrs Langhorn, they were both in trouble.

So, they crossed the path of the King, coming in the opposite direction. Calais was daubed with crossed flags of the two nations and red-white-and-blue bunting (it was lucky the same colours did for both), with a royal train and Guard of Honour drawn up on the quayside.

The cross-channel steamer had been diverted to the other side, and Mrs Langhorn and Ranklin watched as the Royal Yacht *Alexandra* slid cautiously alongside, perhaps a hundred yards away. A band on the quayside struck up "God Save the King". Ranklin and all the other Britons on deck stood stiffly to attention, of course, and indeed nobody seemed to be moving except the poor bugger on *Alexandra's* foredeck who had made a seaman-like choice between securing the mooring rope or standing rigid while royalty drifted away.

There was a bustle of people coming *up* the gangway, a flurry of salutes, and then a short, stocky figure in naval uniform with a lot of gold braid and a flat cap – he was wearing undress uniform – moving among them.

"What's he doing?" Mrs Langhorn asked.

"Dishing out medals to the mayor and it looks like a couple of local generals."

"What have they done?"

"Been here. Easiest honours they've ever earned. And they fight like cats for them."

After a while, she said: "He does it very well."

He leant back from the rail to look at her. She was watching intently across the scummy harbour water and looking...he could only describe it as "pleased".

The party on the *Alexandra* broke up and trooped ashore. There were a lot of them, most of the men in uniform, and several women, including the unmistakably old-fashioned figure of the Queen. Then nothing for several minutes except some military shrieking. "What's he doing now?"

"Inspecting the Guard of Honour on the quay."

"And what'll he be doing in Paris?"

"Meeting the President, of course, driving round in a carriage...big dinners here and there, seeing some army manoeuvres, some show at *l'Opéra*, the races at Auteuil, opening some exhibition..."

"Keeping pretty busy."

"Not much time for a cup of coffee and a browse at the newspapers," Ranklin agreed.

"I don't think I'd've liked it much," she said matter-of-factly.

There was a burst of cheering from the far quay, then the train let off a blast of steam, chugged hard and began to pull out. The band started "God Save the King" again and they all had to stand up straight. The train snaked slowly around the inner basin of the port and was gone, just a moving plume of smoke rising above the rooftops.

Their own steamer woke up with shouted orders and clanging bells, and passengers wandered away to the saloons or to wave goodbye to friends on the land side. Mrs Langhorn lingered by the rail and Ranklin waited politely.

"He wouldn't know you were watching, would he?" she asked.

"No."

"I bet he doesn't even know what you've been doing for him."

Ranklin just nodded.

"He certainly wouldn't know I'd been watching."

On an impulse, and because if he didn't ask now he never would, Ranklin said: "Is Grover really his son?"

She looked back at the smoke drifting over the town. And finally, she said: "You know...I honestly don't know." She looked at him and smiled perkily. "A girl's got to make a living, hasn't she?"

SPY'S HONOUR

GAVIN LYALL

CHAPTER ONE

The journalist put down a pad of coarse writing paper on the café table, tilted and shook the chair to make sure there were no bits of broken glass on it, then sat down. A waiter put a cup of thick sweet coffee and a glass of water in front of him and the journalist nodded, but neither of them spoke.

He sipped the coffee, took out a pencil and wrote: *Salonika, November 9.* Then, feeling pessimistic about when the despatch would reach London, completed the date: *1912.* After that, he stared blankly out at the cold morning, past the big Greek flag that hung in limp folds over the door. He knew just how it felt. He sighed and began to write quickly.

Today, after 470 years of Turkish domination, the Greek Army once more trod the streets of Salonika. It has been a great day for the Hellenes, their goal is reached, their dreams realised. And no ancient army returning victorious to its native Athens ever received a more tumultuous welcome than ...

He realised someone was standing beside him and looked up, not moving his head too fast. He wasn't surprised to see a uniformed officer – the city had more of them than beggars at the moment – but hadn't expected the uniform to be of a Major in the Coldstream Guards.

"You are English, aren't you?" the Major said. "Do you know where I can get hold of a horse?"

By the mane, the journalist thought, if there aren't any reins. But he said: "Not so easy, in a country at war. But if you've got money, anything's possible."

"Just for a couple of hours or so."

"There's a stables in the street behind this place, but don't blame me if it turns out the Turks have pinched them all to escape on. But if you want to get out to the Greek HQ down the road," he nodded to the east, "you could get a lift on a supply cart."

The Major was wearing highly polished riding boots and an expression that said he hadn't put them on to go jaunting in oxcarts. He looked around the café as if hoping there was a saddled horse half-hidden in some corner, but only saw an old man sweeping fiercely at the chips of glass and crockery welded to the floor by sticky patches of wine.

"It looks as if you had a bit of a party last night."

"It happens every four hundred and seventy years, I believe."

Unsmiling, the Major went on: "I suppose you didn't happen to run across a chap, a British officer in the Greek gunners?"

The journalist perked up. "No, but I'd like to. What's his name?"

But the Major just nodded and said: "Well, thanks awfully. I think I'll try that stables."

Left to himself again, the journalist finished his coffee, beckoned for more, and wrote:

I spent the evening observing exultant human nature from a point of vantage in the principal café, where a huge Greek flag had replaced the Turkish red and white. The appearance of officers in uniform was the signal for the crowd to rise and give vent to more cries of 'Long live'.

Then he crossed out from 'cries' and wrote simply: 'more Zetos'. If any reader of The Times didn't understand Greek, he wouldn't dare to show it by complaining.

The road across the coastal plain must have followed the same line between the sea and the distant snow-dusted hills for thousands of years. Alexander the Great would have ridden it often, and Mark Antony on his way to Philippi to avenge Caesar's murder. But like so many historical sites the Major had seen, it was frankly just another scruffy place. The road itself was no better than a farm track, soggy and stony at the same time, jolting the wagon at every step the oxen took.

A couple of miles out of Salonika they passed a small crossroads that had been shelled in the last hours of the battle. The road was pitted with small shallow craters that were already filling with rain, and the wreckage of a wagon had been piled at one side. A Greek working party was clearing the scatter of cooking pots, bundles of clothing and prayer mats, and lifting stiff corpses into another cart; one of the dead was clearly a woman. In the field beyond, another group was half-heartedly burying the remains of a horse; obviously the army cooks had had first pick at it.

The Major had never been on a fresh battlefield before and found it difficult to believe that Alexander's or Antony's battles had left so mundane a litter.

He got down near the tents of the Greek headquarters and after a flurry of saluting and schoolboy Greek, found an officer willing to look at the documents he had brought. General Kleomanes, the officer apologised, would much regret not greeting him but, alas, their supposed allies the Bulgarians were sending an army to dispute just who owned Salonika ...

So the squabbling over the loot had begun already, the Major noted for his report. And perhaps Serbia, the third ally, also had its eyes on such a well-established port; what would the Emperor of Austria-Hungary, Serbia's northern neighbour, say to that? And the Czar of Russia say to any interference with Serbia? And the Kaiser say to Russian interference? The dominoes of Europe were all ready to topple, and the Major unconsciously stiffened his shoulders as he stood with Antony and Alexander.

Of course, a European war would be a terrible thing, quite dreadful, however short it must be. But it was for the politicians and diplomatists to avoid it. A soldier's job was to take what came, and if that included action and promotion, so be it. The Major had missed both the Sudan campaign and the South African war.

Good God – suppose the politicians kept Britain out of it!

The Greek officer led him through the neat lines of artillery and machine guns – drawn up not for battle, but to impress the citizens and journalists of Salonika – to a clutch of small buildings beside a railway line. These too had been bombarded, and he thought they were still smouldering until he realised the smoke came from cooking fires and looted stoves.

He paused to look at the shell damage with professional interest. It seemed curiously arbitrary: a patch of wall had been blown apart, some of its stones reduced to a muddy paste, yet a few feet away there was unscratched woodwork and unbroken panes of glass.

A group of officers huddled round a stove glanced at the Major's papers, glared at him, and gestured out through a doorless back door towards a smaller whitewashed stone building. His escorting officer stayed by the stove.

"Colonel Ranklin?"

The man asleep on a folded tent in one corner had a round, childlike face that aged into strained lines the moment he woke. Then he worked his dry mouth and scratched in his limp fair hair, making grunting noises.

"I'm sorry to be the one to demote you, as it were," the Major said, "but it's 'Captain' Ranklin again now. I'm here to reclaim you."

The man levered himself up into a sitting position and

scratched vigorously at his thighs. He was short and, despite the last few weeks, slightly tubby. He wore a long goatskin waistcoat over his Greek uniform and hadn't shaved for some days, but the stubble was so fair that it only showed where it was stained with grime.

"Who the devil are you?" he croaked.

That wasn't the way you spoke to a Major in the Coldstream. "I represent, at some moves, His Britannic Majesty."

"Good for you," Ranklin said, peering at the Major's uniform in the dim light. "How did you get here?"

The Major decided not to mention the ox-cart. "On the good ship HMS *Good Hope*, now anchored in Salonika harbour and waiting, among other things, for you."

Ranklin got stiffly to his feet. "But I'm number two in this brigade."

"Not any longer, I fear. It's all been cleared in Athens."

He handed over the documents and Ranklin glanced at the preambles and signatures.

"But I resigned my commission in the Gunners."

"And now, effectively, you've resigned from the Greek gunners, too."

Then Ranklin said what was, to the Major, a very odd thing: "Did you collect my pay?"

The Major's face stiffened with surprise. "I ... I'm afraid it didn't occur to me."

Ranklin was wiping his face with a damp rag. "Well, I'm not leaving Greece without it."

"I was told, unofficially, to pass on a message that I don't understand: that if you don't return to London there will be civil as well as military consequences. So shall we get a move on, *Captain?*"

It wasn't quite that easy. Having conceded the Major's basic demand, Ranklin made no effort to hurry. A small boy tending a fire by a large hole in the far wall made him a tin mug of coffee, and Ranklin sipped as he sorted through his kit. Most of it, along with battered tins of tobacco and sugar, he gave away to other officers and gunners who drifted in to say goodbye and scowl at the Major. Nobody even gave him the chance to show his haste by refusing a mug of coffee.

"Who's the boy?" he asked.

"Alex? He just adopted us on the road. His parents are probably …" he shrugged. "He doesn't say, doesn't seem to want to remember them … I suppose it could have been our guns."

"Some guns had certainly caused civilian casualties at a crossroads I came through. Don't your chaps look where they're shooting?"

"Of course not."

The Major stared. "I beg your pardon?"

Ranklin stopped in the middle of packing a small haversack and looked at him. "Haven't the Coldstream heard of indirect fire yet? We've stopped the sporting habit of putting the guns and gunners out where the enemy can get a decent shot at them. Now we skulk behind hills and forests and shoot over them." He went back to ramming socks and underclothes into the haversack and said more thoughtfully: "And it works. It really did. Observation and signalling, the clock code, ranging, concentration – everything we've been practising since South Africa. It all came together and it worked. Our guns won."

"Really?" The Major held the low opinion of artillery common among soldiers who have never been shot at. "Well, that's something you can tell them back in London. And that it makes for a pretty messy war in this part of Europe."

Ranklin slung the haversack from his shoulder. "We've been using French guns, the Turks have German ones. How's it going to be different in any other part of Europe?"

The Major didn't know; he just felt that it ought to be. Then he had to wait while Ranklin went in to say goodbye to the Brigadier – and, it seemed, the Paymaster. He came out of the station ticket office counting a roll of worn drachma notes and they walked back to the Salonika road.

Ranklin stowed the money away. "I suppose you've got no idea what they want me back for?"

"Not the foggiest, old boy. But after twenty years in the Army," and he guessed Ranklin had also served nearly that long, "I'm only sure it'll be something you never thought of." He was too well-bred to have put into words his feeling about an officer who fought for money, but now he saw a chance to hint at it. "Perhaps they want you for some sort of job in *Intelligence*."

LOVE AGORA BOOKS?

JOIN OUR BOOK CLUB

If you sign up today, you'll get:

1. A free novel from Agora Books
2. Exclusive insights into our books and authors, and the chance to get copies in advance of publication, and
3. The chance to win exclusive prizes in regular competitions

Interested? It takes less than a minute to sign up. You can get your novel and your first newsletter by signing up here.

facebook.com/AgoraBooksLDN

twitter.com/agorabooksldn

instagram.com/agorabooksldn